THE CASTLE BEHIND THORNS

MERRIE HASKELL

Katherine Tegen Books is an imprint of HarperCollins Publishers.

The Castle Behind Thorns
 For information address HarperCollins Children's Books, a division of HarperCollins Publishers, 195 Broadway, New York, NY 10007.
www.harpercollinschildrens.com

Library of Congress Cataloging-in-Publication Data

Haskell, Merrie.
The castle behind thorns / Merrie Haskell. — First edition.
pages cm
Summary: When Sand, a blacksmith's apprentice, wakes up in a broken castle, he must find a way to put back together.
ISBN 978-0-06-200819-0 (hardcover bdg.)
[1. Fairy tales. 2. Castles—Fiction.] I. Title.
PZ8.H2563Cas 2014 2013021527
[Fic]—dc23 CIP
AC

Typography by Carla Weise and Joel Tippie
14 15 16 17 18 CG/RRDH 10 9 8 7 6 5 4 3 2
❖
First Edition

for Aunt Carol
you were there for me
whether I was kind or prickly

Castle
Boisblanc
N
KEEP
INNER
MIDDLE
OUTER
Portcullis
Smithy
OUTER
Stables
W
E
MIDDLE
Well
Great Hall
Kitchen
INNER
To Crypts
Gardens
To Count's Chambers
Herbary
KEEP
Treasury
Perrotte's Observation Tower
S

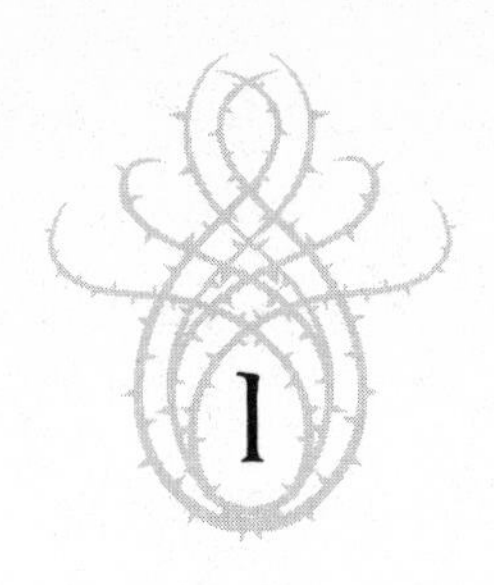

Ashes

Sand woke, curled in the ashes of a great fireplace.

Surprised to find himself waking at all, for he had no memory of falling asleep, Sand scrambled to his feet. Soot billowed from him in a cloud and sneaked up his nose. He sneezed four great sneezes that came back in lonely echoes from the vast room beyond the fireplace.

Sand had never slept in a fireplace before. He never wanted to again. But he hesitated inside the fireplace, one foot suspended in midair, afraid to leave.

In the room beyond, everything was broken.

Every single thing.

The mantel lay in two disjointed pieces on the

cracked hearth. Mixed with the mantel's splinters lay the shattered crest of a great family, their gilded phoenix and silvered swan once entwined, now separated and dismembered.

The enormous wooden tables throughout the room sagged and slumped like beasts fallen to the hunt. Every bench around the tables lay sideways and in pieces. Each cup and bowl was shattered or smashed. All the tablecloths and tapestries puddled in scraps on the floor or hung in tatters, and even the wood and kindling for the fireplace had been reduced to slivers.

Across the red-painted walls adorned with gold phoenixes, long scrapes revealed white plaster. Overhead, a myriad of fissures snaked along the ceiling's timber beams.

Sand stepped over the broken mantel and crest, shedding ashes on the phoenix's and swan's painted feathers as he went.

How had he gotten there? How had he gotten *here*?

For now he knew where he had awakened.

He was inside the Sundered Castle.

Every morning of his life, Sand had stepped out the front door of his house and ignored this broken castle across the valley. Everyone in the village ignored it. It was unreachable. Only the castle's towers were visible above an enveloping thorny hedge, a raspberry bramble of astonishing proportion that had grown up around the ruin after the abandonment. Of course, no one picked raspberries from the hedge.

Though he saw the castle every day, Sand rarely thought about the place anymore. But to Sand as a small child, the split towers were exciting, a place for great adventure, with a lost treasure hidden somewhere inside.

His father had answered all of Sand's ceaseless, little-boy questions with bored detachment. Why did thorns surround the castle? Well, the Count and Countess had planted the bramble to keep looters out, and also to make sure no one got injured by the unstable towers. Why had the castle broken apart? An earthquake some twenty-five or more years ago had cracked the walls, and everyone had run away. Everyone? Yes, everyone, even Sand's father, who had been an apprentice shoemaker in the castle when it was sundered.

The end. Stop asking questions, Sand. No one cares about the castle.

Eventually, the allure of the castle wore off, and Sand did stop asking questions. And as he grew older, he even mostly forgot about the castle, just like everyone else in the village.

But now he was inside.

Sand shook the better part of the ash from his

clothes, straightened his tunic, and studied the hall. He didn't believe he was in danger of imminent death from the roof or walls crashing down, in spite of the cracks in the ceiling. In fact, the long-ago decision to abandon the castle seemed poorly thought out. The towers and walls had remained upright since his father's boyhood. If they had stood this long, the castle must be safe enough for a little exploration.

Eager to see what surprises the place might offer, Sand crunched his way across the broken floor tiles to one of the lower doorways. Even if Sand didn't find any treasure, his father had lived here as a boy, before he'd forsaken shoe leather for the hammer and anvil. Maybe Sand could find some secret answer to his father's strangeness hidden here among the broken and abandoned things.

Sand clambered out of the great hall over the broken door and climbed a short flight of stairs into the kitchen. He stopped and stared in dismay. The disarray here was a thousand times worse than that of the hall.

Here, loaves of bread ripped in half lay strewn across the floor. Sand picked up one of the half-loaves, finding it lightweight and rock hard. It had dried out, but had never become green or fuzzy with mold. He turned it over and over in his hands, wondering: How had a loaf of bread been pulled apart by an earthquake?

He found other small lumps on the floor among the shattered crockery—lumps that looked like dried apples, more or less, but not the sort of apple that had started out as a slice, more as if . . . as if these apples had been ripped in half, just like the bread.

Bread, Sand supposed, *could* be broken if it fell to the floor during an earthquake. Maybe. But apples?

Sand sniffed an apple chunk. He detected no odor, no faint tang that a dried apple should have. He tossed the apple lump to the floor and brushed grit off his hands. He took a deep breath. The room smelled of nothing but dust.

The kitchen housed four big hearths with cauldrons, hearth cranes, and spits, and four baking ovens along a wall. Everything except the stones of the ovens and hearths were broken; those were merely cracked.

Sand couldn't even imagine the force it would take to rip an iron kettle in half without heating it to glowing hot, yet it had been done, over and over. He shivered.

The other door out of the kitchen was split down the center, but still standing. Sand pushed aside the unhinged slab of heavy oak and slipped through the narrow exit. He found himself in a little kitchen garden, where smashed cold frames held rattling dry leaves that might once have been cabbage. Sand thought that the cabbage must have reseeded itself year after year within the frames for it not to have rotted away to nothing in over twenty-five years.

A doorway across this small courtyard led to an herbary. Sand poked his head inside. Drying racks for herbs sat crushed on the floor, and pottery shards lay about as if flung from every direction. Nothing of interest here. Sand backed out of the room and went on.

The small garden courtyard had exits at each end, both with sagging, metal-bound oak doors. One had stood open and one had been closed when the castle broke apart. Sand chose the open door, passing through a dark, narrow tunnel to find himself at the head of a flight of stairs leading down into another courtyard.

This courtyard was much darker than the upper ward, due to the towering raspberry bramble that loomed a full man's height over the castle walls. Sand gawked at the hedge for a moment. It was one thing to see these thorns from a distance, where they appeared as nothing but vines shrouding the castle. It was another thing to see the hedge from inside, crowding above the walls, blocking light and wind.

Sand shook himself. Beyond the castle's well lay a long low block of buildings that must have been lodgings for servants and guests. He ducked inside the first door he could find, just to get out from the cold shadow of the thorns.

Sand wandered from broken room to broken room. For a quarter of an hour, his lonely investigation was pleasant. Sand had lived too long in a too-small house with two half sisters not to enjoy the quiet and the aloneness for a moment. But underneath this pleasure grew a dim sense of unease.

Nothing was whole here, nothing at all. Not a spoon, not a toothpick, not a bed, not a door. No room had been exempted from the destructive force that had overtaken the castle.

The outer walls were largely intact; many of the windows and doors, though cracked, remained in place. The inner parts of the castle had been fairly protected from the elements, though this was not true of every room; in some places, wind and rain had reduced fabrics to thread and dust, had dried out and warped wood, and had washed away paint.

After the third such room, Sand realized the true oddity of the Sundered Castle. There were no signs of life. No leather had fallen to mouse teeth. No rafters were homes to swallows' nests.

Everywhere was silent and still. Sand expected a certain amount of peace—the place had been abandoned by humans for decades. But there was *nothing* here, no noise, no life anywhere. Not a single rat or snake. Not even a gnat. Not even a spider.

Sand's desire to wander cooled. He should stop exploring and find the fabled lost treasury.

Sand returned to the innermost ward of the castle through the small garden courtyard. He tried the closed door on the other side, but it had rusted shut. He strode back through the kitchens and into the great hall. There he found a more amenable door and entered the central courtyard of the castle.

Over this larger, irregular yard loomed the four-towered keep, the castle's last bastion against attack. Here, finally, Sand saw the true sundering of the castle: Daylight shone through a giant crack running north-south through the keep's walls. The crack crossed the courtyard from the keep's base, splitting the earth with a slender rift in the ground—not wide, but immeasurably deep.

The rift led straight to the castle's chapel, which Sand easily identified from the remains of its colored glass windows. The chapel too was divided, in line with the courtyard's rift.

Sand stared down into the dark fissure on the ground. It appeared endless. Sand had a feeling that if he looked too deep, he might find the Devil staring back.

Sand's scalp prickled, and he backed away. He faced the cleft keep again. Cracked in half though it was, it looked safe . . . enough. And if he left now, if he just ran away from the castle, he would always regret not discovering the treasure inside. What's more, if he brought some of the treasure out—well, he couldn't keep it. Not to spend, anyway; no one would believe a village boy could come by gold honestly, and they'd be right. But if he returned what treasure he found to the dowager Countess, he might receive a reward.

But on the ground floor of the keep, he found no treasury, just a bunch of small rooms with no discernible purpose—rooms filled with tapestries and chairs mostly. Heart thumping nervously with every creak of the stairs, he climbed to the next floor.

There he found the library, doubtless once the jewel of the countship. All the castle's broken rooms had been well appointed and impressive once, but the library amazed Sand the most. How many books were represented here, in this sea of jumbled and torn parchment? One book was more than he could imagine owning, despite his father's aspirations for him. Well—maybe two.

Sand picked up a few pages from the floor and read them haltingly, for in spite of his father's efforts and wishes, Sand was in no way a fluent reader of Latin or any vernacular. He let the pages drift back to the floor and moved on. He found rooms where ladies once sewed, rooms where important people once slept, all sorts of rooms, but no treasury.

He gave up on the keep. He hurried cautiously down the stairs, afraid every second they would crumble beneath his weight, but they held.

He felt that a treasury, a proper one, should be underground, and perhaps a bit hidden.

Maybe the treasury door lay somewhere inside the chapel? He crept inside, admiring the way the sun shone through the colored glass windows depicting a saint's life, and cast patterns in pease-porridge green and marigold yellow on the floor. After a quick genuflection, Sand had to look away from the broken altar and the cracked crucifix. He scuttled past them, feeling guilt for not putting these holy things to rights.

Beyond the altar, he saw a passage leading down into darkness. He grabbed half a beeswax taper and lit it using the pieces of fire striker he found lying next to the candle fragments. Chunks of flint and steel still made fire, no matter how broken.

The stair led to the crypt. He forced himself to enter the dark recesses, candle held high, where he found the worst damage yet. The rift in the courtyard penetrated down to the crypt ceiling. A matching fissure snaked across the floor.

The fissure ran straight through one tomb in particular, which lay now in shattered pieces of undecorated limestone.

The body that had once dwelled inside the

fragmented tomb must have been ejected by the same force that had rent earth and stone throughout the castle. Scraps of a shroud littered the floor. It was strange, like some great outside force had tried to free the body. But to what end? To just let it lie in a heap on a dirt floor?

The body hunched in a haphazard pile of withered skin. *Like one of the apples in the kitchen*, Sand thought disjointedly, altogether horrified. His candlelight should have been steady in the still air below the earth, but it trembled with his shaking hand. Even the quivering light showed the details too well.

The corpse had been a girl. Her clothes were, perhaps, the only thing in the entire castle that were not ripped or torn; they were fine fabrics, deep saffron velvets and russet silks that had not faded with age.

And the corpse was whole as well, though clearly the body's bones were broken beneath its powdery, dried-out skin. The neck was tilted at an odd angle, and the arms and legs were bent horribly akimbo.

Sand's first impulse was to run back upstairs, out into sunlight and spring air. He should forget all about this crypt and the desiccated body. He should give up entirely on the castle's lost treasury and just go home. Shielding his candle flame, he sprinted for the stairs.

But he paused on the first step back up to the chapel.

He shouldn't leave her like that. He should put *something* to rights in this broken place, and she deserved it; she had been a person once.

Reluctantly, he turned to face the tomb again. He dripped a blob of melted wax on a stone, planted the candle there, and set to work. He cleared away the stone crumbs from the niche where the tomb had once rested on a raised slab. Squeamishly and holding his breath, he lifted the girl's broken body and laid her in the niche.

He breathed shallowly through his nose at first, and then normally. The girl had not rotted at all, just as nothing in this castle had rotted since its abandonment. She smelled like . . . nothing, really. Stone, maybe. He carefully straightened the girl's bent legs and arms. He aligned her head, though it would not stay in the spot he chose for it. He shrugged and left her chin slightly tucked to one side.

Once she was arranged in proper repose again, he repositioned the other loose and broken sarcophagus lids on their cracked bases. No other bodies had fallen onto the floor, to his relief.

With his duty done, he fled up the stairs into the sunlight. He was ready to leave. He'd seen enough, maybe too much, and he wanted nothing more from this place. Its treasures could stay hidden. Its secrets could remain undiscovered. He had to get out.

This place hadn't suffered from some earthquake. Something else had happened here. Something that cut leather, ripped apples in half, and tore apart cast iron kettles. Something that broke bread and tossed bodies from tombs.

He descended to the lower courtyard and found an open gate. An uneasy race through a dark passage ended in yet another courtyard, faced by stables on one side, and the workshops and lodgings of the castle's craftsmen on the other. He didn't pause to explore; he just headed directly toward the castle's gates.

Sand threw open the man-size night portal to find himself in a dark tunnel pierced by arrow slits and larger openings that he'd heard called "murder holes." In theory, if an enemy entered the castle, he could be trapped between the inner and outer gates and simply killed by raining death down through these openings. Sand shivered, thinking how glad he was to be alone in the castle—alone, he knew for sure that he couldn't be trapped in this tunnel.

He reached the outer gate and opened its night portal—and stopped. The portcullis was down, but he could raise a portcullis. What he could not raise was the nasty snarl of thorns beyond the portcullis grate. The brambles covered the whole of the gate, so dense and thick that he could not see daylight through them.

And these were no ordinary raspberry brambles, as he'd always been told. The thorns were ten or twelve times as long as a normal thorn. Fascinated, Sand reached for one of the sharp spikes, just to test its sturdiness. He meant, of course, to touch the smooth side of the thorn, not the pointy bit. But one thorn twitched over and jagged into his wrist, piercing the skin deeply.

"Ouch!" Sand cried, jerking his hand away.

The thorns reached for him.

2

WOUND

SAND JUMPED BACK, SLAMMING THE NIGHT PORTAL shut. He threw the bar down and backed away from the door.

His wrist pulsed. He wasn't bleeding—though he sort of wished he were. Bleeding he could understand. Bleeding he could stop. His flesh around the wound puffed up, round and red.

He swore, and went to find something to bandage his wound.

Torn bedsheets made good bandages, and there were plenty of linens to choose from. But bandages didn't make Sand's wrist feel any better, and they didn't lower the thorns. How was he going to get out of the castle?

He steeled himself and opened the night portal again. Immediately, the thorns reached yearningly through the grating of the portcullis. Sand yelped and closed the portal. He backed away, heart racing.

He could try cutting them, but he imagined the thorns grasping his knife or shears and pulling him in—or just stretching to reach past the length of his blade and sinking more sharp ends into his tender flesh.

Fire?

Torn bedsheets also made a good torch, when coupled with scrap wood. He had no pitch or resin for long burning, but he needed only to set the thorns alight. Quite possibly, the thorns would even flee from his fire in the same manner they moved toward him.

He found another broken fire striker, and tinder that couldn't really be broken, only scattered. He managed a spark, and he managed to catch it, and shortly, Sand had a proper torch. But when he opened the portal and thrust his torch into the heart of the bramble and leaped backward, the brambles pulled together swiftly and smothered the flame.

Sand slammed the portal shut and left the tunnel.

The Count and Countess could not have planted this bramble. That story was wrong—had to be wrong.

Of course, the story also said that the castle had been evacuated and abandoned because of an earthquake. But he was here, where clearly some magical force had done this work, sundering apples and iron kettles as well as buildings.

Stories didn't know everything.

Maybe he could find a way over the thorns. Cautiously, he climbed the keep's tallest tower all the way to the top, where he found a cozy room with windows in every direction, and an odd ceiling speckled with numerous hinges and latches. Unlike the rest of the castle, though, nothing was broken within this room—because it contained nothing.

He leaned out one of the broken windows to look at the thorn brake. The hedge was easily three times as thick as the outer wall of the castle itself. The only place in the castle high enough to see over the hedge was the keep, which was far from the castle walls.

There was no getting *over* the thorns. It was as impossible as going through.

Sand was trapped here, in this broken castle, surrounded by a deadly briar.

The sun's rays were growing long and red. Below, the courtyards had fallen into shadow. Sand's stomach growled in anger over its neglect.

He went to the kitchen and sorted through the debris to find enough withered apples to make a pathetic meal. Then, wrist throbbing from the thorn wound, Sand looked about for a place to sleep.

His first, daft impulse was to crawl back into the

fireplace. Grandpère always said it was human nature to want to return the way you came, but that was dangerous sometimes—at its most extreme, that's how people got trapped in burning buildings, unable to think to try a new way out; at its silliest, that's how people got stuck doing stupid things like sleeping in a fireplace two nights in a row.

So, instead of crawling back into the cold, dirty fireplace, Sand swept aside the ashes and gathered together all the bits of broken wood lying nearby—except for the pieces of the phoenix and swan crest, which he propped against the chimney stones in some semblance of restored order.

Sand made another fire. He built it up, warming his hands for a bit, then mended three or four of the broken wax candles that were lying about. Mending candles was dead easy, since all it took was remelting the broken ends together. Though he supposed he didn't even need to mend them, as a candle stump burns just as well as a whole candle. But Sand *wanted* to mend the candles. He wanted something in the Sundered Castle to be right again, whole again.

He slept there, the first night, by his fire, under the eyes of the phoenix and the swan. He shivered a little, but it was with the oncoming fever of his thorn wound, not because he was cold.

⚘

THE NEXT MORNING, SAND'S wrist had swollen around the once loose-fitting bandage, the skin purplish where it wasn't red. His mouth tasted foul, and he was thirsty.

In all of his poking about the day previous, he had not seen one single whole bucket, pot, kettle, cup, or bowl. He looked again, though, just to be sure. He had already guessed that a bottle of wine or a jug of ale left intact was out of the question, but that did not stop his hopeful investigation.

Eventually, Sand found himself staring into the castle's well without a bucket or a rope. He couldn't see the bottom, of course, but he could smell the mineral tang of the trickling water below. Not that it mattered. No rope, no bucket: no water.

He climbed slowly to his feet and began searching the castle for *anything* that could hold water. He had no luck. Every single thing that could haul water from the well, from butter churn to chamber pot, was broken in the exact way that made water-hauling impossible without major repairs.

With that thought in mind, Sand forced himself to go down to the outer courtyard to the craftsmen's workshops. Though reluctant to seek the castle's smithy, fearing what he might find there, he knew if he were ever going to repair anything for real, he would need a working forge and proper equipment.

Sand pulled aside the remains of the door to the long-abandoned blacksmith's workshop and stopped, staring in fascination and alarm at the anvils that lay wrenched apart on the loose dirt floor. Sand took a deep breath that shook with more emotions than he could name. The iron kettles and pots that lay broken in the kitchen—Sand could almost, *almost*, imagine that. He could certainly imagine the forces that overturned and smashed the bricks of a forge, or split apart hammers and tongs and other tools that were now nearly useless. He picked up a split bellows that sagged, half bent over the edge of a fallen forge. Bellows split now and then in a smithy, even without a great magical devastation.

But an anvil—a hefty, proper anvil, pulled apart into jagged, chunky metal, so that he could see the fibers of the iron inside . . . It was unimaginable. Or it *had* been unimaginable, before today.

The workshop had been a large one with numerous forges, as befitted a count's seat, with space for armorers and swordsmiths to work, as well as areas for the forging of more mundane articles, like spoons and forks. Sand could tell: This smithy had once been magnificent. And now it lay in total ruin.

Sand backed out of the smithy, dread creeping over his shoulders with chilly claws. There was nothing here to help him.

Disconsolate, he returned to the middle courtyard. Thirst was on his tongue, in his throat, in his jaws.

He slid down the well post into a hunch, chin on chest. The early spring air was chilly for resting, but the sun warmed his shoulders as it crossed overhead. He sat for a long time, watching the light and shadows change with the movement of the day. It was strange not to hear birds. There were none in the castle, and none in the thorns. All around him was silence.

"Nothing lives here and nothing dies here," he said, speaking just to break the quiet. "Except me."

After a time, Sand poked at his wrist. Still swollen. The faintest of red lines had started a march up his arm, the first telltale of blood poisoning.

He prayed then to Saint Eloi, who watches over blacksmiths: "Please don't let me die here, alone. I don't even know why I came to be here—but it can't have been to let me die, can it?"

The prayer reminded him of the night before he'd awakened in the fireplace. He had fought with his father, their biggest argument yet. Instead of going to bed when his father ordered him to, he'd taken off for Grandpère's house, running by frosty moonlight over the well-worn path.

And then? He had paused at the shrine to Saint Melor, where a small spring pooled and people threw in bronze pins and silver coins with their prayers.

His memory lingered on that shrine and the way the offerings there had glittered in the water under the full moon. He'd had no pins or coins, but he'd made a handful of nails that day at the forge. He'd had a nail in his purse; he'd pulled it out and tossed it into the pool, offering it with a prayer to Saint Melor, who had lost a foot and a hand that were replaced with bronze and silver appendages. "Oh, holy Saint, intercede for me. Help my father to understand my heart, help us to repair the love between us. Do not make me to go the university."

He didn't remember anything after that until the ashes in the fireplace.

He forced himself to his feet and went to the kitchen, half convinced he was hungry, not thirsty, and picked through the debris for bite-sized morsels of shriveled carrots, desiccated pears, even a dusty crust of a pie.

But eating just made his thirst worse. He had to find a bucket, or something that could act like one. He should look everywhere he had not yet looked. He pushed himself first to the stables, where he found all the saddles slashed; all the reins, girths, and straps cut; and every single piece of straw bent in half. No whole buckets here—just another reminder of the strangeness of the castle's sundering.

The sun was near to setting when he stumbled into

the rooms that had once been the private retreats of the Count and Countess. In the Count's sun-washed rooms, all was decorated in phoenixes—or once had been. Goose-down stuffing trailed out of three long slashes in the mattress, as though a giant trident had been swiped down the length of it.

A great wave of tiredness overcame him. Sand looked in the mattress for signs of rodents or any other small animals that might be enjoying such a cozy home, but of course there were none. He straightened out several widths of shredded linen sheets, overlapping them across the torn mattress to contain the stuffing. He collected strips of blankets and sheets and bed curtains from around the room and made a little nest. He prayed to his name saint to watch him through the night; then, shedding his ash-covered clothes, he crawled into the nest.

In the rosy rays of the setting sun, the red lines marching to his heart looked even more inflamed. His wrist throbbed. "Well, I guess it will be a race," he said to the silence. "Am I going to die first of blood poisoning, or of thirst?"

He shucked his old bandage and took a length of sheet to wrap tightly around his wrist. "Perfect bandage material," he said, wearily winding and winding and winding. "I must have a hundred yards of bandage here. A thousand."

That thought jolted him fully awake.

Sand crawled from his nest and stumbled into his clothes. He ran from the room, pelting from bedchamber to bedchamber in the darkening castle, gathering torn bedding as he went.

He carried his pile of cloth down to the well, where he tied a mass of bedsheets together into a rough ball shape, then tore the remaining sheets into long strips, and knotted *them* together in a long cord. He attached ball to cord, then threw the ball into the well, holding tightly to the end of his makeshift rope.

The cloth ball didn't hit the water, but Sand knew he was close. He pulled the ball back up dry, as expected, and ran upstairs to find more sheets.

He collected another wad of bedding and carried it down to the well, air rasping like a metal file through his dry mouth and throat.

His fingers fumbled together another length of sheets. He glanced at the cornflower twilight sky, trying to judge the approach of night, and whether or not he should stop to light candles. He forged on though, testing the broken windlass, and found that at least half of it was still rooted firmly in the ground, planted in cement.

He tied the end of his rope to it, and tossed the cloth ball into the well once more. This time, his effort ended in a splash, albeit a quiet one. He waited a moment, and hauled up the rope.

It was heavier than he expected, and even his smith's muscles burned by the time he hauled the ball out. It flopped, sopping, onto the flagstones of the courtyard. Sand eagerly picked up a segment of sheeting and wrung it into his mouth, then another, then another, then dunked his sheet-ball into the well again, so that he could drink until his thirst was quenched.

Relief spread through his body, like the warm relaxation that overtook him just before sleep.

Perhaps he should have gone to bed then. But now that his desperation for water was gone, he suddenly, intensely, missed his family.

Driven by the notion that he might see the sparks from his father's forge if he just climbed high enough, he lit a mended candle and entered the keep. Blacksmiths did some work best in the darkness, when it was easier to see the gradations of color change in hot metal. That was why his father's smithy was high on a hill, on the far outskirts of the village—so that his hammering didn't keep people awake when he worked at night. Sand and his family were used to it.

Stomach sloshing, Sand dragged himself up the stairs to the odd, empty room in the tallest tower. Outside, the sky was nearly dark, the dimmest of ruddy reds clinging to a cloud bank in the west, the exact color of heated iron just before it became bendable and began to glow.

He looked out across the village to the dark shape of a small house on a hill. No fire shone through the smithy's open door. So his father was not working tonight. Because he was worried? Agnote, Sand's stepmother, certainly would be, would be worried right out of her mind for Sand right now. No matter how his father felt, she would have sent him off to look for Sand, first to Grandpère's, then probably along the road to Paris.

But then what? No one had seen Sand. He had disappeared from the world. What did his father think? What was he going to say to Agnote when he returned home without Sand?

Sand crept back down the stairs to the comfortable nest he'd made in the Count's rooms. It took a long time to fall asleep. His thorn-pierced wrist sent wave after wave of pain up his arm, and he kept thinking about his father, his stepmother, his sisters, the forge, his home. Agnote and his little sisters must be crying. But Agnote, even Agnote who had blown breath into him when he arrived blue from his mother, would never, not in a thousand years, think that Sand lay restless and ill inside the Sundered Castle.

KITCHEN

WHEN SAND WOKE THE NEXT MORNING, THE SUN was far above the thorn brake, and he felt clammy. His head and wrist throbbed. "I'm alive," he groaned. "But I'm not doing a very good job of it."

He looked at the red streaks snaking halfway up his arm. Agnote was a midwife, and she had treated poison in the blood often enough, but with mixed results. What had her treatments looked like? There had been tisanes and tinctures, of course, and poultices with green leaves—wet, stewed-looking leaves, pale green . . . slightly scalloped, with big veins. Cabbage? Not dock or mullein, but cabbage like people ate?

Only, nothing but thorns grew here. It was early spring; beyond the castle, things were greening nicely, but inside the walls the land was empty of even the tenderest shoots of green *anything.* Nothing grew in the gardens. Even the fruit trees stood dead and barren, never having regrown even a little from their shattered trunks.

Sand made his way back to the courtyard where ancient, dry leaves of cabbage still lay under pieces of glass in the smashed-up cold frames. He no longer believed they had reseeded themselves—he believed that they were the same cabbages that had been here the day the castle had been abandoned. How they had managed to survive as long as they had, as well as they had, Sand didn't know, but if no insects came to eat them, that must have helped. He collected the dry, rustling leaves and carried them into the kitchen, pondering how he might boil water and stew the leaves without the benefit of a pot.

In the end, he decided to use half a pot, tilted on its side. It would be a very shallow stewing pot.

It worked well enough; the stewed cabbage leaves, even with as little efficacy as they must have retained after years of sitting around, felt very good on his wrist. Sand's body felt lighter, like he'd taken off the heavy goatskin coat he wore in winter. He wasn't going to die of thirst—not soon. And though he might still die of poisoned blood, it would take a while, and the cabbage helped the pain.

Sand went looking for a surgery. There had to be some place for healing in the castle beyond the mess of an herbary—a place where a barber had once practiced dentistry, lanced boils, and cut hair.

He did find what could have been such a place, eventually, tucked away in a corner of the middle courtyard. He found dried-up old leeches in a broken bucket and a handful of sharp tools split into fragments. He carried a selection of damaged barbering tools back to his kitchen fire and settled down to work on his arm.

He selected a broken lancet, and wrapped a bit of linen around the severed handle. His breath came in quick gasps. The lancet's small, two-sided blade made him nervous. He'd never guessed he could be afraid of a bit of iron.

But he went on with it anyway.

Sand pressed the blade point into the dark spot at the center of his wound. The pain was agonizing. He bit down hard on his lips, willing himself to break through the swollen skin and release whatever poisons lay beneath.

But the lancet's tip slipped a fraction and pressed deep into his wound without splitting the skin. Out squirted a needle of thorn almost half the length of his little finger. It was just *there*, poking out of his wrist, like a ground squirrel in its burrow, popping up to look for danger. With the thorn came no small measure of blood mixed with pus.

Sand plucked out the thorn carefully with his fingertips and threw it into the fire.

He almost thought it might not light. He could imagine the thorn holding itself intact and piercing him again as he swept the ashes out of the fireplace in the future. But he watched, and the thorn burned just fine.

Immediately, the throbbing in his arm took on a new pace. He hoped it was a healing rhythm.

SAND, FEELING BETTER, BECAME curious to see the shop where his father had worked as a boy.

He strolled down to the outermost courtyard and found the shoemaker's area. The ruin of wooden lasts and torn shoe leather told him nothing. Sand could no more imagine his father in this room when it was whole and orderly than he could imagine his father at age thirteen.

He wandered away, looking aimlessly into other areas just to see what he could find among the rubbish. The kennels were as empty of dogs as the stables were empty of horses—the animals had gotten out. Likewise, the only bird he found in the mews was a tiny stuffed falcon—a once-loved hunting bird that someone had decided to preserve?

The brownish-gray falcon had gotten odd

treatment during the sundering. One of his legs was broken, and he rested on his face as a result, but all in all, the stuffed bird was almost undamaged. Sand scooped up the bird and fiddled with the falcon's leg for a bit. He splinted the leg with a stick of kindling and a bit of twine, and it worked—the falcon could stand upright again.

"Nice to see a friendly face around here," Sand told the falcon, stroking the dark stripe on its cheek. "Now all you need is a name. Of course, I'm not entirely sure what sort of falcon you are. You might not even be a falcon at all. Are you a hawk? You're no eagle or owl. What else can hunting birds be?"

He tucked the bird into the crook of his arm, and took it on the rest of his exploration of the outer courtyard, too glad for the company of the bird to consider how strange this action was. The bird didn't talk back, but it had a face to talk *to*. "I hope you're a merlin falcon," Sand said. "I think I'll call you Merlin, even if you aren't one. It makes me feel more hopeful." Like he had a powerful wizard on his side, even if the wizard was trapped in a stuffed falcon body, just as Sand was trapped in a broken castle.

HUNGER BECAME SAND'S NEXT concern. He stood Merlin on a slumped kitchen table while he looked for something to eat.

He found some surprisingly well-preserved olives

beneath two halves of an amphora, which had held in some of the moisture of the oils within the olives. Sand's discovery became a salty and unexpectedly tasty lunch.

But that was just one meal, and Sand was resolved never to come as close to disaster again as he had with his thirst. He had to figure out his food now, before he ate everything easily scavenged and had nothing left to eat.

He looked around the kitchen, deeply discomfited by everything about him lying broken, shattered, and disarrayed. Was there anything here he could make whole? Was there anything he could repair easily?

The spits were all broken, but not all in the same way. With little difficulty, Sand put together a whole spit out of just the unbroken parts. He did this quickly—it was, after all, just some metal pieces that rested on other metal pieces—and when he put the reconstructed spit in place at one of the hearths, he felt a bubble of satisfaction in his chest, kind of like a big cabbage burp.

"Merlin, we should definitely roast something for dinner," he said.

The question was . . . *what?* The kitchen and pantry held enough food to feed hundreds for weeks, but though nothing was rotted or spoiled, the food remained scattered, split, dried, browned, shriveled, and stale. The challenge was making it edible.

He set to work. Bit by bit, Sand brought order to the kitchen. The big kitchen worktables were all broken—of course—but a smashed bench was just about the right length to prop up one of the tables. The table surface wasn't perfectly level—a dried pea would certainly roll off—but it would suffice as a place to work.

He found half a bucket here and three-quarters of a bowl there—anything that would actually *hold* material—and placed them on the table, and then began sorting foodstuffs into these jumbled containers. Onion chunks. Cracked cheese wheels. Dried peas mixed with gravel. Lentils mixed with ashes. Almonds mixed with grit. Bread crumbles. Apple bits, fig bits, and pear bits. Withered and halved lampreys, eels, salmon, pike, and trout.

And turnips—endless ruptured turnips. Had the kitchen just received the turnip delivery for the whole year when the castle was sundered? It was the only explanation he could think of to account for the excessive numbers of turnips in the kitchen's root cellar, buried in layers of sawdust. Someday he might have eaten everything else in the castle, but there would still be turnips left.

Sand soaked half a haunch of venison in water until it plumped, then roasted it between two half-onions. "That'll be quite nice," he told Merlin.

❦

A FEW DAYS LATER, Sand felt comfortable with his food supplies. The larders and pantries were refilling with his salvaged foods. He had eaten well every day, meals meant for a king, or at least a count. The night before, he'd roasted half a rehydrated peacock, and eaten broken pigs made of marzipan and sugar.

He decided to make a second pass around the kitchen. He sorted the nonfood items—the many, many nonfood items—he didn't think he'd ever be able to return to their original purpose, and tossed them into piles according to the material they were made from. Wood, after all, could be burned, whatever shape it was in, and iron was infinitely reshapable.

Afterward, Sand scrubbed the kitchen from top to bottom. He doused the floor with water painstakingly wrung from his well cloths, and swept the accumulated water, dirt, and debris out the door with a broom he'd mended with strips of leather.

When he finished, he gazed at his clean, drying floor; at the tables filled with food that he was salvaging, sorting, and storing; at the nearly neat stacks of half-bowls and quarter–cooking pots; at the apple fragments he had soaked in water and now roasted on a spit with dustings of nutmeg and cinnamon; at the heaps of splintered firewood stacked in the corner; at the ripped dishcloths neatly folded and arranged on the mantel next to his falcon.

He, Sand, had done all this. He had saved these things, sorted them, repurposed them, and made them work again.

With his mended broom held above his head like a sword, he shouted: “I am Sand, lord of this kitchen!”

Even though when he said it out loud, he could hear how silly it sounded, he knew that was incomplete. There was no one here to challenge his rule, no one here to tell him otherwise.

“Lord of this kitchen, and lord of this castle!” he yelled. It wasn’t even a bit satisfying; the kitchen had high ceilings to let the heat rise, but the sound didn’t really echo.

Broom still held aloft, Sand ran into the great hall, and stood before the broken phoenix and swan crest. “I am Alexandre!” he shouted to the rafters. “And I am lord of this castle!”

His voice rang out and returned. It was incredibly satisfying.

And no one disagreed.

Yet.

DARK

PERROTTE WOKE IN DARKNESS IN A CRYPT OF STONE, with no memory of ever having died.

She knew she woke from death, not from sleep. This knowledge dwelled with her, dwelled *within* her, deep in her bones, and even deeper in her mind.

She did not move for the longest time. She did not think that she *could* move. She felt dry, withered even, and she felt that her skin drew moisture from the stones around her.

She knew it was dark, yet she could see the minutest details of the stone of the niche where she lay. Darkness did not matter. Strange; there had been a point not that long ago, when she was small, when she had been frightened of the dark, when she had been scared to death—

Well, not *to* death. She had died of something else entirely. She knew that; she knew fear had not killed her.

Yes, she had once been afraid of the dark, but now the dark was friendly. She had spent much time in the dark, and it was no enemy. Darkness had simply been a place to rest before returning to the world.

It was troubling. Why had she not been in Heaven? Had she been such a sinful child after all, that she had been consigned to Purgatory instead?

Before waking here, now, Perrotte would have been frightened or troubled by this line of thought, but nothing really frightened her anymore.

Timeless time passed. Her fingertips twitched at her sides, then her wrists moved. Her chest rose and fell. Her lips and throat were so dry. She swallowed convulsively, barely finding the moisture in her mouth to do so. A taste lingered on her tongue, a flavor left behind in a mouth so arid it might as well be a tomb in a desert. What was the flavor? Sweet yet tart. Fresh yet moldering. Living yet dead.

Memories flashed through her mind like summer lightning. They were there, the memories of being dead, waiting to be coaxed down from the clouds.

And before *that*? Before being dead, what did she remember of dying?

Those memories are behind the door.

She imagined climbing off the stone couch where

she rested and staggering to her feet. She didn't move her legs yet, though. She lay still, breathing, remembering how to breathe, remembering how to live, and trying not to dwell too much on the whys and wherefores.

She had died, and then she had undied. That was all there was to it.

5

ANVIL

BY THE NEXT MORNING, SAND WISHED THERE REALLY was someone else in the castle, someone to challenge his dominion over it. Just a little bit.

He was terribly lonely. Growing up in the little house attached to the smithy across the valley, with his stepmother's drying herbs hanging from every rafter and a pair of younger half sisters constantly underfoot, he had always longed for just a little quiet and privacy. But now he drowned in quiet and privacy, and found himself talking out loud—to himself, to his falcon, to the objects he repaired, to the rooms he set right.

Sand stayed as busy as he could, because when he wasn't busy, he found himself climbing to that empty, highest room of the castle, to look out across the valley of cherry orchards and asparagus fields to his parents' house. It was too far away to see his father, Agnote, or either of his sisters with any clarity, but he could sometimes make out figures moving around, and the sight comforted him.

In the other direction, he strained to catch sight of his grandparents' house but he could only see the chimney and the smoke from Grandmère's kitchen fire.

Discontent, he turned back to studying his father's house, squinting to see more clearly. Would anyone ever look across and see him staring back? Would anyone ever see the smoke from his fires and think: Perhaps that is where Sand has gone?

He wished that he had not spent the last year arguing with his father.

For twelve years, he had agreed with his father about his life's plan. He was not meant to be a blacksmith, no matter how much he wished it so. He worked in the smithy when he could, learning as much as his father would allow; but most days, he was forced to walk down the hill to study as much reading, rhetoric, and philosophy as the village priest would provide—which, thankfully, was not much. His father wanted him to go to university someday, and Sand never disagreed.

But then Grandmère had sprained her ankle, and

Sand had been sent to spend a few weeks helping out his grandparents. Commonly in a smith's household, all its able-bodied members helped out with the forge from time to time; Grandmère herself and Sand's own mother had both been accomplished smiths. Likewise, Sand had been pumping the bellows for his father since he could remember, and had first struck hot metal before he could write his own name. So Sand was able to stand in Grandmère's stead in the smithy, and help Grandpère with his commissions.

Those weeks at his grandparents' house, uninterrupted by his father's constant talk of university, had changed his life. After working with his even-tempered grandfather and learning at his side; after hearing the stories of his mother, who had died of fever when he was young, and his uncle, who had died in the League War; after hearing his grandfather's profound and resolute sadness that none of his blood would carry on his work, Sand wanted nothing more than to become a blacksmith.

When he returned home, Sand told his father: He would not go to Paris or Angers. He would not study at a university. He would become his father's apprentice. And if not his father's, his grandfather's.

They had fought about it that day, and for many days to come. It had been a most unhappy year in the little house across the valley.

Their last fight had come to pass because his

father had turned down a huge commission, claiming he didn't have the hands for it. His father wouldn't take an apprentice, nor would he let Sand work on the commission with him. Sand didn't see the sense in it.

"You're too busy with your learning to help me with the job. So don't think about it," his father had said.

"It's all I think about!" Sand had cried, before he ran from the house. Once out on the grass silvered with winter's last frost, he felt like he could breathe again. So he kept running, toward his grandparents' house three miles away, until he stopped at the spring of Saint Melor.

Agnote must be so worried.

He prayed to Saint Eloi to send his stepmother a sign. "Let her know I am safe. Let her know I am well. And if you have time, let her know I require rescue! Let her look to the smoke here at the Sundered Castle and worry on it!"

WITH THE KITCHEN IN hand, Sand wanted to figure out the other necessities of life, like bathing and sleeping and fresh clothes. Everything depended on tools, however. For half of the castle's mending, Sand needed a working smithy; for a quarter, he needed needles and thread; and for the final quarter, he needed all manner of things he didn't even know about.

What Sand knew of needle-making, he could balance on the end of one finger. Fortunately, he found a few needles that were only bent, not snapped, and those he put to good use with the longest segments of thread he could find, sewing up his bedclothes and a few outfits to change into, as his ash-rubbed clothing grew smelly.

Getting the smithy back together, however, would take time. Charcoal burned just as well in halves as it did whole, so that was one problem avoided. The magical force that had sundered everything in the castle had occasionally made some very odd choices in its destruction—Sand found a hammer that had been broken only at the wooden handle and not any of the metal parts, and another hammer whose handle was whole while the metal was broken. He spent what seemed like endless hours fitting the right parts together.

Reconstructing one of the forges wasn't so hard, either—Sand just had to stack the broken bricks and wet some clay to line the forge. And fixing the bellows presented little difficulty; he'd mended bellows with Grandpère before. As for an anvil, unless he could figure out how to weld one back together or recast a new one, he was going to have to work with what he had. He had seen blacksmiths work off metal-wrapped bricks in a pinch, and half an anvil was better than *that*.

Smiths working with very heavy items used small wooden cranes to raise those items into place onto their anvils. Both of the cranes in the smithy were more like firewood, postsundering, but with a little tinkering, some braided linens acting as rope once more, and a great deal of effort, Sand managed to raise one of the anvils into place on the only ash log left mostly whole in the smithy.

Sand almost danced a little jig as he untied the rope from his new anvil, then stepped back to examine his nearly orderly corner of the smithy.

"Well, you're nothing special," he told the anvil, grinning. "Just a plain, square anvil, and one worse for wear." He rubbed the corner that had been sheared off in the sundering. "But you have a smooth face, and you're ready for hot metal and heavy hammers."

His grin faded slowly as he realized something.

"And you're ready for cold metal and lighter strikes as well," he said, smacking his forehead. He picked up his hammer. "I—I'm an idiot."

He strode away from the forge, stomping into the kitchen with anger that was directed only at himself. He collected a half dozen broken copper things, and whacked them quickly into a shape. Copper required no heat to reshape, just a strong hammer—and he could have had a strong hammer his very first day in the castle, if he'd taken the time to mend one.

"Idiot," he said again, sighing, even though he was glad to have a cup to drink from, and a proper cooking pot. Coppersmithing was no less an art than blacksmithing—he just hadn't thought of it.

His ill humor faded as he took his first drink from a proper cup. Then he returned to the smithy and fired up the forge. He set to work on repairing a set of tongs, dreading how slowly the work would go. He would have to let the metal completely cool every so often—for he had no tongs to save his fingers. But once he was striking orange-yellow iron again, and watching black scale crowd to the surface of the steel and fall away, he felt like himself for the first time since he'd awakened in the ashes of that long-dead fire.

The hammer blows seemed to match the beating of his heart, or maybe his heart was timing itself to the hammer. It didn't matter which. He had a smithy, and everything he needed to do some proper mending.

DAY BY DAY, SAND's wrist improved, and by the time he had a working forge, all he could see of his wound was a raised, red-purple scar where the thorn had gone in. Sometimes, in the middle of the night, he would awaken with a start, as a flash of pain shot through his wrist. But for the most part, his scar was quiescent.

It was time to challenge the thorns again.

He tried burning them a few more times, but it didn't matter how big he made the fire, the thorns immediately extinguished it.

Now that he had a forge and an anvil, though—he could mend a shovel and dig underneath the wall.

But he did not dig far before he realized that the thorns had roots as deep as the branches were high, and as lively. He backfilled his hole of squirming, reaching roots as fast as he could, and turned the shovel to another purpose.

Spring warmed the ground, and outside the castle, signs of new, green life dotted the distant trees and fields. Sand harvested seeds from inside dried apples and pears, whole kernels of grain on wheat sheaves, partial onion bulbs and garlic sets, and peas in broken pods, all dried. He planted them carefully in the gardens and watered them, hoping he might someday have fresh food.

But the next day, it snowed, a return to winter in the midst of early spring.

The chill in the air wasn't very intense, in spite of the layer of wet snow. The early spring mud hadn't hardened at all underneath the layer of white, and Sand left dark footprints everywhere he walked in the wetness.

Sand scooped up a handful of snow and packed it into a ball. His fingers numbed quickly, but he held onto the ball for a long moment, wondering to what purpose he could put it. If he had a pressing need for ice in midsummer, he could take a bunch of these snowballs to the dungeons and store them layered with cloth or sawdust. But to what purpose? What did he need ice in midsummer for? And he would have to store *many* snowballs to keep them from being lost to melt too quickly. It was cool in the dungeons but not cold.

"Still, something to remember for next winter," Sand said. His own voice startled him—not so much that he was talking to himself, for he did that several times a day just so he wouldn't be so lonely.

What startled him was the fact that he was thinking he might be here through next winter. And that next winter, he might want to think about preparing for the following summer.

It made a dull ache in his belly, to think like that.

So he didn't think like that. He stopped thinking about *time* and *people* and *loneliness*. He might have to plan for years, for winters and summers to come, and he had to plan on relying on himself—but he didn't have to *think* about it.

Sand's work continued. He mended tools in the smithy. He made nails. He mended some of the furniture in the great hall, haphazardly and with more nails than a good carpenter would use.

Slowly, he learned how wood and fabric fit together. They had their own rules, less complicated than the rules governing metal, but important rules just the same. He mended privy seats and doors, cushions and pillows. Life became more comfortable as he worked his way through the castle, focusing on the rooms he used the most.

In the evenings, he told Merlin the falcon all about his day's works, and felt the better for having something with ears to talk to, even if he couldn't see the ears beneath feathers, even if the ears didn't hear him.

His scrap piles grew, and he felt that the number of things left unrepaired seemed much larger than the number of things he managed to repair, and yet rooms began to fill back up with mended things. Anything that couldn't be fixed could help fix something else.

Piece by piece, room by room, Sand slowly cleaned and repaired, sorted and mended the castle.

In the castle's chapel, he restored the crucifix and resewed the altar cloth. He levered the two halves of the altar back into place.

He saved the most uncomfortable task in the chapel for last, which was attending to the relics. The chapel was the home to the partial remains of two saints: Sainte Trifine, a mother and princess who had died and been brought back to life, and Saint Melor of the bronze foot and silver hand.

The relics had not made it through the sundering intact. Spilling out of a silver, oval reliquary were the old, wizened lumps of Sainte Trifine's heart, split into two; and mixed with the shards of a larger golden reliquary lay the broken head of Saint Melor.

Sand could do nothing, really, that didn't feel horribly sacrilegious, but leaving these things broken seemed worse than sacrilege. So he poured a few hot drops of beeswax between the bits of Sainte Trifine's heart and, steeling himself, pushed the halves together with his fingertips. Then, with a small hammer, he beat back into shape the silver reliquary that housed her heart.

For Saint Melor, he did not think candle wax would be the proper medium for putting the skull to rights, so he simply repaired the reliquary and set the pieces of the skull back inside.

He wiped his fingers with his shirt hem for a good ten minutes after, and he never did quite get rid of the waxy feeling of Sainte Trifine's heart that day.

His stomach grumbled, and he turned back toward the kitchen. He'd mended the door at last, and when he opened it, a flurry of feathers flew at his head.

Sand yelled in surprise, and ducked. A line of fire sprang into being across his face. The noise of wings passed into the courtyard, and he turned, tracking a frantic little falcon as it circled the courtyard twice, then flew up, up, up, straight into the sun.

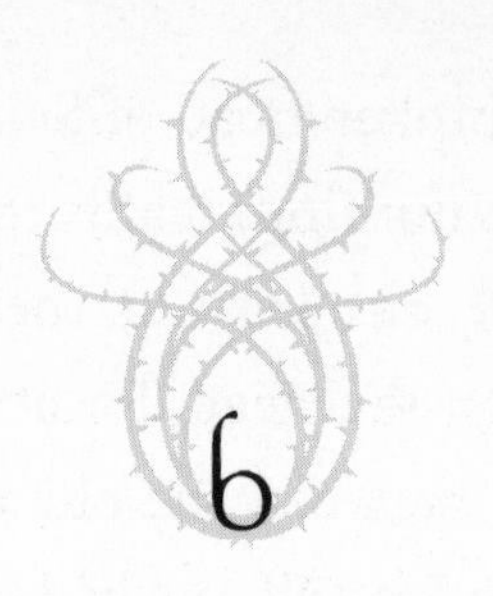

6
Water

SAND STILL COULDN'T ENTIRELY BELIEVE THAT Merlin the falcon had come to life and flown away, but there were two indisputable facts that proved it: No longer did a stuffed falcon sit on the mantel, and a thin scrape from the escaping bird's claw now lined his cheek.

He could not think overly much about it. What logic was there to follow? The falcon had been dead—indisputably dead, stuffed and mounted and then broken in the sundering—and now it was alive, the first living thing that Sand had seen inside the castle. It made no sense! Not a single, solitary lick of sense.

Sand went on about his day of mending and cleaning and straightening, while the scratch on his face went from burning pain to dull stinging and then to vaguely annoying. Spring returned by noon. The snow melted everywhere that the sun reached, and feeble winter hung on only in shadows.

Sand settled down with pieces of several different buckets and finally considered how to take them apart and mend them into one, good bucket. He was no cooper, but the hard parts of bucket construction, the parts he knew little about—the selection of wood, the cutting and dressing of the staves, and all the words of the trade that he'd heard but didn't really know, like flagging and jigging—were already done for him. He just had to bring the staves tight together again so that water couldn't leak out.

"And what does it matter?" he muttered to the bucket staves laid out before him as he inexpertly tried to fit them. "I'm no worse off than I was before if this doesn't work."

The first few times, it did not work. Buckets were sized by eye, and none of the staves from the candidate broken buckets quite fit together. Sand cautiously shaped a few of the staves with a half-chisel, knowing it wasn't exactly the right thing to do but not sure how to do what he needed to. The real craft of coopering lay in this part of the process, but the magic of it lay in the next step, when coopers used steam heat and iron truss hoops to shape their barrels and buckets. Since he possessed no real artistry with wood, Sand decided to move on to heat and iron. He understood heat and iron better than he understood anything else.

One of the buckets still had a proper base hoop intact and in place. Sand added staves from other buckets, and added an upper hoop from yet another bucket, slipping it down over the outside of the staves. He dug out a small pit in the smithy and built a good fire in it, then set half a tilted cauldron of water to boil. He placed the bucket over the cauldron, waiting for the steam to soften the wood. It took a while, but when eventually he started hammering truss hoops, driving them down over the widening staves, it all came together.

It should not have worked. His joins between staves were terrible; he did not possess the right tools; he did not fully understand the principles of making a watertight bucket; and this sort of work took at least a journeyman's eye to supervise a raw novice like him. But somehow, once he had hammered the last truss into place, he had made something watertight.

Or so he assumed. The bucket held his small amount of test water just fine. But when he threw the bucket down the well, attached to his bed-linen rope, the weight of the full bucket was too much, and the linens drew apart. He lost half the rope and the whole bucket down the well.

He wasn't sure if he wanted to laugh or cry. A whole day's work on one bucket, and it was gone down the well! And yet—the bucket had obviously held enough water that it had been too heavy for his makeshift rope.

He laughed first. It had hardly been a rope at all; just some tied-together sheets, not even braided, let alone twisted and back-twisted as befit proper rope.

And then he cried, just a little. Agnote would have pointed out his rope problem long before he lost a bucket, and kept him from such a stupid mistake. Grandpère would have suggested taking the time to braid the sheets on the first day, even when he'd been so thirsty—just in case his first linen sheet-ball had likewise been too heavy and snapped his line.

His father, though—if he had been the one to supervise this whole experiment, he wouldn't have warned him about the rope. He would have said, "Do you think there is anything you are forgetting?" and if Sand had said, "No," he would have just nodded and let Sand proceed, watching from under his heavy brows. He would have let the rope snap, yes; and afterward, he would have shrugged, saying, "And what sort of caution would you have learned if I had stopped you?"

And then his father would have had Sand make a better rope while he went to look for a hook, and together, they would have tried to fish the bucket out of the well.

He missed his father then, keenly, so keenly it was like a hundred knives pierced him. In spite of all the arguments, in spite of his father's ridiculous ambitions for Sand that made no sense . . . he wished he could be home.

Sand crossed himself and prayed to Saint Eloi and his name saint and to the Seven Founder Saints of Bertaèyn: "If the Lord grants me the gift of leaving this place, if I ever rejoin my family, I will not gainsay Papa again. I'll go to university, as he wants. I will obey him in all things."

The feeling of the knives didn't go away entirely—in that moment, he missed his grandfather and Agnote. He missed his little sisters, too; they were such pains at times, but right now, all he could think about was the way they blinked at him with their large blue eyes, so adoring and fond, as if he could do anything.

He pushed the feelings away. He didn't really have time to mope, did he? He'd better go about fishing that bucket out of the well.

Unfortunately, there were no hooks to be had—but the castle housed plenty of metal, and a half-functioning smithy, so he would make his own hook. *After* he reworked his bedsheets. Having no rope jack or a ropewalk to twist linen into rope, he decided that a double-thick braid was the wisest course. He settled in, thinking that he would work on the rope until sunset.

But Sand finished no rope that day. That day, everything changed.

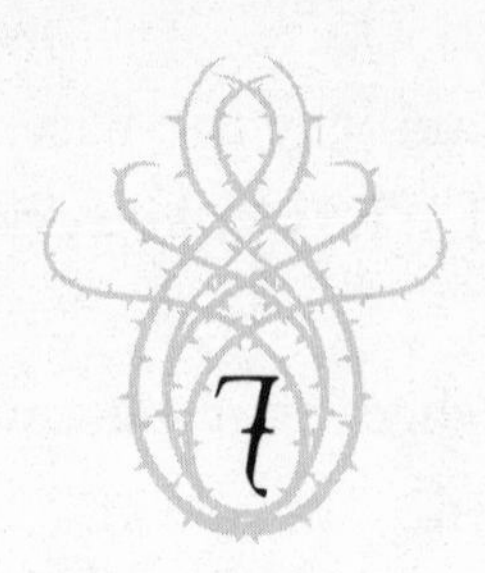

7 Stone

A CRACK IN THE CEILING DIVIDED THE CRYPT IN half, Perrotte noticed. The crack crossed above her, in line with her waist, and her creeping fingertips discovered that the line crossed beneath her as well—a hairline in the stone under her, though much wider above. Light came from the crack in the ceiling, she decided, the dimmest, faintest of lights through the slenderest of cracks, but it kept her from total blindness here in the dark.

She imagined climbing out of her niche and walking upward into the light. She would come to the surface, and oh, how surprised people would be! She imagined her father's and her nurse's happiness at seeing her alive again, and imagined her father's wife's shock and perhaps dismay.

Slowly, Perrotte pulled herself to sitting. Even slower, she put a hesitant foot to the floor. She half stood, a false start, and sat back down. She waited, then tried again. This time she stayed on her feet, and started forward in the dim dark, hands outstretched for balance and to ensure she did not run into something in the shadows. Odd piles of rubble lay about, piles she did not remember.

She reached the stairs out of the crypt and ascended them, stumbling slightly over broken stones. In the chapel, sunlight poured through the colored glass windows depicting the strange life of Saint Melor and his metal foot and hand. She noted without understanding that the glass was cracked.

She wandered out to the courtyard, squinting into the brightness of the sun. She tried to make sense of what had once been her home and was now a shattered ruin. Confusion gave way to bewilderment, which in turn gave way to astonishment. This was Boisblanc, the castle where she'd been born, lived, and grown. Now it was an empty shell, broken in half. The keep was cracked, the earth itself was cracked, and nothing was as she'd left it.

The memory of comforting darkness was fading. She could barely recall those early moments of wakefulness in the stone niche in the crypt. Those memories slipped behind a door in her mind. All that she felt now was thirst. She stumbled to her knees, forced herself up, and went on. Warm blood—living blood—ran from a scrape on one knee, but she tried not to mind. She needed something to drink. She could not think past that need anymore. Wine—in the cellars—cider—in great barrels—ale—

Her feet carried her toward the pantries, and she found nothing there to drink, either. Water. Water. *Water.* She struggled to keep on, staggering out of the kitchen and into the bright sun again, heading down the stairs toward the well.

Water. She might have said it; she might not have. The word was like a call within her. With the well in sight, she fell to the mud.

8

Porridge

A GIRL, DRESSED IN SAFFRON VELVET AND RUSSET silk, with frizzled golden-brown hair flowing from under a small cap, staggered toward Sand across the courtyard. Her hazel eyes were glassy, and her mouth was open.

"Water," she croaked, and fell.

Sand had never moved so fast, but still he didn't manage to catch her before she reached the ground. She thumped sideways into the mud, and Sand felt a twinge of guilt that he hadn't somehow been faster.

A *person*. A *girl*.

The girl from the crypt—yes? She wore the same—

The *dead* girl from the crypt.

Almost, he did not touch her. Almost, he was too

afraid of her sunken eyes and hollow cheeks and the fact that she had been *dead* when last he saw her. But he forced himself to touch her. He turned her over. Her breath was labored, her eyes closed.

She had spoken before she fell—one word. "Water."

He had water. He ran to the kitchen and filled his copper cup. Hand over the cup to catch sloshes, he ran back. He knelt beside her in the mud and dribbled water in her mouth, hoping it would revive her; her eyes fluttered, but did not open. She swallowed the water, though, swallowed all of it, and immediately her sunken skin plumped and brighter colors came to her cheeks and lips.

He dripped more water into her mouth, until she would swallow no more; then, unwilling to leave her in the mud of the courtyard, he hoisted her awkwardly onto his shoulders. She was taller than Sand but lighter than he expected, as light as one of his sisters.

He carried her to his bed in the Count's room, tucking her into his comfortable nest. He built up a fire to take the chill from the air, then hurried down to the kitchen to make her some food. He did not want to leave her alone too long, in case she woke.

He put a good porridge on to cook in a copper pot. He combined oats with dried bits of plum, pear, apple, raisins, and some carefully picked-over crystals of honey. He heated water for washing, then carried porridge and water up to the Count's room. He drew up a stool next to the bed. Dampening a scrap of fine toweling, he washed the girl's hands and face.

This woke her. She stared up at him with frightened yet imperious eyes.

"Who are you?" she asked.

"I am Alexandre, son of Gilles Smith," he answered, withdrawing his hands and folding the bit of toweling he'd used to clean her.

She frowned, sitting up. He pushed back the stool a little, giving her space, while she cast her gaze around the chamber. Nothing broken remained in the room; only items that had been mended had been brought back in.

"Where is my father?"

"Pardon me, but *who* is your father?"

"The Count of Boisblanc, of course." She sat up slowly. "You are here in Boisblanc, and you do not know this, Alexandre, son of Gilles Smith?"

Sand blinked. "Call me Sand," he said, but his mind was ticking over and over. The ruler of Boisblanc was a countess in her own right, but since her husband was a prince of France, most everyone referred to them as the Prince and Princess, not the Count and Countess. The woman everyone still called the Countess was the dowager, the mother of the Princess.

As for the Princess's father, Count Derien of

Boisblanc had died before Sand was born. This girl looked Sand's own age, about twelve or thirteen. She might be the daughter of the Prince, he supposed, but she could not be the daughter of the deceased count. . . .

Well. Except for the fact that until very recently, this girl had been *dead.* And who knew for how long? Maybe her father was a Count of Boisblanc from a hundred or more years ago.

"Um," Sand said, and stood.

"Um," she mimicked, swinging her legs out of the bed, but not yet standing.

"You . . . you were dead, last I saw you," he said.

". . . my lady," she said.

He frowned.

"Address me as 'my lady,' " she said.

He swallowed. She was awfully prickly. But he nodded, trying to maintain an amiable face as he said, "You were dead last I saw you, my lady."

A number of expressions chased across her face in quick succession, and he felt like he only recognized any of them long after they had been replaced. Fury, sadness, grief, despair—he knew those, but there were a dozen others.

"I was," she said, and closed her eyes. "I was dead, and I thought I remembered it—but it's only a memory of a memory anymore."

"How long ago?" Sand asked, but he knew it was a stupid question. "Um, who was the king when you—?"

"The King?" Her lip curled the way only a Breton's lip could when the King of France was mentioned. "Charles. Laughably called 'the Affable' by his sycophants."

The flesh above Sand's eyes prickled. "King Charles the Affable died some twenty years ago. Or so. He hit his head on a doorway and died."

Again, expressions fled across her face so quickly that none ever landed. Humor, perhaps, for the way in which Charles died, and some sort of triumph, but also grief again. Always grief.

"Twenty years?" she whispered. "I've been dead for twenty years?"

Sand was a truth-minded person. "More. It's been more than twenty-five years since the castle was sundered." Then he regretted what he'd said, so he added a late "My lady" to make her feel better.

"What of my duchess?"

"You mean Queen Claude, who is also the Duchess of Bertaèyn?"

"Queen Claude? I mean Duchess Anna!"

"*Queen Anne* died . . ." Sand counted on his fingers, trying to remember the seasons since he and his father had come in from the smithy to find Agnote weeping at the news. "Some three years back."

The girl lay down on the bed and buried her face in his pillow. "That can't be," she said, muffle-voiced. "How old was she when she . . . died?"

Sand had no notion. "She was near to my father's age, I think."

"That is impossible!" The girl sat up again. "Anna and I were born the same year. In another month, I was going to her court to wait on her! She can't be old *and* dead."

"Not so old, when she died, and she had been Queen of France twice over, and mother of two daughters . . ."

"Queen of France." She appeared devastated by this, which Sand understood. The duchy had been trying to slip the yoke of the French for years; Sand's own uncle had died for Bertaèyn's independence. It had been a blow to all her subjects when Anna Vreizh was forced into marriage against her will, to become Anne, Queen of France.

The girl blinked, looking around the room as if seeing it for the first time, eyes lingering on the scratched walls. Her gaze fell to his painstakingly crafted bowl of fruit porridge.

"My lady, I have food for you." He picked up the bowl—more than three-quarters of a bowl, in fact, and a lucky find—and handed it to her.

She wrinkled her nose. "What is this?"

He hesitated to tell her the particulars of where he got food, fearing her disgust. "Porridge?"

"Are you asking me or telling me?"

Abruptly, he was tired of her rude manner. Certainly, she was the daughter of a count. But he was the son of a blacksmith. Blacksmithing might be the craft of a peasant, but smiths had an important lineage and many secrets. And many royals had worked a forge as well; Grandpère used to tell him stories about how Richard the Lion-Hearted of England had worked side by side with his smiths, improving techniques for shaping armor.

He decided: He wasn't going to call her "my lady" anymore. While they were both trapped in this castle, they were on the same footing.

No. Not the same. *Sand* was the lord of this place. He was the one who had started mending it. He was the one setting it aright.

"Eat it or don't eat it," he said abruptly, setting the porridge on the floor beside the bed, tilting the bowl so it didn't spill. "It's as good as any food you can find around here. What's your name?"

She blinked owlishly at him, looking small and young and lost all of a sudden. "Perrotte," she said. "That's my name." And then hesitantly, in a tiny voice, she said, "I'm sorry. I am not treating you well. My mother would be most upset with me. She taught me greater graciousness than that."

Sand had heard plenty of stories about the Countess from other villagers, and he had a hard time imagining the Countess teaching anyone graciousness. But he didn't say anything.

Her voice grew tinier still when she asked, "And my father?"

"The . . . Count of Boisblanc?" Sand stalled.

"Yes," the girl said, eyes narrowing.

"If we are talking about the same Derien, Count of Boisblanc . . . he is dead."

In comparison to her reaction to the news of Queen Anna's death, Perrotte remained much calmer—on the surface. But the way her face went completely calm made him think she was extremely disturbed underneath it all.

He knew only one other person who generally appeared calmer the worse she felt, and that was his stepmother, Agnote. He'd learned how to read the signs of that kind of control. Perrotte's eyes gleamed; she blinked rapidly, and then her eyes were normal again. She breathed deeply, and said in a voice only slightly thickened, "He was injured in the League War. He never healed fully—he was quite ill, and had been for some time, before I—" She stopped speaking abruptly, her face still as composed as if it were shaped from metal.

Sand never knew the right thing to do when faced with grief. He cast about for something else to draw the girl's attention. He handed her a cup of water, and she drank it, wrinkling her nose slightly.

"And my sister?" she asked, returning the cup to him. "Rivanon was newborn. Does she live?"

Her sister, Rivanon! That was the Princess. "Yes. She married a prince of France—we call her the Princess, though she is also our Countess. Your mother yet lives, and though she is the dowager, we all call her the Countess still—"

"She's not my mother," Perrotte said sharply. Sand realized she was shivering. He pulled a mended blanket from the foot of the bed and drew it around her shoulders, then handed her the bowl of porridge again.

Perrotte bowed her head for a moment; Sand thought she was praying, until he saw that one finger was rubbing the roughness of the bowl's broken lip, over and over.

"What happened here?" she whispered. "The castle is so empty, and so many things are broken . . ."

Sand shrugged with one shoulder. "I don't know. There are stories—stupid ones. Everyone says that there was an earthquake, and the castle was abandoned—but!" He leaned forward a little. "I don't believe that story anymore, not any of it!"

"Why?" she asked.

He gestured at the bowl. "*That* could have been broken in an earthquake, certainly—fallen off a shelf, lost a big chunk . . . But there is so much else here that could never have been damaged that way. Sheets torn into pieces! Saddles and blankets rent in two. And . . . whole anvils, just torn in half! Something happened here, but it wasn't any simple earthquake."

Perrotte stirred restlessly on the bed, then subsided.

"What?" he asked.

"Nothing," she said. "That memory of a memory . . . Or maybe a dream."

She couldn't remember the sundering, Sand thought. She had already been dead—hadn't she? But on the other hand, she had been the only thing in the castle that *wasn't* broken into at least two pieces, so maybe she had been alive when the castle broke—or maybe she had died in the sundering, and they had left her in the crypt and then fled?

He hadn't checked on the other bodies in the crypt, though. He'd been afraid to.

He didn't want to say these things to her, however. It seemed, well, rude, to refer to her dead body, or to mention how he had found her in the crypt, and returned her to the niche and straightened her in her resting place. It felt like touching someone while they slept without their permission. Agnote had many rules in their house, but only one was truly insurmountable: *Keep your hands to yourself.*

Sand suppressed a shudder and forced himself to stop thinking of dead Perrotte. She was alive now, as alive as he was. Though, whatever magic had done this, whatever magic had resurrected this girl . . . it was as powerful as anything he'd ever heard of, outside of the miracles performed by saints. In fact, it was rather on par with those miracles, and Sand didn't know *what* to think.

Perrotte appeared to be done with her thoughtful meditation over the damaged bowl, and had picked up a spoon, finally eating the porridge he had prepared. He watched her carefully, waiting to see if she made a face, but she kept her expression smoother than ironed silk.

She met his eyes. "Well?" she said sharply, through a mouthful of porridge.

"Well?!"

She swallowed her bite and put the bowl back on the floor. "Why are you here, son of Gilles Smith?" She stared, her eyes catching the afternoon sun in a way that made them look more green than brown. A small vertical crease appeared between her brows, and she pursed her lips. "Gilles . . ."

"Pardon?"

"The shoemaker's boy, his apprentice . . ." She narrowed her eyes. "You look a lot like him. His name was Gilles."

Sand almost fell off the stool. "That—that was my father! He worked in this castle when he was a boy."

"My Gilles was no smith."

"No! After the castle was sundered, he apprenticed with my mother's father."

Perrotte shook her head. "I don't think that was him. He would never have given up shoemaking for something as brutish as blacksmithing."

"I beg your pardon," he said stiffly. "But I think I know my own father. And—" Angry words in defense of blacksmithing leaped so quickly to his tongue that they choked themselves off.

"No, *you* don't understand—he wasn't really strong enough to be a smith. Not that you look strong enough, either." She eyed his arms critically. Sand felt heat rise in his cheeks.

"I'm strong enough," he said. "And Grandpère always says blacksmithing takes strength of eyes and mind more than strength of arm. I'm plenty strong enough in arm. *You* are strong enough."

She looked dubious. "Still," she said. "It is hard to see Gilles as a blacksmith, let alone an old man with a boy my own age."

"Then maybe what you lack to be a smith is not strength of arm but strength of vision," Sand snapped.

"I have terrific vision!" she announced. "I can see eight stars among the Pleaides."

Whatever *that* meant.

"Not vision of the eyes. Vision like imagination," he said. "You—" He stopped himself from saying something mean.

Fortunately for both of them, Perrotte changed the subject. Patting her hair, she asked, almost offhandedly, "So, the Countess. She knows I'm alive?"

Sand straightened his sleeves. "That would be impossible," he said. "No one knows you're alive. At the moment, no one knows *I* am alive. We're trapped in this castle. There's an impenetrable wall of thorns surrounding this place."

If he had expected her to have a horrified reaction to this news, he was sorely disappointed. She just made a sideways grimace with half her mouth, and said, "Impenetrable? I doubt that very much, Alexandre."

"Call me Sand," he said, as was his habit when addressed by his full name. He almost swallowed his tongue in an effort not to stick it out at her.

"And *you* must remember to address me as 'my lady.'"

He just bared his teeth in response, a fake smile. He would not stick his tongue out at her. But no way in Heaven was he doing *anything* she told him.

Hook

Even though Sand was sure that Perrotte was his age, he found himself trailing after her like she was one of his littlest sisters and he'd been set to child-minding duty. Certainly she was taller than a toddler, though no less obstinate, and honestly, she walked about as well. She had not regained her full strength, and she stumbled at times, weaving back and forth as she made her way through the castle.

He refused to offer her his arm at first. She would not take his advice to stay in bed, to trust him that nothing she would see today could not be seen tomorrow—just unpeopled rooms full of dryness, stillness, and broken things. But she trudged on, stubbornly clinging to walls to rebalance herself on the way, peering into rooms as if hoping each time to see someone, something. . . .

Finally, he couldn't stand the situation anymore, and offered her his arm for support—but she refused him. She just marched on, all the way from inner courtyard to middle to outer, down to the castle's gates.

At the end of the passageway to the outermost gate, Perrotte flung open the night portal and stared silently at the wall of thorns. When she reached for them, Sand swatted her hand away. "Don't touch!"

Exactly like minding a toddler.

She jerked her hand back and glared at him. "You. Do not. Touch me."

"It's just—" He pulled up his sleeve and showed her the purple-red scar on his arm. It was hard to make out in the dim light of the tunnel, but the scar appeared puffier than usual. It also itched horribly just then. He scratched it. "One of the thorns got me, and I almost died from it." He didn't know how to explain any better.

Perrotte looked dubious, but kept her hands folded as she bent forward to examine the thorns. One branch of the brake lifted slightly—it could have been the wind, but it could just as easily have been some malevolence—and snagged at her head, catching her small cloth cap and a few trailing tendrils of her hair.

"Ow!" Perrotte said, and lifted her hand to her head to disentangle herself.

"No, stop!" Sand shouted, reaching for her hand. He hesitated a bare fraction of a second, torn between helping her and obeying her order not to be touched. She heard him, though; her hand froze just in time, hovering over the thorns twining in her hair.

She dropped her hand and stepped back—but the thorns hung on. Perrotte untied the strings of the cap under her chin, took another step, and then with a vicious jerk, pulled her head away. She grunted. The thorns retained Perrotte's cap and several dozen of Perrotte's golden-brown strands, but she was free.

"God's guts," she swore, rubbing her scalp.

Sand's arm itched furiously. "That was a close thing," he said. "I almost died of blood poisoning when just one thorn got me." He rubbed his old wound, surprised by his casual tone.

At the word "poisoning," Perrotte shuddered, staring at the little scrap of silk that had been her cap. Slowly, it was pulled from view by the shifting brambles of the thorn hedge.

Sand scraped at his arm with his fingernails and regarded her curiously. Perrotte slammed shut the portal, spun on her heel, and left the tunnel. In the outer courtyard, she stopped, staring up at the thorns towering over the castle walls. Her eyes seemed unfocused.

"Perrotte?" he asked. "What's wrong?"

"A memory of a memory," she said absently. Her eyes cleared, and she fixed her keen hazel gaze on him. "Well. Here we are, then, trapped in Castle Boisblanc, where everything is broken."

"I've mended a few things," Sand said.

"Surely," she said, almost arrogant.

"Some of which are at the bottom of the well," he said, remembering the bucket he'd lost just before she'd appeared. He didn't want the bucket to become waterlogged, and he certainly wasn't going to wander around child-minding Perrotte all day. He wasn't quite sure how to take his leave of her, so he sketched what he thought might be a courtly bow, and hurried off toward the smithy, muttering, "Excuse me, then," under his breath. And notably, not referring to her as his lady.

"Where are you—" she called after him, but he didn't stop.

He wasn't angry, he told himself. What did her ingratitude and high-handed manner matter? He had things to do. He had a castle to repair.

He was sorting through his pile of scrap metal, looking for something that wanted to be a hook, when she caught up with him. He ignored her, and chose a likely-looking bar of steel, jagged on one end from the sundering. He no longer remembered what the steel had been, or where he had found it before bringing it to his scrap pile, or even if he *had* found it. It might have been in the smithy's scrap pile from the beginning. Iron was too easy to reuse and too hard to wrest from the earth to ever throw any of it away.

"What are you—?" she began, but he cut her off by noisily shoveling charcoal into the forge.

"I'm doing what I do," he said roughly. "I'm mending." He arranged his tinder and kindling, struck a spark, and pumped the bellows, enjoying the way the flames grew into a blaze and roared.

"Mending?"

He didn't say anything. He piled charcoal around the kindling and pumped the bellows furiously. Smoke died away as the kindling was consumed and the charcoal took light; he spread the lit coals wider, and piled more charcoal on top.

He regretted that building a fire was a relatively slow process—he'd like to be at the stage of hammering things before she asked any more questions.

But a good fire couldn't be rushed, even with a bellows. Fortunately, Perrotte said nothing further. He didn't look at her, hoping she would leave if he ignored her. But when he glanced away from the fire, she was still standing there, watching him work.

Once the fire was burning well, Sand thrust the steel bar into the heart of the white-burning coals, and pumped the bellows again. When he pulled the bar out with his tongs, the end glowed a lovely light orange. He set to work with his hammer, shaping the end with a few well-placed strokes, smoothing out the jaggedness to something a little more pointed and purposeful. But not too sharp. It wasn't meant to be a fish hook.

He put the metal back into the heat, this time pushing it farther so as to heat the center of the bar, and pumped the bellows. He glanced at Perrotte. Still, she said nothing—just stood there, with her arms crossed, watching him, as silent and as still as the stone for which she was named.

He began to feel a little bit guilty for his ire, for ignoring her. She had just risen from death, or something like it. She was more than twenty-five years removed from everything and everyone she had known. So what if she was a little prickly? Wouldn't he be a little prickly in her place?

And he couldn't ignore the truth of their situation. She was the first person he'd spoken with or touched in so many days they might have been weeks, and she might be the only person he spoke with or touched for the rest of his life.

Her mere existence changed his world.

He was about to say something to her, but he didn't know *what*. So he angled his heated metal over the edge of the anvil and started bending it, then set it to heat again. Since he was making a mere hook, and it didn't have to hold up to heavy usage, and also because Sand was in a hurry to retrieve the bucket, he chose not to weld the hook's eye.

He got a little lost in the process of working the hook. He came back to the world during the quench. The bubble and hiss of water meeting hot metal was as satisfying as ever.

He looked over at Perrotte, half-expecting her to have finally left. But she still stood there, watching.

"Sand," she said, and now her voice was polite, not prickly. "I would like to learn how to do that."

"Quench something?" he asked, not surprised. Everyone wanted to quench something, at least once.

"No. *That.*" She gestured at the hook. He stared down at where it dangled from his tongs. Surely she didn't mean that she wanted to learn how to make hooks. Hooks were boring. "I want to smith something." Her voice was smaller and less imperious as she added, "I want to mend something."

"Oh," he said, words failing him. He'd never been allowed to call himself even an apprentice blacksmith, but he was well aware of the importance of keeping his grandfather's craft secrets. But Perrotte didn't have to learn anything particularly secret just to mend something.

He remembered then the story of when his father became his grandfather's apprentice. After his father left Castle Boisblanc and shoemaking behind, he had shown up at Grandpère's house. His father had begged to be taken on as Grandpère's apprentice. Grandpère had asked his father the one question, the most important question.

No one needed to ask Sand the question, of course; raised by a smith and with Grandpère's blood in his veins, everyone had known Sand's answer since he was a toddler. And in the end, they hadn't asked him the question because his father had no intention of letting him become a smith. It still rankled him that he'd never been asked. That he never would be asked.

Even so, Sand asked Perrotte the one important question of blacksmithing: "Do you have an imagination?"

10

Bed

PERROTTE BLINKED LIKE A SLEEPY CAT.

"Of course I have an imagination," she said, sounding prickly again.

"Well, great," Sand said. "I've never heard of a good smith who had no imagination."

Perrotte glanced around the dim smithy and ran her finger through the fine layer of dust and soot on the nearest hammer. "It would take some imagination to think of this place as beautiful. Is that why smiths don't clean better? They can imagine away the dirt?"

He shook his head. Dust and soot were part of the job. "I meant—can you imagine how things are going to shift in the fire and under the hammer? Can you look at four pieces of broken metal and think of a way to put them together into something useful? Turning swords into plowshares? That sort of thing."

Perrotte frowned. "I'd like to turn a plowshare into a *sword*," she said. "I'd cut our way out of those thorns, and then use it to run my enemies through—" She bit off her next words and swallowed them.

Sand stared at her, aghast. She met his eyes, defiant.

"What? You don't like bloodthirstiness?" she asked.

"Pardon? No. I'm horrified that you would dull a sword on that thorn brake. I could make you some pretty good hedge shears."

He laughed inwardly as the defiance on her face changed to surprise. But he did wonder who her enemies were—and how he would make sure never to give her a sword and then get on her bad side.

SAND FINISHED BRAIDING HIS rope. It went fast, because when his hands tired, Perrotte took a turn. Then he spent the better part of an hour leaned over the edge of the well, casting his hook into the water again and again, dredging for the bucket. Perrotte leaned over the edge with him, and gave him completely useless advice. Sometimes he caught the bucket and managed to haul it up a couple of feet before it plummeted into the water again.

"Let me have a turn," Perrotte said, and on her

second try, she hooked the handle and triumphantly hauled the brimming bucket upward.

"Beginner's luck," he muttered, then helped her bring the bucket over the well's lip. That she had completed the rescue in no way diminished his enthusiasm for having a real bucket to haul water in. He grinned, carrying his watertight bucket, full, all the way to the kitchen.

It occurred to him: The bucket was far better at holding water than it had any right to be. He'd had tremendous luck in mending so many things over the last week, working far beyond his skills.

And then there was the matter of the hawk.

And the matter of Perrotte.

When it came down to it, Sand had to admit that some sort of magic was at work in the castle.

"This is what we have to eat, then," Perrotte said, interrupting his thoughts. She eyed the kitchen table's collection of broken and dirty foods.

"There's lots of turnips in the root cellar," Sand said, pouring some of the water from his hard-earned bucket into a copper pot. This was so much easier than wringing water out of bedsheets over several trips!

"You should plant a garden," Perrotte said.

"Thank you for the suggestion," he said formally, putting fragments of venison, turnip, and onion into the pot. "I already have. It isn't working out."

"What does that mean?"

"It means, nothing grows here. Nothing lives. Nothing rots, either. Everything just . . . dries out."

Perrotte shook her head. A yawn overtook her, and she looked taken aback by it. She lifted her hand to her mouth belatedly. "I'm sorry. I'm so tired."

Sand glanced at the unplumped chunks of turnip, onion, and venison sitting in the cold water. "Food won't be ready for a while yet."

"I'm more tired than hungry. I can eat in the morning. Good night."

"But—"

She stopped in the doorway. "But what?"

"I don't know—that is—" Sand had mended only one bed. "You can sleep in my bed," he blurted.

Perrotte drew herself up taller, an affronted expression on her face. "Your bed? *Your* bed, in *my* father's room?"

"My bed," Sand said again, feeling his eyebrows knit together. "The one I mended."

"Why haven't you been sleeping in the servant's quarters?" she asked. "Or above the smithy? That would be the place for you."

He gaped at her. "This is *my* castle!"

"No, it's not. I'm the heiress of this castle! May I remind you!"

Sand blinked. Very well, technically it wasn't his

castle. But she was no more the heir of it than he. "No," Sand said. "This castle belongs to your sister."

"She's not my real sister!" Perrotte screamed, face turning bright red, and a vein popping on her throat. Then she clutched her head. "Oh. Ow."

Sand was frozen. He didn't know how to react to this Perrotte, to screaming Perrotte.

He was reminded again of what it was like taking care of his little sisters. This would be a temper tantrum, then? And he should just ignore it?

"I'm sorry," Perrotte whispered, shamefaced.

Sand shrugged, which wasn't an acceptance of her apology.

Perrotte took a deep breath. "I'm sorry," she repeated. "I don't quite have the control on my behavior that I should. And considering I have more than eight-and-thirty years now . . ."

This startled Sand out of his frozen state. "What?"

"Well, if it's been twenty-five years since . . . and I was thirteen at the time . . . So I'm quite, quite old now. I really should know better."

Sand sighed, and stirred the stew again. He really should know better too. Perrotte had awakened from the dead—today. To find everyone she knew and loved gone, and twenty-five years in the past. More than that. She was probably closer to forty than eight-and-thirty.

Even the people who still lived, like his own father,

had changed, perhaps unrecognizably to Perrotte. And she had also discovered that she was trapped in this castle, this broken castle where nothing lived, nothing thrived, with a boy who apparently thought it was his own castle. . . .

"Of course it's your bed for the taking," he said, feeling weary. He bit his lips, thinking about the smith's quarters. He hadn't even gone to look at them, but she was right, that's where he belonged.

"No. No, no. I'm horrible. Your bed is the one you mended. You shall have it. I'll go sleep in my old bed."

"It's not mended," he pointed out.

"How bad can it be?"

"Bad enough. Take the bed. I'll make do in the smith's quarters, as you suggested."

"No!" She stepped toward him. "I'm sorry, Sand. I don't know what I was thinking. I think . . . I think sometimes, even though I hated everything my father's wife did, and regarded her every word as poison she dripped from her tongue, sometimes I think I'm as heartless as she is. And I don't wish to be. Please, Sand. Forgive me." She reached for him.

Awkward, uncertain, he gave her his hand. She squeezed his fingers.

"There, then," she said, and let his fingers go. "*Do* you forgive me?"

"I—" He wanted to shrug, to hold back his forgiveness like a punishment. But this time, he did forgive her. So he nodded. "I do."

"Come with me, to look at my old room."

He banked the fire and lowered the stew pot toward the coals, then went with her to the keep.

"Let's just look," she urged, entering a room he'd taken no particular notice of before.

Sand had never tried to mend any of the things in these chambers. It looked like a whirlwind armed with sledgehammers had taken the room apart, and then picked up some daggers to finish the job. Sand regarded Perrotte's face.

"None of these things are mine," she said, poking into a broken clothes chest. "Someone else was sleeping here—they must have moved all my things out. How long—how long between when I died and the castle was sundered?"

"I've never been sure about that, myself. More than days, less than years?"

"And they gave my room over to . . . ?" Perrotte looked around, picking up bits of torn fabric and investigating them. "I don't know who. Some cousin, maybe. Some relative of my father's wife. Blech."

Sand shook his head.

"Well, I won't have this room! It's not mine anymore."

"Do you want the Countess's room?" Sand suggested, then almost bit his tongue. Of course Perrotte wouldn't want to sleep there.

But she just shook her head.

"Look, you take your father's room," Sand said. "I really will find somewhere else. Maybe this room. It's quite nice." The castle's silver swans and golden phoenixes were painted on the walls here too, though most were scratched through.

"Thank you, Sand," Perrotte said quietly.

PERROTTE HAD WALKED INTO her father's room and lain down in Sand's former bed with the weariness of someone who had been awake for days.

Sand left her, returning to her old bedroom and putting it in some sort of order for his night's sleep. He pulled the mattress off the broken bedframe and stuffed the feathers back inside. He sewed the mattress, using a nail from his purse as an awl and strips of old sheets for thread, tying each of his stitches like Agnote would knot a quilt.

He wandered back to the kitchen to check on the stew. The turnips were beginning to mush up, but the venison was still tough and dry. He ate dried apples and crumbles of cheese instead, then raised the stew off the fire so it wouldn't burn in the night.

Back in Perrotte's old room, he bedded down. The lonely ache in his chest—it hurt worse with Perrotte here. While he felt relieved to have company, she was strange to him. He didn't understand her, nor she him, and he missed his family intensely.

He curled on his side, trying to force himself to sleep. He must have dozed—but then he heard a scrape and a shuffle, smelled the scent of burning beeswax, and sat bolt upright.

Perrotte stood in his doorway—the door needed to be repaired along with everything else in the room—holding a candle. "Sand."

"What?" He clutched at his chest, trying to still his racing heart.

"Will you—will you stand up?"

Confused, he stood.

She walked over and picked up a corner of his mattress with a grunt, then started to drag it awkwardly toward the door.

"What are you doing?"

She didn't say anything, just continued to drag the mattress along. It was a smaller mattress, which was the only reason she could shift it at all, and while his mending job might have been good enough to sleep on, it hadn't been meant to hold together through this treatment. The mattress leaked a trail of feathers behind.

"Perrotte? Just tell me what you're doing and maybe I can help!"

She continued to pull the mattress along, bent nearly in half and breathing heavily. For the sake of not losing *all* the feathers, Sand picked up two of the other corners and lifted, helping her to maneuver through the door. He carried the mattress along behind her, feeling like an attendant carrying the end of a robe in a coronation ceremony.

She led him into the Count's room, then placed the mattress at a right angle to her own—head to head, but perpendicular, so that just a corner of each mattress touched.

Immediately, she crawled under her blankets and snuggled in.

"Get your covers," she said, yawning. "I'm tired."

"What are you—"

"Please, Sand."

He jogged off to the other room, returning with half-blankets piled high in his arms.

"Lie down, Sand."

Hesitant, he lay on his mattress. Perrotte leaned over, and he thought she was going to blow out the candle. But first she seized his hand and held it tightly.

Then she blew out the candle.

Though it was strange, holding her hand across the corners of their mattresses in the dark, Sand had no trouble falling asleep.

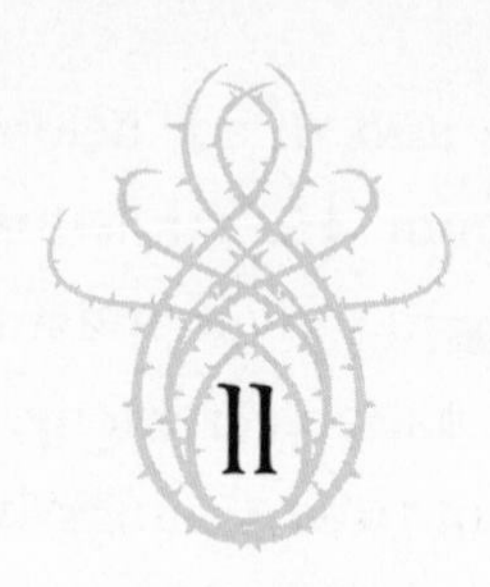

Stars

SAND'S BREATHING EVENED OUT ALMOST IMMEDIately, though his fingers twitched and squeezed Perrotte's in his sleep. Eventually, Perrotte pulled her hand from his, and lay with one palm under her cheek.

She had been so tired before. She had slept only briefly before going to fetch Sand from her old room. Now she was wide awake.

Perrotte had never been a good sleeper, and maybe that was why she lived again. Death was the ultimate night, and she couldn't keep her eyes closed even through that.

Bad sleep was why she had come to be an observer of stars. Before her father remarried, there had been no questioning of her late nights and lazy mornings, or the reason that she needed doors in a tower ceiling and a servant to come prop them open for her, or star charts, or an astrolabe, or a tutor in the natural sciences.

But then her father never recovered from a wound that baffled physicians. The Count felt he needed a son, so he married Jannet, the pious younger daughter of a family from Lower Bertaèyn, who spent more time praying than doing most anything else.

For a while after her father remarried, Perrotte's life had remained much as it had been. But slowly over the months, Perrotte realized that secret ice lurked in her new stepmother's otherwise pleasant manner—narrow ice, tiny ice, that seeped slowly into every crack and crevice between people and widened them.

The plan for sending Perrotte away to some convent had been sprung without warning; suddenly, her tutor, dear old Efflam, was being sent into retirement, while her father's new wife paced around, ordering servants this way and that to prepare Perrotte for a journey. "You need proper religious instruction before you move out into the world of temptations and trials," Jannet had said. "You need time for spiritual contemplation before you go to the Duchess's court."

There had been no time to appeal to her father; the Count had gone to dance attendance on the King in Paris, and wouldn't be back for a month. Perrotte had played chess with Efflam for years; she knew when checkmate was inevitable. All she could do now was guard the supply lines of her retreat, as it were; she had to make sure her special possessions came with her: her books, her maps, and her astronomic instruments. She had packed everything from her tower room, and her chests were prepared when Jannet came in for inspection.

"Sir Bleyz is ready for you, Perrotte. Now, what's all this nonsense?" Jannet asked.

"My things," Perrotte said.

Jannet threw open one chest, then another, glancing with unconcealed disdain for what she found inside. "Unpack them," she ordered Perrotte's maid, Loyse.

Perrotte stepped forward. "No. They are coming with me."

And just like that, Jannet had yanked the first thing out of the closest chest: Perrotte's prized astrolabe, swaddled in silk. Jannet held it against her breast, above her swelling belly.

"I'll be taking this until you learn how to honor your new mother properly. Raoul! Yannig! Come in here. Take these chests away to my rooms. Perrotte will be traveling only with this." Jannet had nudged a single clothes chest with her foot.

The servants had all obeyed Jannet. How could

they not have? She was their Countess; Perrotte would be the heir only until Jannet produced a son, which she might do in the next few months.

Years later, in a room not far from the site of her dispossession, Perrotte pushed the memory away and sat up, groping for her candle. Sand's breathing didn't shift. She went to the hearth and crouched to light the taper from the embers.

Shielding her eyes from the light, she left the room. She wanted to see the stars.

She wondered if her old astrolabe and any of her other possessions were still in the castle. She was afraid to find them, though; they must be broken like everything else.

Perrotte reached the castle's courtyard, and stumbled out into the mud, bare feet squelching coldly. She looked up, finding "the shining Bears at the height of the sky," as one long-dead Latin philosopher put it, the stars that never rose and never set. The constellation of the larger bear, or as everyone who was *not* a dead Latin philosopher called it, the Plough, contained seven stars, by most counts. But Perrotte always looked for, and always found, the two-part star in the Plough's handle, a double star that most people never noticed: a star and her sister.

She thought of her own sister then, who had been newborn when Perrotte returned from the convent.

She felt warmth toward this unknown sister, and guilt. Perrotte had seen Rivanon exactly once, and what she felt now made no *sense* to her, and not because Perrotte lacked imagination, but because it did not seem that anything that could have grown inside of Jannet could cause such feeling in Perrotte's heart. She was a rotten older sibling, a poor protector. Perrotte had been trapped, first by death, now by thorns, and she had left Rivanon alone to be raised by Jannet.

It struck her then afresh, like biting down on a tooth she'd forgotten she'd broken: the overwhelming grief and the horrible wonder of having been dead. The feeling of loss and fear were strong, even though her memories of the darkness and the stone beneath the chapel were fading. Each time she remembered, it was as though another layer had been scraped from a parchment, turning inked words and images into so much dust.

Her memories of the time before *that* also grew fainter. Somewhere, somehow, she had eaten something. Someone had spoken to her, in the darkness of death; a soft hand had brushed her forehead; she had felt a mother's love in that moment, when she had been fed something sweet yet tart, fresh yet moldering. Perrotte remembered: *a woman's face—her brown eyes—a red seed—*

It had all happened in a place so dark that it was

hard to remember anything, a place so deep that it was starless.

Except there were stars.

Her feet itched to climb the tower stairs up to her old observatory room, but her legs wouldn't take her. So she stayed in the courtyard, tilting her head back, back, back, and turned wide eyes to the stars.

She tried to be as still as possible, but her heartbeat rocked her back and forth, back and forth. She swayed on the balls of her feet just a little. At first she fought the rhythm, trying to be stiller than still. But stars were not still; they had their movements just like the rest of the living universe.

So Perrotte let her body rock with the beating of her heart, while her mind whirled with the circling of the stars, until dawn faded them away.

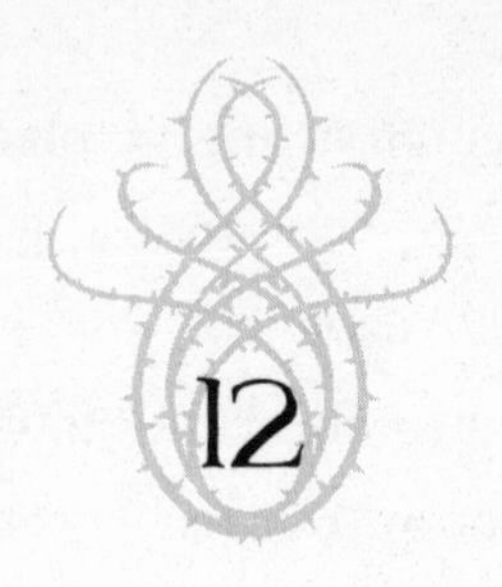

12

Tower

SAND OPENED HIS EYES. HE FACED A DIFFERENT WALL than usual. He frowned, confused.

Then he remembered Perrotte.

He sat up, twisting to look at the mattress cornered with his. Perrotte wasn't there.

He jumped from bed and went to find her, willing his heart to stop its frantic beating. He hadn't dreamed her. He hadn't imagined her. And she wasn't dead again, just because he'd taken his eyes off her for the night. He *would* find her.

He didn't have to go far; Perrotte was in the kitchen, which was warm with the scent of the fire and cooked venison. Perrotte was crouched over the pot, occasionally stirring the stew. She smiled at him when he came in, and his heart settled.

"Good morning," she said.

He nodded, not really sure what to say. He wanted to ask why she'd moved his mattress to the Count's room the night before. He wanted to ask her why she'd held his hand. He thought he knew why, that she'd simply been lonely and scared. But he'd thought he understood things about girls before, and been proved wrong nearly every time.

He served them both bowls of stew, giving her the spoon while he ate with his hands. While he was thinking about how to phrase his questions, Perrotte asked, "Are there any herbs?"

"All dried up and withered away, as far as I can tell," Sand said. "But you are welcome to look."

"Ah. But at least there are onions and garlic. Though . . ." She picked up an onion piece and knocked it against the table. It rustled more than knocked. "So dry. That's how I felt when I woke: dry."

When she "woke." Sand supposed there was some value in talking about it like that, in not saying "dead." Christ and several of his saints had resurrected people. Sand wondered how *they* had all referred to that process of coming back to life. Maybe it felt like waking.

A cold thought overcame him. *He* had woken, in the fireplace. He had not known how he'd gotten there—could he have been dead first?

But—but no. He would know. Wouldn't he?

Perrotte poked at her stew. "What was your life like, Sand? Before?"

He shrugged, sipping broth from the bowl before scooping up a chunk of turnip with his fingers. "I hoped to apprentice with my father, but I guess that was never going to happen."

"How do you mean?"

"He wanted me to leave Boisblanc. He didn't intend for me to become a blacksmith. He made me learn to read, and study every day with the village priest. Papa meant for me to go to a university and study there."

"The village priest? Why not send you to a cathedral school?"

"I don't know. My father never told me. We lived too far from a cathedral school? We had too little money?"

"Cathedral schools are free—but hard to gain entrance to."

"I don't think my father ever tried to get me into one."

"And what would he have you study at university?"

"Papa didn't even know that much! I used to ask him the same question. He would say, 'Study what you like!' And I would tell him that I wanted to stay home and 'study' blacksmithing, and he would get angry. We fought all the time about it. It didn't matter how ridiculous his dream was, he wanted it. But me, go to Paris? Or even Angers? Show up at the city gates, alone? And find tutors? With what money? With what sponsors? Even if someone took pity on me, they would not be inspired by my intellect. I am terrible at reading Latin."

"I could teach you to read better."

"I don't want to read better! Everything I want to know, a smith can teach me. Without a book." Sand laughed, and noticed how bitter he sounded. "I love blacksmithing, and my father refused to teach me any more of it. I used to sneak over the fields in the early morning while my father slept and have lessons with my grandpère."

"Why did your father want you to go away so badly?"

"I've only wondered that my whole life."

"Your stepmother?" Perrotte guessed. "She didn't want you around?"

"Agnote? No! Agnote loves me. She's tried to make peace between us since I was little. She doesn't understand my father either."

"Your mother—died in childbirth?"

"That would be easy to understand, wouldn't it? If my father didn't want me around because I killed my mother by being born? But no—poor Maman died when I was a toddler, from a summer fever." He scrubbed a hand through his hair, noting how long it had gotten since he'd awakened in the castle. Only as he lowered his arm did he realize his hands trembled. "My father doesn't even seem to want my little half sisters around. During our last fight, he said not going to university was selfish, because after a few years, I could find educated men to marry my sisters to." He shook his head.

"Parents never make any sense," Perrotte said, almost to herself.

Sand wanted to disagree, but the specter of his last fight with his father hung before him, and he had no heart to argue otherwise right then.

Perrotte put aside her mostly full bowl. "Have you tried contacting the outside world?"

"I build a fire every day. If anyone has noticed the smoke, it hasn't led to any sort of rescue or even basic investigation that I have seen."

Perrotte looked thoughtful. "We could hang a sheet from a tower window," she said. "In case . . . in case for whatever reason they aren't seeing the smoke, or are just imagining some silly reason for it to exist. A sheet from a tower window would look too strange to ignore or explain away. I think someone would see it and know we wanted rescuing, if we did that."

Sand shrugged. Hanging a sheet couldn't hurt, although he didn't think it would help. He'd lived in sight of the castle his whole life, and no one ever really looked at it, except maybe small children. In addition to the sundering and the thorns, the determined ignoring of the place by the outside world was like part of the castle's curse. "We have sheets aplenty, and no shortage of tower windows," he said.

"Good! Let's go."

"Are you done eating? I'm not done eating."

"I'm full."

He was dubious. She'd had barely five bites.

"You could fetch a sheet while I finish," Sand told her, and she went off.

He grabbed his spoon back. He chewed an astringent chunk of turnip, chasing it quickly with a bite of venison. He did not look forward to a time when turnips might figure more prominently in their diet.

He was licking the last bits of stew from the bowl when Perrotte returned with half a bedsheet. Sand took her to the smithy to scrounge up some nails, then led the way upstairs to the strange little room at the top of the tallest tower.

He went directly to the window overlooking the valley, inhaling the fresh breeze from the fields. But when he turned to ask Perrotte to hold one end of the sheet, she was standing stone-still at the edge of the stairs.

"Perrotte? Are you all well?"

"This room," she whispered. He drew closer, and saw tears brimming in her eyes. "This was my most favorite room in the whole castle. This room was my observatory."

"Observatory?"

"I used to study the stars from here. Until *she* took it all away. What did she do with my things?" She made a half-hearted gesture, as though waving at objects that were no longer there.

"She who?"

Perrotte shook her head confusedly. "My father's wife."

Her stepmother? Sand could not imagine Agnote taking away his favorite things. Not more than temporarily, as a punishment for a true misdeed. It was against her nature.

But the suddenness of Perrotte's stone stillness and her tears made no sense to Sand. "Did you just remember that all your stuff was gone?" he asked. "Had you forgotten about it until we came up here?"

"No." Perrotte twisted her hands together. "I remembered that. I wanted to see this room again anyway. What I didn't remember . . ." Her breath caught on a deep, shuddering sob.

Sand's heart wrung itself for her. He didn't think he had cried that hard since he was a small child, but he still remembered how it felt.

"What I didn't remember 'til now," Perrotte said at last, "is that this is the room where I died."

Forge

"I'm sorry," Sand said, his voice roughened by he knew not what emotion. There were too many feelings inside of him to know which one was making it hard to speak. Mostly, though, he did feel sorry for this girl who had been dead—or had she merely been broken, like the things in the castle?

"It's not your fault. You didn't do anything," Perrotte said, wiping away the last of her tears. She looked around the room as if suddenly, all the missing things would reappear.

"I meant, I feel sorrow *for* you."

She choked on whatever she tried to say in response to that, and turned abruptly, leaving the room. Sand returned to the task of hanging the sheet out the window before heading down after her.

Sand didn't know if Perrotte wanted to be alone or not, but he knew *he* did not want to be. He had spent too many days by himself to give up on even prickly Perrotte. But he didn't know where she'd gone. He looked for her in the kitchen, in the great hall, in the Count's bedroom, but each room was as silent as when he'd haunted the castle alone. Where had she fled to?

He tried the chapel next. Perhaps she had gone to pray. But no one knelt there before the repaired crucifix, or the cracked statues of Saint Salomon and Saint Melor, or any of the relics.

Sand peered into the dark rectangle of the entrance to the crypt, then closed his eyes, listening for any sign of her presence. He heard nothing, but—what *would* he hear, exactly? Her breathing, from all the way down the limestone stair?

Reluctantly, he descended a few steps. The darkness seemed to reach for him. Panic thrummed in his chest. He hurried back into the chapel and lit the stub of an unmended beeswax taper. Armed with light, he descended into the dark to find Perrotte.

He crept all the way to her niche where the crack in the earth ran: empty. He let out a chuffing breath of relief. Turning away, he wondered what he had expected to find—Perrotte crying? Perrotte praying?

Perrotte lying on her stone slab, arms folded as if in eternal rest?

He hurried upward into light, chiding himself. Really? He had expected her to go to the crypt? If *he* were awakened from death, the last place he would go was down *there*.

He shivered. "Never mind that thought, Sand," he muttered.

But as he searched the castle without finding her, his worries grew. He began to wonder not where Perrotte was, but if he had imagined her entirely, both dead in the crypt and then come to life? Was he so lonely that he'd begun to have waking dreams just to feel less alone?

He decided to start over, in the last place he'd seen her, in case she'd stolen back to the observatory while he searched elsewhere. But that room remained as empty as ever, the only movement from the bedsheet gently lifting and falling on the early spring breeze.

Perplexed, Sand stared out the window at the land all around. Had she gotten free of the castle somehow? But no—thorns still surrounded the castle. No small figure in a russet and saffron dress crossed the asparagus fields below, either.

In the distance, the wide ribbon of the Liger River shone like quicksilver in the bright afternoon sun. The cherry orchards between the castle and the river were turning yellow-green with oncoming spring. Sand leaned out of the window, staring at the wide-open world, longing to be a part of it once more. He took a deep breath of the fresh, promise-filled air—

He paused. The fire in the kitchen should have gone out; there really should be no lingering scent of fire on the air. But the scent came to him, and a thin line of smoke from the smithy drew his eye.

He took the circular stairs two at a time, then burst through the door at the bottom. He raced his own thoughts into the smithy, where he found Perrotte pumping the bellows and staring into a pile of kindling and charcoal in the forge.

"Wh-what are you doing?" he panted.

"I want to mend something," she said fiercely. "Anything in this castle that's not broken is something that you've mended, right? This hammer? These tongs? The bellows here?"

"Except for the outer walls of the castle, yes, everything."

She nodded, a grim sort of satisfaction on her face. "Including me. Yes? You did something to me."

He flinched. "That, we don't know. I—I can't believe it was me. All I did in the crypt was straighten everything up, put your—put you back to rights. You'd been knocked over in the sundering. But . . . nothing else."

She turned her keen eyes on him. "Nothing else—nothing? Tell me the whole story."

He took a deep breath, eyes darting around the smithy as he tried to think of something to distract her from this question. Nothing in the piles of scrap metal and broken tools around him led to any new thought. He blew out his breath and told his reluctant truth.

"Your tomb was shattered. I'm no stone mason or sculptor; I didn't know how to put that back together. I didn't even try—just shoved the rubble into a pile. Other tombs, they're cracked, the lids were loose, but none were as destroyed as yours. I put them back to rights. But for you, all I could do was . . . your body . . . You were on the ground, all . . ." He mimed the broken and awkward position of her arms, before realizing what he was doing. He dropped his hands. "All I did was set you to rights. Nothing else."

She was silent for a moment, still pumping the bellows meditatively. Sand kept an eye on the rate of burn, fretting for the lost charcoal. The castle held a lot of charcoal, but when they ran out, they would be out forever, and he'd never smithed with wood fires before. He wasn't sure he could.

"I'm sorry," Perrotte said. "I was rather caught up in my resurrection. It never occurred to me to ask—how did you get into the castle, Sand?"

"I woke up in the fireplace," he said. "In the great hall. I don't know how I got there—but the night before, I was running to my grandpère's house after a fight with my father, and I stopped at a shrine of Saint Melor. Do you know it? There's a spring and a small pool. People leave bronze there, sometimes silver."

"Saint Melor is the patron of the Boisblanc family," Perrotte said. "And you are the son of a boy who lived here in this castle. There's some connection there."

He shrugged. "I don't see how."

"That sounds like someone who lacks imagination to me," she said.

If she thought that would make him angry, she didn't know anything about blacksmiths. Sand just laughed.

But maybe she wasn't trying to pick a fight, because she grinned at his laughter, appearing pleased with herself. "Well, Sand of the Fireplace, let's not worry about it right now. Instead, teach me how to mend."

"Certainly," he said, eager to think about and do things he understood. "In that dress, though?"

She stroked the fabric of her smooth, soft-woven dress, frowning. She sighed. "I wonder if anyone saved my clothes."

"They'll be torn even if they were saved."

"Well, I guess this will have to be good enough for

now. My sleeves are tight enough not to trail in the fire . . ."

"It's your only whole dress," Sand pointed out. "In any case, you need a leather apron to protect from sparks, like mine." He patted his apron. "So we have sewing to do, any way you look at it."

"Ugh, fine," she grumbled, and stalked off. Sand banked the fire, then settled down tailor-style in the dirt with an awl and two halves of a smithing apron.

Perrotte returned faster than he would have expected, wearing the intact bodice from a sleeveless gown that she'd laced tightly in place, and a whole skirt torn from a different gown that she had belted on with some cording from a curtain or tapestry. She had knotted her hair in the back with a braid wrapped in more cording.

Sand nodded to her, his lips compressed over his awl while his fingers tied the smithing apron together with fragments of thin twine and leather.

"I wasn't sure if I should look for boys' clothing or girls'," she said.

Sand spat his awl into his palm. "My grandmère wears a skirt when she works in the smithy. It seems no better or worse than what my grandpère wears. The important part is not to wear good clothes that you'll be sad to see burned, or trailing sleeves."

While he finished repairing the apron, Sand told

her how to build up the fire: how to arrange the charcoal and for what purpose. Then he showed her the important parts of the forge: the air pipe that ran from the bellows, and the so-called duck's nest that caught the ashes and cinders as they fell from the fire.

"They should call it a phoenix nest," Perrotte said.

Sand grinned, handing her a simple piece of steel to learn with.

"What will this be?" she asked, running her fingertips over the triangular corners of the metal.

"You'll need your own spoon, I'm thinking," he said. "All the other ones are broken, but for my own. A spoon's a good and useful thing to learn how to make."

He set her to taking out the corners from the broken bit of steel, which had been fresh from the foundry twenty-five or more years before. He instructed her on heating the metal and using the tongs, on swinging the hammer from her shoulder and not her wrist, on not letting the metal get too hot in the forge, nor trying to work it when it had grown too cold. He taught her the colors in the order that meant increasing heat, from faintest red to sparkling white.

Perrotte never appeared scared of the glowing metal, and that was a good sign. Sand told her what he had been taught since he was a baby: Only a fool burns himself on bright metal. Iron lost its light long before it cooled, and a smith should have a care for dark heat.

He worried that once the work started, and she grew tired and dirty, Perrotte might think herself debased, a noble girl learning a peasant's craft. But when she looked up at him from her first bout with the hammer, trembling with effort and exhilaration, and bearing a streak of ash across her brow, he saw only fierce happiness on her face.

He answered her grin with one of his own. "Good work," he told her. "Now put your iron back in the fire until it is heated again."

AFTER PERROTTE'S FIRST LESSON at the forge, during which she turned out a credible spoon, even if it was a bit small in the bowl, they went to the kitchen to find something to eat. Well, Sand wanted to eat; he was unconvinced that Perrotte would eat much. He worried about her.

In the kitchen, she poked at dried apples without swallowing more than a mouthful. Sand wondered what he could make to tempt her. Inspiration struck: There were oats in the pantry, which he sorted from stones and debris by tossing the mixture in water and letting the oats float to the top. Then he mixed the grain with tallow from a melted candle. He formed the grain paste into patties and set them to fry.

"Hm." Perrotte watched Sand's progress with his little bread cakes. "Those smell good."

"Would be better with butter," he couldn't help but point out.

"Or jam."

"Or venison gravy."

"Or red-wine sauce."

"Or milk and honey."

"Or sugar and cream."

Sand didn't respond. His cheeks ached from salivation.

They ate the oat cakes, and while they were better than anything Sand had eaten in the castle so far, except for the long-gone marzipan pigs, they still weren't good.

"I'd love a fresh apple, a fresh carrot, a fresh . . . anything," he said.

Perrotte nodded.

"Is that why you won't eat? Nothing fresh?" he asked.

She frowned. "I don't know. I'm just . . . not terribly hungry. I have more appetite today than I did yesterday. But . . ." She hesitated. "I hardly slept last night. Maybe an hour, if I were to judge from the stars."

That worried him too, but maybe that's what happened when a person was recently deceased. He didn't know.

"The thing is, we need to try to break through the hedge," she said.

Immediately, his scar came alive, a shooting ache through his wrist. He clutched it. Her acute eyes followed his gesture.

"One thorn," he gasped, speaking against the tide of pain. "One thorn tried to kill me, and it does not want me to forget."

She shook her head, obstinate. "I'm not afraid."

"Well, I am. I've tried everything, Perrotte. I've tried digging under. I've tried burning them. They are . . ." He didn't know how to finish the sentence. Smart? Evil? Determined?

"If you made me a pair of hedge shears, and I had, say, some armor—gauntlets, perhaps?"

"No."

"Then I'll just try it without your help. With a sword. With a broken sword."

"No," he said again, not because he believed he could talk her out of it, but because it was the right thing to say.

"We can talk about it," Perrotte said. "For as long as you like. For days. For weeks. But I'll get my way."

He was a little surprised that she hadn't already tried to order him to help her, on the basis that he was a peasant and she was a lady. But since she didn't . . . he was actually considering it.

But still—no! It was too dangerous. She had no idea, she really did not!

He had his mouth open to argue, when from the kitchen door a gentle *thump* interrupted him.

Perrotte and Sand both froze, staring at each other.

Thump. Thump, thump. A long pause, then: *Thump.*

Wordlessly, Perrotte shot to her feet. She ran across the room and jerked open the door. She ducked just in time: a drenched falcon flew over her head, landed on the mantel, then started to preen its feathers.

14

Heart

"What in Heaven is that?" Perrotte asked, hands protectively braced over her head.

"Merlin!" Sand exclaimed. "What are you doing here?"

Was Sand *talking* to the bird? "Sand! Are you listening to me?"

Sand faced Perrotte with a smile of true joy, but when he opened his mouth, his eyes clouded. "I heard you," he said. "It's . . . well, it's Merlin."

"A falcon. I can see that. I thought you said nothing lived here?"

Sand's face went blank. "There *was* nothing alive, except for me, until Merlin. And then you."

Perrotte bit back her exasperation, and said simply, "Go on."

He twined his blunt-tipped fingers together, staring down at them. "I, erm. I found the falcon in the mews."

"So, it's not true that there was nothing alive in the castle?"

"The truth is . . . Well, the truth is the truth, and thus worth telling, but sometimes truths are so complicated that it's exhausting to get them out in the right order." He glanced up at her.

That sounded like an evasion if ever she'd heard one. She raised an eyebrow.

"The falcon was dead!" Sand blurted out. "Stuffed and mounted, and then also damaged in the sundering. I mended him, and put him on the mantel, so I'd have something to talk to. But a couple days before you—you came upstairs—" He gestured helplessly at the bird, who stopped stripping water from its feathers just long enough to glare at the humans.

Perrotte stared. "The bird came to life," she whispered. "After you put it to rights, this falcon came to life. Just like me."

"Well . . ."

"It's true, isn't it?" Her gaze landed on an iron pot on the table. She seized it and turned it over in her hands. "Look at this. This was broken too, wasn't it? But it's perfect now."

"That's just some wrought iron, it was easy enough to—"

"Fine, fine—you're a blacksmith. But you're not a cooper!" She pointed to his mended bucket. "Or any sort of carpenter! And certainly not a tailor. But everything you've mended is as good as new!"

"That's not exactly true."

Her eyes wandered over the things he'd mended in the room: the shiny copper kettles, the window latches and hearth crane, the bucket. Her mind went back over the repairs he'd made to the mattresses. Yes, some things were obviously kludged together—the tables in the kitchen were prime examples of things he hadn't repaired with any attempt at artistry. But when he *tried* . . .

"It's like . . ."

"Don't say it out loud," he said, a pained frown creasing his face.

"Magic," she said quietly.

His lips were a thin line. He didn't respond. He simply turned on his heel and walked away.

Perrotte let out a huge sigh. She should let Sand spend some time alone; obviously, he didn't want to talk about the magic.

She wandered about the castle, investigating the extent of the sundering. After staring at the enormous rift in the keep and the ground of the courtyard for some time, Perrotte went to the herbary, determined to find something she could turn into a hot drink.

Luck was with her. She mentally scolded Sand for not having looked harder in the herbary. Certainly, the herbs she found were practically dust, but most of the dust retained enough scent to identify. Chamomile, mint, linden blossom, calendula—a bounty of herbs, and though Perrotte didn't recognize everything, the few herbs she salvaged made her feel useful and smart.

Triumphant, she carried her spoils back to the kitchen. Loyse, who had been her nurse and then later her maid, had brewed a nightly tisane for them to share. Apparently, Perrotte had absorbed more about the herbs than she had realized. Not that she remembered what each of these herbs did, besides promoting general well-being. Except chamomile—Loyse was always giving her chamomile in hopes that it would help her sleep.

Had given. Not *was always giving*. Perrotte felt a pang. Was Loyse still alive? What had happened to her after Perrotte died, after the castle was sundered? As with her unknown sister, Perrotte felt a dark knot of guilt in her chest, thinking that she had left Loyse behind to suffer unprotected under Jannet's rule.

Perrotte heated water and set a bowl of mint tisane to steep. She settled down on the hearthstone and tucked her feet beneath her, leaning against the chimneypiece and absorbing the heat from the hearth. She had gotten chilled, wandering around in the reluctant spring weather. Since her awakening, it seemed Perrotte only noticed she was cold long after she should.

Another effect of death or resurrection?

"Are you cold, Merlin?" she asked, then startled herself with a big yawn. She picked up the mint tisane and sipped. The drink warmed and cooled at the same time. When it was gone, she held the bowl in her lap—the same bowl that Sand had filled with porridge the day before.

Her eyelids felt weighted with lead. She leaned her head against the chimney stones and let her eyes close.

When Perrotte opened her eyes again, dark night showed in the high windows, and the room was lit only by the low fire. Perrotte jumped up. Her forgotten bowl fell to the stones of the floor and shattered.

Her wordless cry disturbed the falcon on the mantel; the bird shot up with a flurry of wings and perched in the rafters, shooting Perrotte a baleful look for the disturbance. She wanted to yell at Merlin, but she bit her tongue. The anger inside her felt endless, and she didn't know how she would stop yelling if she ever started. And the falcon hadn't done anything. Perrotte was the careless one who broke things in a place that could take no more breaking.

She stooped to pick up the pieces of the bowl, fighting back hot tears. A few slipped free nonetheless.

How was she going to tell Sand that she had broken something that had been nearly whole?

She took a deep breath. Sand wouldn't be angry. Or disappointed. Or anything bad. He was kind, understanding. Her tears receded as suddenly as they'd come on—not because she remembered Sand's kindness, but because she remembered how Sand had been so upset when she mentioned his strange abilities. It was obvious, wasn't it? He was gifted in ways that a normal boy would not be. She didn't understand why the magic was so hard for him to talk about. It wasn't like he'd been dead or anything. *That* was hard to talk about.

She heard a comforting sound in the distance: *clang, clang, clang, ring.* Perrotte set aside the pieces of the broken bowl and headed for the door.

Clouds obscured the stars above, to Perrotte's dismay. She worried that her nap on the kitchen's hearth meant she wouldn't sleep at all that night—and now there were no stars to watch. She hurried on, cursing the clouds and trying to believe she would fall asleep and stay asleep through the whole of the night like a normal person. Like a girl who had never died.

Inside the smithy, Sand stood at his anvil, shaping metal effortlessly. Before she had a chance to see what he was making, he plunged the metal into the ashes piled beneath his forge.

When he saw her standing at the door, he banked the fire, put down his tools, and went up to the keep.

They barely spoke, but nonetheless he climbed the stairs to the Count's bedchamber with her. He didn't argue about where to lay his head that night, to her relief.

After she blew out the candle and rolled onto her side, she did not have to reach far into the dark for his hand; this time it was there, on the corner of his mattress, waiting for her. He said nothing and she said nothing, as his warm fingers twined with hers. She gave a relieved sigh, and quite easily fell asleep.

BUT SLEEP DID NOT last for long. A dream woke her, or a memory: an anguished voice that cried, *This wasn't gentle*.

She didn't want that memory. She pushed it behind the door in her mind.

Perrotte wondered how close dawn was. Without stars or moon, she couldn't be sure, but she didn't think she had slept more than an hour. She was wide awake, no longer tired—and yet, she had been exhausted when she climbed into bed.

Maybe—just maybe—she couldn't sleep because she had slept for twenty-five years or so, while her friends grew up and had children and—in some cases—passed away. Twenty-five years of death might function like twenty-five years of sleep.

A sleepless night and a starless night were an ill-matched pair, as far as Perrotte was concerned. If there were stars out, she might dare the tower just to be closer to them, even if it meant braving the memories of her death. As it was—remembering how she died was almost as hard as remembering what it was like to be dead, though for different reasons. The memories of being dead were there, though sort of shrouded in darkness, but remembering what it was like to die . . . that would hurt.

But hurt how? Would it be hard to remember the physical pain, or was there something more?

It was odd, to be able to ask these questions of herself, and yet not conjure up a single memory to answer them. Perrotte imagined the door in her mind: thick oak, triple locked, and barred with iron. On her side dwelled questions and worries. On the other side of the door lived memories and monsters. She'd much rather live with worry than with monsters.

She crept down to the kitchen. The falcon's eyes shone in her candle's light from across the room.

"Did I wake you?" she asked. "Or can't you sleep, either?"

The falcon did not answer. She found that reassuring. Sand's magic was frightening; she was pretty certain it even frightened him. Sand's magic meant that death was no longer a permanent state, and anything broken could be mended. But at least animals hadn't started to speak.

It occurred to her to pray, for the first time since she had been brought back to life. She glanced around the kitchen. Not here.

Perrotte's feet carried her to the chapel. She knelt at the altar, clasping her hands. Her candle's flame seemed tiny in the night, and the way the darkness pressed around her reminded her of something—

—a dark-haired girl, a red seed, an iron throne—

Memories crowded at her, if they could be said to be memories. They were more ghostly than thoughts, less substantial. Like memories of memories. Like dreams of memories. There were not always threads to connect the moments.

First there was darkness and stillness. Relief that her death was done, that the fight to live was over.

That memory trailed away and another rose to take its place.

She awakened in a place where darkness was light. She walked for some time, a march without end—until, abruptly, it did end. She reached a hillock covered with lilies that glowed like tiny suns.

Beyond the hill, a river ran both fast and slow, smelled both fresh and dank. She felt drawn to the water. But when she reached the shore, she turned away, only then noticing the thousands of shadowy people walking beside her, shades who did reach the river, who passed her, knelt down and scooped the water greedily into their mouths. They drank and forgot and faded, then marched on down the riverside, sliding into a distant fog.

In that moment, Perrotte knew: She would not drink. She could not. She burned, and could not fade, could not disappear into fog. The flames that consumed her were anger, sadness, and regret. Her life had been stolen, and she would not forget that.

She fought her way backward, against the tide of shades that yearned toward the river of forgetting, until she found a tree, a tree that gleamed white in the darkness—a birch. Like the white forests of her family's name. She clung to it, turned her face to the bark so as not to see the march of shadow people around her, and held fast.

Perrotte came back to herself with a shudder, her head snapping up. Had she been asleep—and was that a memory or a dream?

She crossed herself and said a prayer for her father's soul. She could not imagine how he had felt when she died; she was having a hard enough time understanding how she felt about his death. Mostly, she regretted the time they did not have together. How were either of them to know that the last time they saw each other their leave-taking would be no more than a kiss on the cheek and a tweak of one of her braids while admonishing her to mind her stepmother and her tutor?

Her thoughts turned as they became too painful. She rested her forehead against her folded thumbs, trying to think of a prayer to say for Sand. Her heart beat too loud in the stillness, though. She took a deep breath, trying to calm her pulse. But instead of slowing, the thumping remained steady and still so very loud. She touched her chest wonderingly. Was she ill? Was she . . . dying?

But once she felt the rhythm of her own heartbeat there, beneath her bodice and skin and flesh and bone, she shook her head in confusion. Her own slow, steady heart shared no rhythm with the thrumming beat that filled the chapel.

The noise was coming from one of the reliquaries resting on the altar.

Slowly, Perrotte got to her feet. With dread, she reached for the silver, oval box that held the holy relic of Sainte Trifine and loosed the clasp.

There, inside the box, lay a beating heart.

Thorns

In the morning, Sand found Perrotte in the kitchen, sitting on a hearthstone and stirring porridge. She scooted aside, making room for him on the stones beside her.

He lowered himself to the warm hearthstone, making care to keep a proper distance between them. He propped his elbows on his knees and folded his hands between them.

He wasn't really sure what to say to her. He wanted to apologize for being so silent and skittish the day before, but he wasn't sure he was done being silent and skittish.

If only she wouldn't talk about him doing *magic*.

Perrotte gave the porridge a final stir, and then

tapped the spoon against the side of the pot to get the porridge off. "I think it's ready."

He stood and served himself a bowl. It was lumpy, and not in an interesting way. He swore he would make all the porridge from now on.

"Sand," she said after a moment. "What's wrong?"

He was silent. How could he say that he was afraid he was a witch? Because admitting that meant admitting her awakening was unnatural and wrong. It was all to the good that they were trapped in a castle surrounded by impenetrable thorns—it saved them both from interrogation, accusation, trial, and possibly even burning.

"Something is wrong," she persisted.

"How do *you* know?" The words burst out of him with heat, and it felt good to speak so forcefully. "You've only known me for three days."

Instead of whipping back a comment just as rude, she was silent and frowning, arms clutched over her chest. It occurred to him then: That had been the most unfair thing he could say. He barely knew her, either, and yet he had been rude on purpose, hoping to provoke a fight. Fighting would feel good. He could say mean things, harsh things, things he'd never gotten to say to his father—and he would feel that she would deserve every one of them.

But she didn't.

He didn't want knowing that to stop him, though. He wanted an argument.

"Don't," Perrotte said quietly, and threw him all off guard.

"Don't what?" He said it less aggressively, but he still hoped there might be a good fight.

"Whatever you're doing. Don't . . . don't pretend that just because we're trapped together that we—" She broke off, biting her lip. "Look, I was mean and rude to you at first, and now you're being mean and rude to me, and I was horrible, and now you're horrible . . ."

Shame welled up within him, though he wanted to tamp down. He already knew that if he picked a fight with her, if he said all the mean things he shouldn't say, he would regret it afterward. As he already regretted what he had said—or maybe not *what* he'd said, but *how* he'd said it, with such contempt.

"We're all we have," Perrotte said.

"Well!" He gusted an explosive sigh on that word, only then realizing he had been holding his breath. "When did you come to this conclusion?"

"When I dragged your mattress down the hall," she said. "And I'm sorry. For how I was. For acting like the Queen of Earth condescending to her servant."

He said stiffly, "You are a lady, and the daughter

of a count. I am a peasant."

"God's body," she swore, opening her arms wide. "Do you think there were counts and peasants when the world was populated by Adam and Eve?"

He felt his cheeks heat at that comment, and kept his eyes on his porridge lumps. "I'm sorry too."

"I accept your apology. Do you accept mine?"

It was so needlessly formal, as if she were reminding him—in spite of her words—that they were in fact lady and peasant, and not equals. "Yes, I accept your apology," he said. He bit back a sarcastic "my lady" at the end. That wouldn't do.

"So, then." She waited, arms folded, staring at him. "What's wrong?"

"I don't know how to feed the falcon," he blurted. Which was true; feeding Merlin was indeed something that bothered him, that worried him.

Perrotte's hands flexed where they held on to her upper arms, a slight flutter of fingers. "We'll take Merlin outside to hunt. Problem solved."

"Have you ever hunted a falcon?" he asked.

"Of course." She said it so offhandedly, and Sand cursed inwardly as he felt his cheeks heat again. Perotte studied the bird. "Merlin's a lady's falcon, anyway, one that small."

"Of course," Sand echoed. "What if you hunt him and he doesn't come back?"

"Then we really don't have to worry anymore."

Sand wanted Merlin to come back, needed him to. With only three living things in the castle, it was too much to lose any one of them.

"I made a tisane," she said, and gave him a cup. He sipped: It was weak, not at all like the tisanes that Agnote brewed, but Agnote was diligent with her herbs, and kept nothing past its first year unless it was very dear or hard to get. These herbs were probably almost as old as Agnote herself. But the tisane was tastier than plain water.

Several times during their meal, Perrotte opened her mouth as if to speak, and then subsided. After the fifth time, Sand looked at her crankily. "What? What do you want to say to me?"

She opened her mouth again. For a long, awkward moment, nothing came out, and then she said in a rush, "I'm going to make a run at the thorns! With or without your help."

He nodded, setting aside his bowl of porridge. "I know." He stood up, shook out his legs, and went to the smithy without even looking to see if she followed.

She did follow, and Sand pulled out the things he had mended the day before. "Hedge shears," he said, pulling them from the ashes and placing them on his anvil. "I just need to temper the blades so they can be sharpened."

Her eyes were alight with eagerness for battle. He remembered the first time he'd watched Grandpère make a sword, how excited he'd felt; when Grandpère had stepped away, he'd snatched up the hiltless blade by its tang and swiped the air with it. Grandpère had returned—and it was the first and only time Sand had seen his placid grandfather angry.

"Put it down!" Grandpère had cried, and Sand had obeyed immediately.

"I'm sorry! Did I ruin the blade? Did I cost you the commission?"

Grandpère had sighed and sat down, rubbing his leg, and told Sand then the story of his uncle Taran, who had gone so eagerly to fight for Bertaëyn's independence from France the best way he could—as a blacksmith. His uncle had never seen battle, had never been *meant* to see it, being quite busy repairing armor and weapons, but he had worked closer to the battle lines than was safe. A poorly aimed cannon killed him and two other smiths working field forges.

"Battles seem grand to children," Grandpère had said. "And wars can seem righteous and just, even to the oldest among us. But before you ever march off to fight, should the opportunity come to you, or even before you run off to *help* a fight—think of the old folks like me and your grandmère with no children living, who know the secrets to great arts and have no blood to pass them to."

While this had troubled Sand—was blood so very important? Did it not matter at all that Sand's father had been passed the secrets of the craft?—he understood Grandpère's sorrow. Sand wanted to learn smithing because he loved it; he loved it for many reasons, but one of the reasons was that the craft sang in his veins, and his heart beat in time to his hammer's blows.

Remembering that moment when he'd angered his grandfather so, Sand went with great reluctance to pull out the other items he'd mended for Perrotte: a pair of armored gauntlets and a breastplate.

She clapped her hands with pleasure. Sand just sighed.

"Please, leave the thorns alone, Perrotte," he begged.

She shook her head. "You'll thank me, when we're free," she said.

He grunted, and set to work hardening her shears, while she tried on her armor.

When the shears were cooled, filed, and sharpened, he followed her down to the gates, while he alternately clutched and scratched at his wrist. The way his scar changed from itching to pain and back to itching—it was like nothing he'd ever experienced.

"Raise the portcullis for me? Please, Sand?"

"Don't do this, Perrotte."

"Sand," she said, pleading. "We can't live here for the rest of our lives. We can't just let Jan—we can't let the thorns win. Or the curse on this castle. *Whatever* it is that's keeping us here. We have to get out."

"I want to get out too! But—" The pain was unbearable. He ground out a curse, a proper one, one that he should confess to a priest if there were a priest to confess to. He clawed at his wrist, even as the pain drove him to his knees.

"We can't let it win!" Perrotte said, and dashed inside the gatehouse to raise the portcullis.

He fought the pain, slowly staggering to his feet. "No, Perro—"

But the iron bars were up, and she was back, running straight at the thorns, swinging open her hedge shears to cut into the bramble.

He thought it might work, for a brief, mad moment. But these were no simple thorns, and while a few small branches fell away in the first heat of Perrotte's attack, the bramble regrouped, twitching only slightly to reach for her. And though thorns could not penetrate her breastplate or her gauntlets, bramble runners snaked their way around her ankles, wound around her upper arms, and wormed into her hair. Perrotte didn't scream, but she did struggle, grunting, against the thorns. She lost the hedge shears, her fingers spasming open as her skin was pierced. The bramble engulfed the hedge shears and pulled them deep inside the brake.

It was worse than Sand had imagined.

His own pain had not subsided; the ghost of the thorn in his wrist still stabbed to the center of his being, but he forced himself from his knees. He had to reach Perrotte. He had to pull her away before the thorns swallowed her too. He grabbed her arms, and sucker branches of the bramble reached for his fingers in turn. Perrotte may not have screamed, but *he* was not so shy. He yelled as he pulled her away from the thorns. Her clothing ripped. Her skin tore. His skin tore. And she left huge chunks of her hair behind.

But they were free.

They fell together in a heap. Her metal-covered fist drove accidentally into his upper thigh, just missing a more tender area by inches. The curved edge of her breastplate smashed into his cheekbone.

And the thorns—the thorns were *following* them, slinking into the passageway after them.

The brambles were still plants, though, and while they could twitch inches in midair with lightning speed, they couldn't travel along the ground terribly fast. Sand shoved Perrotte off him, rolling her away from the thorns, and scrambled to his feet. The thorns that had embedded themselves in his fingers screamed pain; the scar on his wrist echoed it. He reached the night portal and slammed it shut.

Three bramble runners remained, trapped under the door. Sand stomped them into the earth with his boot heel, and swore to come back and take care of them. With hot metal.

Perrotte struggled to her feet. Sand rushed to grab her elbow and help her upright. She leaned into him and let him propel her back inside.

"Bed or kitchen?" he asked. He couldn't imagine how much pain Perrotte was in. Everywhere the brambles had touched, her skin was puffing—a ring around her neck, a lash across her cheek.

"Kitchen," she croaked, and clutched at her swelling neck.

One thorn. One thorn had given him such grief, and she had been assaulted by dozens. Scores. Hundreds?

He dropped her to the kitchen hearth and ran off to draw water to heat, to grub bedding for bandages, and to find the lancets he had used on his own thorn. Wait. He'd left the lancets somewhere in the smithy, intending to repair them eventually, but he couldn't remember where. He'd look for them once he made Perrotte comfortable.

He hurried back to the kitchen with the water and

bandages. Perrotte opened bleary eyes. "Gilles," she said. "Did I forget my gloves?"

"What?" Sand asked, startled.

She shook her head, closing her eyes again.

"I'm not Gilles," he said, pouring water into a pot and stoking up the fire beneath it. "I'm Alexandre. Sand." His stomach, already clenched in knots of worry, took on a new and additional discomfort, a rolling tightness that . . . was it jealousy? For his own father?

He dismissed the thought, and turned to evaluate Perrotte. She wasn't bleeding. This worried him. He hadn't bled from his thorn wound either, not until the thorn came out. Did that mean all the thorns that had attacked her were still inside her, under her skin?

Poultices, first; then he would lance the wounds and pry the thorns out. But poultices of what? The cabbage leaves he'd used on himself were long gone, and what few medicinal plants could be found in the castle were well past the point of possessing curative powers.

But just heat and damp would help, wouldn't they?

It would be better if she were lying down. But he didn't know if he could get her up the stairs to her bed by himself. He was strong, but she was an inch or two taller than him, and now felt just as heavy, heavier than the day she'd stumbled up from the crypt.

"Then bring the bed to her," Sand muttered, and ran upstairs again, this time grabbing pillows and blankets to make a pallet for Perrotte on the hearth. She opened her eyes as he slid her into the comfortable nest. "What happened to my gloves, Gilles?"

"You're going to be all right, Perr," he said, placing a pillow under her head. "We'll get you better. You're going to be all right."

He knew she didn't understand him. He was glad. Even if she understood, she wouldn't believe that she would be all right. He didn't even believe himself.

Gloves

THE CASTLE WASN'T EMPTY.

It wasn't broken, either. That had all been a nightmare, and Perrotte felt silly for ever having believed it. Gilles was going to laugh at her when she told him that she'd awakened twenty-five years in the future and met his son. He was going to laugh when she told him he wasn't a shoemaker anymore. He was going to laugh even harder than that when she told him that she had *believed* all of it.

She climbed out of her bed and went down to the shoemakers' workshop. Gilles was the only one there, waiting for her. "You've come for your scented slippers, my lady?" he asked.

"You're scenting my gloves, too," she reminded him.

"Oh, am I?" he asked with a self-assured grin. He was the only one who dared tease her. And because he was the only one, she let him. "It's not enough that you're the only girl in all of Bertaèyn who'll have scented slippers at court."

"Every footstep will be like a petal falling. You know I plan to set the fashion."

Gilles reached under his workbench for a cloth sack. He donned a pair of work gloves, and pulled out a slipper, holding it up for her to examine.

She sniffed the oiled leather. "Rose and orris."

"As you requested."

"Perfect," she said.

"The gloves aren't done yet, but I'll start them now." He put the slippers back in the bag, then pulled out her gloves.

"Why not? You've had time!"

"Have I?" He didn't sound perturbed or angry, nor subservient and apologetic. "I don't think I have, actually." He measured out a dram each of sweet oil and clove oil. "Hand me that gray amber."

She did so, and he mixed it all together.

"Who will scent my gloves at Anna's court?" she asked, watching him dip a cloth in rosewater and wash her gloves with it.

"I'm sure Anna has pleasant-enough shoemakers in her service. Perhaps even a glover. Probably more than one." He started rubbing the leather of her gloves with the amber and oil mixture, using the rough texture of his own gloves to buff the soft leather of hers. The scent of almonds rose up, bitter and sweet, and reminded her of—

—a place, so dark and dim she could not see.

A place beneath the earth.

A woman's breath on her cheek, and a gentle kiss.

A soft hand brushing her forehead.

"Eat this, daughter, and become remade."

Something sweet and wet passed between her lips, a seed, a red seed—

Sometime during this memory, Perrotte had fallen to the floor. Gilles nattered on, talking about glovers and court, appearing not to notice her sprawled at his feet.

"Don't mind me, I'm just lying here, remembering what it was like to be dead," she said.

He didn't even look at her, just kept working on the gloves and talking.

And that was how Perrotte finally knew this wasn't a memory, it was a dream.

Wake up, Perrotte told herself. *This is a stupid dream. Wake up, and find Sand.*

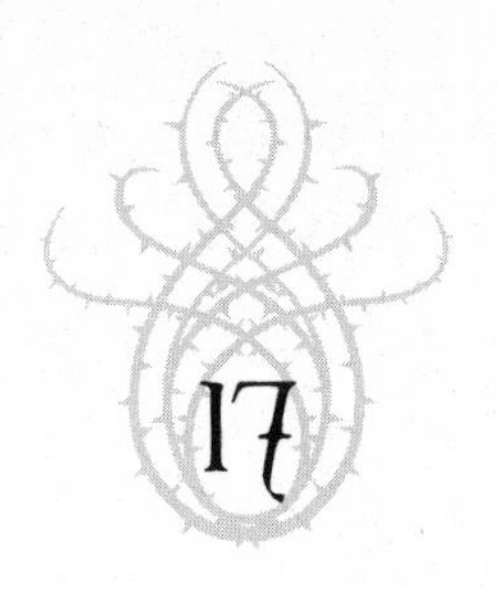

17

LANCET

WITH DELIRIOUS PERROTTE POULTICED UP, SAND hurried to the smithy to look for the lancets. He tore his scrap piles apart; broken iron lay everywhere, with no seeming sense to any of it. Sand cursed, real curses, with proper, sinful swearing by God. The kind of swearing that would have gotten him a slap from Agnote.

"If Perrotte dies . . . ," he muttered. Then, "If Perrotte dies *again*, I mean."

Finally, he found the broken lancets he'd set aside after he'd taken his first thorn out. Why hadn't he repaired these tools immediately? Why hadn't he at least mended them in preparation for Perrotte's planned attack on the thorns? She had so many wounds. He couldn't use broken lancets for all of them. He must take the time and mend these tools, so that he had proper equipment and didn't hurt Perrotte further.

He forced himself to focus.

HALF AN HOUR LATER, his first lancet, now cooled, was ready for filing. He flaked off the gray-black fire scale that had collected on the outside of the metal during his working. Beneath, the steel was shiny and silver-colored. He shaped out a proper edge and point of the lancet so that it was suitable for piercing skin, then continued polishing the surface. Fire scale could not hide the glowing colors of iron. But the rainbow of tempering colors could only be seen on clean steel by bright daylight.

He put the lancet back in the fire for an even heating. It felt maddeningly slow. He could make a dozen nails, maybe two dozen, in the same time it would take him to draw a temper on this lancet.

He took a deep and steadying breath, calming his agitation. Lancets were thin and heated quickly. This was no time for impatience, or for making more of his problems than what they were. He pulled out the tool and quenched the tip. Then he waited, watching the colors change as the heat slowly crept back into the cooled area. He was waiting for the edge to turn palest straw yellow.

Tempering always reminded him of oncoming dawn. The shift in the colors of the sky was very similar, and perhaps that made sense. The sun was the sky's fire, driving color before it like a forge fire drove color through metal. It always seemed to Sand that some great sound like a giant, ringing bell should accompany the sun's rising, and likewise some smaller bell should toll for the colors that shifted in the steel while drawing a temper.

He'd tried to explain all this to Gilles once, and his father had told him to keep his eyes on his metal. He'd tried to explain it to Grandpère another time, and Grandpère had nodded thoughtfully, his half-burnt and bushy eyebrows drawing together as he considered Sand's words.

"Like watching your grandmère move from angry to humored when I tease her," Grandpère had answered. "And her laugh is the bell." Sand knew that to be true as well. He wanted to tell this story to Perrotte, though he might leave the part out about how he found himself watching her face like his grandfather watched his grandmother's.

He thought about her face contorted with pain. How could Perrotte bear it? How could she survive this? Sand's fingers curled overtight around his hammer handle. "*If* Perrotte dies . . . I'll mend her again."

Finally, the lancet tip turned palest straw yellow.

At last. Sand quenched his first lancet in his slake bucket, and began the next one.

PERROTTE WAS AWAKE WHEN Sand reached her, the second lancet still forge-warm in his hand. Her eyes were wide and luminous with unshed tears.

"I'm sorry I didn't listen to you, Sand," she said.

He felt his mouth fold into a grim line. He didn't want her apologies. She was brave, stupid brave; that was a fault, perhaps, but not something she chose to be just to hurt him.

"You didn't know," he said, placing the back of his hand on her forehead, trying to feel if she had a fever. She felt cool to him, but he'd just been at the forge, and his heat sense was skewed.

"But you knew," she said.

"I didn't know." He went over to the pot he'd put on to boil earlier. Of course the water had boiled out, and now the pot baked drily in the embers. He sighed, filled it back up, then returned to her side.

"I was *afraid*, Perrotte. I didn't *know.* You and I both saw the thorns move before, but really . . . what if that was the worst they could do, or would do? What if you were right and I was wrong? I hoped you were right. If you had been, we'd be standing outside the castle right now, laughing our heads off with relief, and wondering why I was so stupid as to be trapped in here for weeks just because of one little thorn prick."

She smiled at him then, a sad, sideways smile. "You're the kindest person I know, Sand," she said.

"I haven't been as nice as I could be," he said.

"I said *kind*, not *nice*," she said. "Jannet could be perfectly nice, but she was never kind."

He was silent for a long moment, thinking about the difference, then forced himself to blink when he realized he was staring at her.

"Then I'm sorry for you," he said gently. "My grandparents are far kinder than me. And Agnote—my stepmother is the kindest person I know. I wish you had known more kind people."

She didn't say anything, just closed her eyelids. Tears slid from the corners of her eyes.

"Perrotte?" he asked, alarmed.

"It hurts, Sand," she said. "And it doesn't get easier to bear with time. I feel the thorns all over me, and they're pushing in deeper. They want my heart. . . ."

"I'm going to start cutting them out," he said. "As many as you can stand."

"All of them."

"It'll hurt, Perr."

"It hurts *now*," she said, opening her eyes. "Cut them all out. If I faint—then good."

He bit his tongue against a sharp answer, trying to keep his face calm and comforting, to look like

Agnote would look while working with a patient. She was a midwife, but lots of people in the village came to her for little bits of healing that didn't require a barber or a physician.

There had been a time when Sand had believed that Agnote was calm always; during all the arguments with his father, she would get that comforting, listening expression on her face and try to mediate between Sand and Gilles, never once raising her voice.

But eventually, Sand had figured it out. She was most upset when she appeared most calm. This became clear after she sent home one of her pregnant patients, who was having blood and pains well before her time. Calm Agnote reigned as she gave the woman strict orders to go home, to lie down, and to have her husband wait on her. Calm Agnote gave the woman a packet of herbs and a promise that she'd follow in an hour to check on her. Calm Agnote had watched her patient walk away, then closed the door.

Calm Agnote had crumpled into true Agnote a moment later, her face a mask of misery. Sand had gone to hug her, then. His little sisters, Avenie and Annick, never wanting to be left out of any hugs ever, crowded in on them, each embracing one of his thighs and one of Agnote's. Agnote had just hugged him back for a long moment, then slid her arms around his sisters' shoulders. "Goodness, children . . . Is this a plea for your suppers?"

Once she'd diverted the little ones away, though, Agnote had gripped his shoulder, and just smiled at him. A sad smile, but a real one, and Sand had appreciated some things about his stepmother that maybe he'd never understood before.

It was hard to keep a calm like Agnote's, but he forced himself to do it now. He wasn't much of a healer, but he was all Perrotte had.

He pulled a poultice off a line of raised bumps on Perrotte's ankle. When he glanced at Perrotte's face, her jaw was clenched. She suffered.

Sand set his own jaw, and pressed the lancet tip into the heart of the first bump. He dug the thorn out. It was more difficult to remove than his thorn, which his body had been trying to reject. Blood came with this thorn, and no pus. He wiped the blood away with a hot cloth, and moved on to the next thorn, and then the next.

Sand wondered how Agnote bore the things she had to do as a midwife. He caused Perrotte pain, even as he helped her. She tried to be brave. She did not scream. But she could not hold in all of her gasps and whimpers.

"Let's take a break," he said, wiping sweat from his brow with the back of his hand. "And then we'll get you up to bed, then try again." He wasn't sure, but he felt like he had missed thorns. And possibly they wouldn't know it, until the thorns worked to poison her.

It was daunting.

"A break," she murmured. "And then I'll tell you about the heart." She crossed herself and started to pray, lips moving silently.

The heart? Was she talking about the thorns wanting her heart again? Sand left her to her prayers.

Merlin watched from the rafters with bright, intelligent eyes. Sand held the kitchen door open and whistled to the bird.

"This is your chance. Go get something to eat," Sand said.

The falcon would have none of it.

"Fine," Sand muttered, slamming the door shut after him. He returned to the smithy, where he stoked up the forge and mended a handful of items from his pile of broken things, losing himself in the rhythm of striking metal, the rhythm of the bellows, the rhythm of heat-cool-heat-cool. How was it possible that his father did not love this work with all his heart? How was it possible his father didn't realize how much Sand loved this work? How much it was in his blood and under his skin—

Under his skin.

In all the turmoil and worry, he'd forgotten about the thorns that had torn his own skin. He raised a hand to his neck, feeling the lumps swelling there, and groaned.

18

CHILD

THE LONG, HORRIBLE DAY FINALLY ENDED. A PILE OF thorns lay in a bowl next to Perrotte's bed where they glistened malevolently in the moonlight that spilled into her father's bedchamber. Sand had not gotten them all in the first round, nor the second, nor the third, but he had gotten as many as either of them could stand.

Perrotte rolled onto her stomach, unwilling to look at her enemies in the bowl.

She had slept longer than she'd ever done since waking in the crypt, but it still wasn't very long. She must have made it past midnight, though, judging from the moon. Four days past full, it was still quite bright, and drowned out many stars.

She wondered if she would ever find the bits of her

astrolabe around the castle, and if Sand could mend it if she did. It seemed unlikely. She was going to have to guess at how to construct one, and enlist Sand's help to do so. Blacksmithing appeared easy, on the surface of it—heat metal and bend it!—but it had so many rules and tests, what little she had learned made her think it as exacting a science as astronomy.

Perrotte told herself the astrolabe didn't matter. She didn't want to go back to her observation tower, anyway. The last time she'd been there, the urge to either vomit or tear her hair had overwhelmed her, and she'd almost remembered dying for a moment.

She didn't want to return to the tower room. She didn't want to remember dying.

She wanted to forget it all forever. Some days, she thought she could.

But the memory of the tower—not the last time she had been there with Sand, but the time before that, when she'd died—was *right there*, just a left turn through a doorway in her mind. The door was always trying to jump open on her, and she was always holding it shut. *I don't want to know. I don't want to see what's behind there.*

Sometimes, when she wasn't attentive, the door cracked open too long, and she heard a voice from beyond.

This wasn't gentle, the voice said.

If she could figure out how to lock the door forever,

though . . . And she thought maybe she could. Perrotte had trained for years in something her tutor called the "method of place." In her mind, she had laid out an entire village, full of houses and fields, with a castle overlooking from a hill. It resembled the village and castle of Boisblanc. But instead of people living in the houses of the village, in each one she mentally stored the layout of the night skies in different seasons. In the rooms of the castle dwelled declensions of Latin and Greek.

This room that she'd built in her mind to store away the terrible memory of her death, though—she had built that when she was dead. Perhaps. Or maybe she had constructed it as she'd come back to life? It didn't really matter *when*. The door was there and always trying to leap open. It was exhausting, to keep holding the door shut. But in time, she might be able to build a wall across it.

Perrotte shook herself. She wanted to see the stars. She slid from bed, giving the bowl of thorns a wide berth, and found her way down and out. She climbed a tower, a different tower, not one of the tallest, but one of the guard towers. She leaned out the window to study the stars.

It wasn't the same; she couldn't fold back the roof and observe whatever section of the sky she liked this way. But it was *something*. The layers of blue-black darkness calmed her. The varieties of stars calmed her too—the way the light of some stars pierced and others glowed more dimly; the way some blazed reddish and others gleamed blue-white. It reminded her of blacksmithing, and the colors of heated metal. She wondered if the colors meant anything.

The stars began to fade away, the fainter ones first, until only the brightest remained in a sky that knew more shades of blue than any painter could mix. Perrotte had always wanted a dress that made her think of this kind of sky, a dusky, dark blue silk that she could sew over with a net of silver and diamonds. If she wore a dress like that, what could she not say or do? To feel like the queen of a vast field of stars would be to feel greater than the Queen of France.

The colors of the sky shifted from blue to rose, and in the distance, Perrotte saw something unexpected.

A child of perhaps eight years drove geese through one of the asparagus fields below.

Perrotte waved.

The child waved back.

Shocked, Perrotte called out, but the sound of her voice must have died long before it reached him.

The child waved again, then turned and left. She watched him until he was out of sight.

The sun finally peered over the horizon. In the rosy dawn, the child had seemed a ghost, a flight of imagination. In yellow sunlight, he seemed impossible.

But the sunlight wouldn't stay golden for long. Clouds rolled in from the direction of the sea, and Perrotte could make out gray sheets of rain in the distance.

She yawned then, a sudden gape, and she was overcome with swift tiredness. The thorns, still plying her with their subtle poisons, no doubt. She crept back to her father's bedchamber, and lay down on her bed. Sand didn't even stir. She put her head down to sleep again. The voice came to her, as she drifted off.

This wasn't gentle.

But Perrotte kept the door closed, and slept, and dreamed.

A woman came to her where she clutched the birch tree, a woman dressed in black even deeper than the darkness, a woman without a face, with just a red, empty scar where her face should have been. The woman asked her why she would not drink.

Perrotte said: "I will not drink. I will not go on."

The woman said: That is your right, as one whose blood was spilled unjustly.

Perrotte felt fierce. "Yes. That is my right."

When she woke, she was feverish, and she felt she had dreamed the whole of the night.

19

Library

SAND WOKE TO A GUSTY RAIN; THE BREEZE THAT SANG in through the cracked window panes smelled of the ocean. Before he opened his eyes, he could hear gulls calling to each other as they rode the winds, and he thought he should climb a tower and look for the birds. But then he remembered Perrotte.

He opened his eyes. She still slumbered on the mattress that cornered with his.

Sand rose and carried the bowl of thorns cautiously down to the smithy. He made the hottest fire he could, pumping the bellows until charcoal burned yellow-white with welding heat, then dumped the thorns into the dazzling center of the fire. The thorns crackled and popped, and Sand swore that inside his neck, the thorns still lodged there wriggled in sympathy.

He brought food and water up to Perrotte and woke her. Her eyes were glassy with fever.

"Drink, Perr," Sand said when she wrinkled her nose at the plain water. It was high-born snobbery that made her look down at the cool, pure well water. "It's not iced and flavored with parsley seed, but it will do you good."

She drank.

He removed more thorns, and she looked a bit better after that. He still wasn't sure he'd gotten them all.

"I need you to get well so you can remove *my* thorns," he said, touching the hot lumps on his neck.

She blanched. "Oh. I didn't realize . . ." She lifted her hands in the air and studied them.

"When they tremble a bit less," he said. "I got the ones from my knuckles, and mostly these don't pain me." This was not entirely a lie; knowing that they could be removed, and that he would feel better afterward, made them easier to bear. Much like the difference between the first time he'd been stung by a bee, and the second.

He gathered the array of dishes that had collected by Perrotte's bed to take down to the kitchen. To his shock, Perrotte pushed back her covers and stood.

"What are you doing?"

"I can't stay here. I'm . . . I've had enough of bed. I'm going to the library. I want to find my missing books."

Sand wasn't sure what books she meant, but then he remembered the ruin of parchment that swamped the room. "The library is in bad shape."

"Of course the library is in bad shape. I don't imagine that the forces of destruction that took apart this castle spared the library."

Sand watched her movements, glad for this sign of recovery but not trusting it. She walked creakily, and sported two bright red spots high on her cheekbones.

Nonetheless, he followed her from the room, and almost ran into her when she stopped in the library doorway.

"It's worse than I imagined," Perrotte said.

Sand nodded. What else was there to say?

Perrotte hovered, almost stepping into the room several times, but always stepping back. Sand understood the problem—she didn't want to crush anything underfoot.

He leaned into the room and scooped up a handful of pages. "Why don't we start out here?" he asked, gesturing at the library's anteroom, whose purpose he couldn't quite discern. It held lots of broken tables and chairs, the requisite shredded tapestries, but not much else that was useful. "I wish I'd at least fixed a table in here," he muttered, hunkering down to spread the pages out, then answered himself with, "If only wishing made it so, Sand."

"Do I need to even be here for this conversation?" Perrotte asked.

He looked up, startled. It was not that he had forgotten Perrotte was there. It was more that he'd forgotten that he didn't have to answer himself when he talked.

Certain that a blush now stained his cheeks, he simply turned back to the pages. "What books are you looking for?" he asked.

"My personal collection. My books on natural philosophy, mainly. Books on mathematics too."

"No histories?"

Perrotte shook her head. "Works of the heathen philosophers, I might be interested in. But the books I owned were Ptolemy's *Almagest* . . ." She ticked them off on her fingers. "Pliny's *Natural History*. Macrobius. Calcidus. Martianus Capella's *Marriage of Philology and Mercury*."

Sand shook his head. Not only would he not know what those looked like when he came across them, he'd never heard of any of the authors she'd just listed, except Pliny. Just more proof that he was utterly unprepared to go to the university, in spite of his work with the village priest. Why did his father think he could go?

"And a book called *Astronomicon*. Press printed. My last birthday gift from my father."

"What about a history of dragons?" Sand finally found a title page. "By Mathilde von Erlenbach."

"Hardly meaningful, when there are no dragons left in Europe."

Sand nodded. They had been driven away some centuries before. He wished he could have seen one, at least once, like this German woman had.

Pages stacked up. Perrotte bossily rearranged their piles. Everything written in Latin went on one side of the room. Greek received a small home near the empty fireplace. Vernacular texts were placed in another area, subdivided into languages and dialects. Each language section got split into scribed or press-printed areas. The final subdivision was the category of "interesting to Perrotte" or "not interesting to Perrotte."

"'Fixed stars,' 'luminaries,' 'spheres'!" Perrotte read from one page. "This could be from one of my books! Or, at least, I found some Ptolemy!"

"Wonderful!" Sand said, though he couldn't understand this level of excitement over books. Certainly, organizing the library was a fine preoccupation for a rainy day—though the smithy had a roof on it, last he checked. He didn't *have* to be here. But here is where Perrotte wanted to be, and he couldn't quite imagine letting her out of his presence for more than a trip to the privy closet.

That was when he remembered the bargain he had offered the saints. If he ever did get out of this castle, he had promised to go to university. He may as well accept it and prepare himself. He had a lot to learn about scholarship and natural philosophy.

Though . . . for the first time, Sand could imagine something he could bear to study at university. *Medicine.* He'd hated removing Perrotte's thorns, but he could see the value in caring for people, far more than he could see the value in studying theology or law.

Medicine wasn't blacksmithing. But it wasn't becoming a priest, either.

Silence came from the other side of the room for a while. When Sand finally looked up from his work, he saw that Perrotte was seated cross-legged on the floor, chewing on the end of her thumbnail while she read over something. Her eyes scanned the page—and her lips didn't even move.

"What did you find there?" he asked.

"*The Life of Sainte Trifine.* Well, part of it."

"Sainte Trifine? Like the relic in the chapel?" Whose heart he'd mended with beeswax? "Is it . . . interesting?"

"Yes. Listen to this. After Trifine was strangled and beheaded by her husband, 'her body was brought to her father's palace. Her father went to Gildas . . .'"

Perrotte looked up. "Gildas was the monk who persuaded her to marry her husband."

"But Gildas also resurrected her." That was really the only part of the story that Sand knew.

"Yes!" Perrotte said, scanning the rest of the page and flipping it over. "Very well, you know the . . . that part. Do you also know the bit where Gildas went to her murderous husband's castle and prayed over a handful of sand—then threw it against the castle walls? The castle collapsed and was swallowed by the earth."

Sand imagined a spinning vortex of earth opening up like a great mouth and sucking down the whole of a castle. He knew only one castle, this castle, and the picture in his mind was disturbing. Sand shuddered. "No. I've never heard that before."

Perrotte's eyes glittered over the edge of the page. "Doesn't it sound—just a little bit—like the sundering of *this* castle?"

"A bit," Sand said, turning away to pick up more debris from the library floor.

"There's more," Perrote said. "Trifine is my mother's family saint. The Cygne saint."

He stared down at the topmost of the pages he'd scooped up. It was scribe-written, some sort of treatise on healing. He thought Agnote might like to read it. He missed her so much—the whole family—even his father. His lost home was like a dark hole, an endless well inside him; all his interior organs kept falling toward that center nothingness.

"Sand, are you listening?"

"The Cygne saint," he repeated. *Cygne* meant swan. "Is that why there are swans all over the castle?"

"Yes. The Boisblancs were in dire straits, financially; they pleaded for the Cygnes' fortune. My mother was the last child of that line, so it was agreed that she and her fortune would come to my father when he married her, if he adopted the swan into his crest and took their motto as his own." Perrotte gave a slightly cruel smile. "The swans everywhere drove my father's wife mad."

"What's the Cygne motto?"

"'Fidelity, Sacrifice, Love.' It's boring."

"You think that's boring?"

Perrotte wrinkled her forehead. "I think it is . . . the opposite of interesting."

"Well, what motto did 'Fidelity, Sacrifice, Love' replace?"

"'*Ex favilla resurgo.*' 'From the embers, I rise again.' Phoenixes rise from embers, of course."

Sand frowned. "I thought phoenixes rose from their own ashes."

Perrotte rolled her eyes. "Embers, ashes . . . What's your family motto?"

He raised his eyebrows. "We're blacksmiths,

Perrotte. We don't have a motto. Unless it's, 'Please kindly pay us on time, for services rendered.'"

Perrotte's cheeks flushed. "Sorry. I . . . I guess I forgot."

They spent quiet time sorting pages, while the rain tapped the distant roof and ran off the ends of broken gutters. Sand despaired, realizing how few books he'd actually known existed, let alone read—while on the other side of the room, Perrotte made small, pleased noises in the back of her throat whenever she found something she recognized.

Sand felt they'd made only small inroads into the library by the time Perrotte called for a break, yawning and clutching the small of her back. But she said she was pleased with their progress.

"I don't think we're that far from assembling at least a few whole books," she said.

Sand looked at the anteroom lined with neat piles of parchment and vellum, then back in at the library's giant pile of chaos. He could step inside the library now without treading on pages, that much was true. It still didn't seem like much.

"I suppose."

"Why so glum, Sand?"

He looked around at the piles of pages. "I don't . . . who can learn all of this? How can I possibly go to the university when I never knew a tenth of this existed?"

Perrotte stood beside him, hands on her hips, and surveyed the piles with him. "Sand, do you have a memory storehouse?"

He gave her a sideways look.

"Sorry. Look. My tutor, Efflam, taught me how to build a memory storehouse. In your mind, you imagine a room with all the things you need to remember in order there. As you walk through the room in your mind, you see things that remind you of what you're trying to remember. Say you needed to remember the names of the stars of the Pleiades."

"Of course. I'm always trying to remember those," Sand said, trying not to sound *too* sarcastic.

Perrotte just rolled her eyes at him. "Well, every Breton knows the names of the Seven Founder Saints of Bertaèyn—so you might imagine a room with the founders' statues, and at the foot of each statue, you would imagine carved one of the stars' names. Maybe under the statue of Saint Maloù, you have carved the name of the star Merope. It helps that Maloù and Merope start with *M*. Like that. It doesn't matter—no one else can really tell you how to build your storehouse. It's *your* mind. Anyway, that's a good way to remember things that you have a hard time with. Not that you need bother—clearly you are a blacksmith and a mender born."

He nodded slowly, staggered by this whole notion:

Storehouses in your mind? He was thinking through all that, when he realized Perrotte had gone silent and was just staring at him.

"What?" He rubbed self-consciously at his nose.

"In the chapel, the saint—" she said, and stopped.

"In the chapel, the saint *what*?"

"I know you don't like talking about the mending magic," Perrotte said in a rush. "And maybe it's not magic at all, because maybe it's a miracle, like a saint would perform."

It came to him, then. The memory of the relic he'd mended: Sainte Trifine's heart. He'd stuck it together with beeswax, then repaired her reliquary. Fear prickled at his chest.

"What about the saint in the chapel, Perrotte?"

"The relic of Sainte Trifine—her heart. It's alive and beating."

20

Falcon

SAND LURCHED TO HIS FEET AND MADE FOR THE door. He strode through the falling rain with grim purpose.

The chapel sounded deathly silent after the weather outside, and his boot steps echoed loudly against the stone vaults overhead. It wasn't a very big chapel and in just a few moments, he was crossing himself and opening the reliquary.

He stared in horror at the heart moving inside the box. He dropped to his knees before the altar.

Perrotte's footsteps sounded behind him. He waited. Her hand touched his shoulder.

He was quiet, thinking before he spoke. He didn't want to speak of this, actually, but he knew he must.

"Magic should have some purpose to it," he said. "There's no purpose in what has happened to this heart."

"I think mending is your magic's purpose, Sand." She stood beside him, staring down at the relic.

"So, I'm some sort of witch? Who made a heart beat inside a silver box?"

"You really think you're a witch, and not someone blessed by a saint?"

"Blessed?" His voice cracked on the word and he stood up.

She shrugged. "It doesn't really matter to me."

He drew back. "I'm sorry," he said stiffly. "I thought you would care."

"Oh, Sand, that's not what I meant! I do care. I just . . . I don't think your mending magic is evil, if that's what you're worried about, but I meant that it doesn't *matter.* You are good. You do good things. My guess is . . . I mean . . ." She frowned, and stared at her hands for a moment, before saying, "Well, you know, strange things happen to saints before they're made saints."

A laugh escaped him in one big bark. "I'm hardly pious enough for sainthood."

She shrugged, smiling a little. "Stranger things have happened."

"I don't like that notion. I aim to be a smith. And

have a family someday."

Now it was Perrotte's turn to laugh. "I said 'saint,' not 'monk.' And I thought you were going to Paris to university, to please your father? Don't most men who go to university end up priests?"

"Some do. And I'm going. But I'm going to study medicine, not theology." He felt muted and flat: he'd figured out how to make the best of that bad situation, but learning to heal people still wasn't blacksmithing.

"*If* we get free of here," Perrotte pointed out. "So far, the thorns are winning."

Sand went to the chapel door to stare out at the rain. From the ground level of the inner courtyard he couldn't see the thorns. "I prayed at Saint Melor's shrine the night before I woke here."

"Saint Melor, patron of my father's family, and Sainte Trifine, patron of my mother's family," Perrotte said. "Maybe you should mend Melor's skull and see if it has answers for you."

Sand glared at her—then over her head, caught sight of the colored glass windows depicting Saint Melor's life. The glass was cracked, and some of it was missing—but most of the story was there.

Perrotte turned to see where Sand was staring. "Saint Melor's father was Saint Meliau."

"Was everyone in Bertaèyn a saint, back in the day?"

"Everyone who didn't murder anyone, maybe," Perrotte said. "Saint Melor was only seven years old when his uncle, Riwal, murdered Meliau for his kingdom. Riwal wanted to kill his nephew as well, so the inheritance would be undisputed. The law in those times was that the heir had to be able to hold a sword and ride a horse. Some bishops persuaded Riwal to just maim Melor, to cut off his hand and his foot so he could neither hold a sword nor ride."

The first colored glass depicted Melor receiving a new foot from a bronzesmith and a new hand from a silversmith; the second showed him going about his studies at a monastery with his metal hand and foot. The legend said that the appendages moved at his command and grew with his body.

Sand said, "I'm pretty sure you can ride a horse without a foot. And Melor could have learned to fight left-handed."

"Riwal didn't think of that," Perrotte said.

"I don't know why they didn't get a blacksmith for the job, either," Sand said. "I think steel would have made a better hand than silver. Same for the bronze foot."

The next glass showed Riwal ordering Melor's guardian to kill the boy and bring Riwal his head.

Well, there was no replacing *that* with silver or bronze, Sand thought. Or even steel.

The final glass showed the guardian's journey with Melor's head.

"That's the selfsame head on the glass that's in this chapel?" Sand asked, though he knew the answer.

"Yes. Melor spoke to his guardian through it. He asked to be buried near a spring that he called into being, and there they built a shrine—"

"The shrine I prayed at not to go to university," Sand said.

"I guess your prayer was answered," Perrotte said.

Sand strongly considered throwing something at her—but there was nothing to hand that wasn't sacred.

"You should get some rest," he said roughly, and stalked off to the smithy. He hoped Perrotte would go back to bed. He needed some time to himself.

In the smithy, he built up a fire and started mending. He worked on anything that came to hand, piece after piece, thrusting finished items into the ashes to cool while his mind churned his thoughts to butter.

If they ever actually broke free of the thorns, he would have to go to university, which was bad enough—but he wasn't entirely sure that Perrotte wouldn't end up accused of witchcraft. He wasn't sure *he* wouldn't be accused of witchcraft. Or heresy. Everyone knew Jehanne d'Arc was a well-regarded martyr *now*, but she'd claimed to hear God's voice and they'd burned her at the stake. Neither he nor Perrotte heard any voices, but they surely had done things that would make people nervous. Things that made *him* nervous. And neither he nor Perrotte had any political patrons to save them. In fact, just like Jehanne d'Arc, Perrotte had political enemies.

Added to this was the constant worry that if they did not break free, they would someday run out of food. And more immediately, what about Merlin? The falcon was just sitting in the kitchen, watching them from the rafters. The bird needed to eat, but showed no sign of departing the kitchen on his own.

Of course, Perrotte hardly ate anything—hardly slept, either. Was that what happened after . . . the sort of awakening she had experienced?

Sand also worried about the thorns in his neck. It worried him that they were there, biding their time, though he didn't feel them terribly often. As if they heard his thoughts, a dozen light licks of pain shot out from the thorns.

He hung over his anvil, panting, until the pain passed. His resolve strengthened. He needed to remove the thorns; he needed to finish removing Perrotte's thorns too. But later. First, he needed some time with his hammer and anvil.

Recovered, Sand worked steadily, mending hinges and bolts and door latches, andirons and fireplace pokers and hearth tongs, toasting forks and spatulas and stirring spoons. His piles of broken iron shrank, and that made him feel good.

Daylight was fading by the time he reached the end of the pile at his feet. His last act was the mending of a chisel—a complicated task, one that required hardening and tempering. Fortunately, he could skip a few steps: The metal's quality was assured—this chisel had been a chisel once already—and since he'd found it in the carpenter's shop, he even already knew at what point he should perform the final quench, which was when the chisel's filed surface turned the color of rain-dampened straw. A wood chisel must be quenched at a different color than a metal chisel.

But in the end, he'd left it too late in the day. He could no longer clearly see the colors in the steel by the time he reached the last step in mending the chisel. Disgusted with himself, he tossed the chisel down with his tongs, and left the smithy to dusk. Night was a good time to see the gradations between the glowing colors, but the tempering colors were subtle, possessed no glow, and required proper daylight to distinguish.

Sand's stomach grumbled, and his feet carried him to the kitchen. It was not that he'd forgotten to eat; it was more that he'd refused to break his concentration from things that made sense. Constant work was the only remedy for forgetting what had happened in the chapel.

The kitchen was cold when he got there. He built

up the fire and heated stew. Perrotte showed up a short time later.

"We have to figure out what to do for Merlin," he said, handing her a bowl. "He's not eaten anything since he returned."

She handed the bowl back, and at first he thought this was a protest against the turnips. "I can hunt the falcon," she said, and tore off a strip of her outer skirt to wrap around her arm. She lifted her arm, chirping oddly toward the ceiling.

Not immediately, but soon enough, Merlin swooped down from the rafters and landed on Perrotte's skirt-covered arm.

"Well done, Merlin," she said in a low and even voice. "You don't have any jesses, do you?" She glanced at Sand. "Thin leather ankle straps for falcons," she explained.

Sand shrugged. "He wasn't wearing any when I found him."

She pursed her lips. "*She*, really. A male falcon would be much smaller."

"Oh," he said, entirely unsure what response was required for that.

"Let's go," Perrotte said. "I might need your arm at some point. I'm still sometimes unsteady."

He hurried after her. She descended to the middle courtyard, which had a ring of guard towers along the outer wall. The falcon blinked, but showed no signs that he—*she*—wanted to fly off. Perrotte headed for a nearby guard tower, and slowly climbed the narrow stone steps to the top.

"Can we, maybe, tie a message around Merlin's leg and see if anyone contacts us from the outside world?" Sand asked Perrotte's ascending back.

"She's not a pigeon," Perrotte said sharply over her shoulder.

He wasn't sure if Perrotte meant that messages were beneath Merlin's dignity, or if it was just not possible.

"It's against her nature," Perrotte explained more gently when they reached the top. "She'll hunt for us, but she's going to come back to us, if the bond is strong enough. She's not going to fly off to—I don't even know where you think she might go—and wait and carry a message back. Or however pigeons do it."

He just nodded, looking down at the thorns from the tower. They didn't loom over the castle walls quite the way they used to. In fact—the thorns used to stand a man's height above the walls, and this tower would not then have been able to look *down* on the thorns at all. He was sure they were much lower now. Weren't they?

Beside him, Perrotte thrust her arm upward. Disturbed by the motion of her arm, the falcon took flight, winging up and away.

"Oh," Sand said, a small disappointed sound. Merlin was gone. He was going to miss the bird. He—no, she—wasn't friendly or cuddly or much of anything other than a distant, lurking watcher, but still, she was something else alive in the castle.

He stood beside Perrotte and watched the falcon fly out over the asparagus fields beyond the castle. The muddy fields were greening, like everything else in the world that he and Perrotte were no longer part of. Even the thorns had leafed out and now displayed five-petaled, pinkish-white flowers.

The thorns. They really had been much higher than the castle walls. Hadn't they? He ran through his memories of his time in the castle. He couldn't really remember, but on his first day in the castle, yes, the thorns had been a man's height above the walls. Afterward, they hadn't loomed quite so high, but he'd attributed that to the fact that everything had been new and strange on the first day, and he'd since grown accustomed to the thorns looming.

But at some point, they'd become less looming, and at some point after that, less looming still. Which brought him to this day, and the fact that they were lower. They really were. Only a few feet above the castle walls, really.

"The hedge—" he began excitedly, but Perrotte was

watching Merlin fly off into the deepening hyacinth-colored dusk.

"I don't think it's a concern for Merlin."

"No—the hedge is *lower.*"

Now she looked at him. "Lower than what?"

"Lower than it *was.*" He told her how the thorns had looked on his first day. "How high did they look when you first—woke?"

"Somewhat over my head, were I standing on the walls. I guess."

He nodded. "And now?"

She stared down at the hedge. "Well, the thorns *are* lower. You don't think it's because I cut any of them at the night portal, do you?"

He frowned. "Seems unlikely. You cut hardly any. That's the other side of the castle, anyway." He had returned to lower the portcullis and burn back the thorns creeping under the night portal. The thorns seemed willing to be stopped at the gate, but they were no less thriving outside.

She shrugged, and scratched her neck where a thorn branch had lashed her. She palpated her skin gently. "I think there's a thorn in there," she said.

"Will you be able to find it again tonight?"

"Probably."

He nodded. "We'll get it." That's how the final thorns would be ousted: one by one as she discovered them under her skin, or if either of them noticed any mark of blood poisoning. "I'll need you to work on mine as well." He pointed at the lumps on his neck. "Are you ready to go back down?"

"Back down?" she asked.

He glanced at the wall of the inner courtyard, where smoke from the dinner fire wafted. "I know turnip stew is not your favorite—"

"Merlin isn't done," she said.

Sand frowned. Perrotte raised her arm. A distant dark spot, low over the ground, raced toward them, growing larger. And then Merlin was there, dropping a lark onto the stones between them, and landing on Perrotte's outstretched arm.

"Did you know she'd come back?" Sand asked.

"No, of course not—but I saw her strike, and saw her turn toward us. Bring that lark with us. It's her supper."

Sand stared with longing at the lark. It would have gone so well in the stew. Or in a pie, if he could figure out a way to make a crust.

"Don't worry," Perrotte said, almost laughing. "Once she's fed, I'll teach you to hunt her from up here—and then you can have as many larks as you like."

He laughed uncomfortably, wondering how much his hunger had shown on his face. He hadn't tasted fresh food of any sort in weeks. But of course, Merlin had the right of first refusal. He picked up the lark by its feet and led the way down the tower stairs.

On the way across the garden courtyard, something new caught his eye—something in a long-abandoned garden bed.

Something green.

He ran to it.

"Sand!" Perrotte called. "What are you doing?"

"Green," he said. "Green!" He pointed at the dirt.

She followed more slowly so as not to disturb the falcon on her arm.

"Asparagus spears," she said reverently.

"Asparagus spears," he agreed. "I think . . . in about a week . . ."

"We'll have something fresh to eat." The longing in her voice matched the longing in his whole body. Something fresh and *green*. He wanted green even more than he wanted the lark he carried.

"I thought nothing grew here."

"Well. Nothing did grow." He glanced at her. "Until now." It had to do with her; he felt it in his bones. She had come alive, and things started to grow.

That was when he noticed the buds on the broken apple, pear, and cherry trees across the courtyard. He started for them eagerly, waving her to join him.

"We'll have fruit this autumn!" he said with

satisfaction. They wouldn't have to figure out how to pick raspberries off the deadly thorns, at least.

"This autumn?" The quaver in her voice was unmistakable. He glanced at her face, which sported a range of uncomfortable emotions. "You think we'll be trapped here that long?"

"I don't know how long we'll be trapped here," he said. "I hope for the best. But I'm also preparing for the worst."

"But the hedge is shrinking."

"And we don't know why."

Perrotte pointed up at the tallest tower with its sheet hanging out the window. "Someone must see that!"

"I thought someone would see the smoke from my cooking fires, too. But so far, nothing and no one has ever approached the castle."

"Have people lost all curiosity in just one generation?"

Sand spread his arms out, encompassing the whole castle around them. "Don't you think that's part of it? In a castle torn apart by an unknown force, surrounded by a thorn brake that attacks people? That's part of the curse, something that keeps people from investigating."

"When you lived outside, didn't you ever come and look at the place?"

"Nope." Sand shook his head. "Not even once. When I was little, if I asked questions about the place, everyone shushed me, or told me not to think about it. So I stopped asking, and I stopped thinking about it. Mostly."

Perrotte harrumphed. "Still, I would think someone would come look."

"They might." Sand sighed. "But they haven't yet, so I think we should carry on. Make sure we have enough to eat, and warm clothes to wear. And that all the doors and shutters are mended to keep out winter cold."

She frowned. "We might be here in winter."

He nodded soberly. "Winter. Or the rest of our lives."

21

KNIGHT

After the red-mawed woman left her, Perrotte walked away from the birch tree. She moved more easily in the dark-bright world now that she had refused the water of forgetting and been granted the right to stay.

Eventually, she found herself beside a sedge marsh, where the water reflected stars that were not in the sky. She counted blades of grass where they broke the water's surface, and she counted stars where the water was smooth and grassless. She found it a good task for a time, one that soothed the rages within her; she counted to some very high numbers.

Sometimes, though, her thoughts drifted away from the stars and from the grasses, and she remembered that she had died. "I don't think this is Heaven," she would think.

"I do not think it is Hell, either. But surely I was not so bad that I am truly in Purgatory. Is this Purgatory?"

And then she would remember the conversation with the woman, remembered saying, "I will not drink. I will not go on," and being told that it was her right.

And she would remember that her death had come unjustly, and for a time, she would forget to count the stars.

PERROTTE'S EYES FLEW OPEN.

She got up to peer out the window. She had managed perhaps an hour of sleep, but no more than that. She rubbed her fingers over random parts of her skin, but felt no thorns—perhaps the last effort had gotten them all. She didn't feel feverish or sick anymore.

Restless, she left the bedroom. She wanted her observatory back, but death had taken it from her—death and Jannet. She also wanted her astronomic books back; so far, she'd found no hint of them in the library. There were other works of natural philosophy that she could read and enjoy, but it saddened her that not only had Jannet destroyed her closely read and annotated texts, she had likely also destroyed all Perrotte's notes on her observations.

She would begin again. She found some blank parchment fragments in the library, suitable for jotting notes while she observed the stars. All the ink had been lost in the sundering—spilled and then dried—but she had discovered most of the supplies for making ink throughout the library: green vitriol and gum couldn't be destroyed by being halved, and oak galls needed to be crushed to make ink anyway. She even found quills long enough to use as pens.

Perrotte would choose a new observatory in another tower of the keep and take the roof tiles off. She wouldn't have a fancy hinged and closable roof, but an observatory was an observatory.

And she had something else important to observe, besides the stars: the thorns. She wandered around the castle with a bit of chalk from her purse, climbing guard towers and looking out at the dark mass of thorns, until she found the perfect spot to make her observations. She drew an X on the floor of the tower, so she would be sure to stand in the same place every time. As dawn lightened the sky, she quickly jotted down: "From the fourth window on the east-most tower, the thorns reach halfway up the fifth stone block to the left of the arrow slit on the right guard tower."

The next night she wrote: "One-third of the way up the fifth block."

Perrotte considered her measurements against other factors in the environment. Did the spring leaves growing on the hedge weigh it down? Possibly, but the hedge had grown its leaves long before anything started growing within the castle. According to Sand, the hedge kept time by the seasons of the outside world, ignoring the magical spring that had just begun within. Perrotte did not think the hedge bowed beneath the weight of its leaves simply because the leaves were not new.

Perrotte wrote down the day's activities, in case something she or Sand did affected the magic. Or in case some magic of Sand's affected the hedge. She didn't really think it had anything to do with her. Sand was the wizard, or possibly the saint, who had the mending magic.

Mending magic. Perrotte considered Sand's peculiar magic. The castle's sundering . . . It *meant* something. It was a curse, enacted by something or someone. It had to be—castles didn't just spontaneously break apart. Well, certainly, earthquakes occurred, but not in Bertaèyn very often, and Sand was right, no earthquake would do what had been done to the interior of the castle. It was magic, or a curse, or something along the lines of what Saint Gildas had done to the murderers of Sainte Trifine, when he caused their castle to be swallowed up by the earth.

And the bloodthirsty thorns just proved it, didn't they? Those grew, without question, because of *some* magic.

So what would make the thorns shrink? What

would lessen their power in this broken place?

What was the opposite of breaking?

Mending.

The sun peered over the horizon, breaking her meditation. She took a deep breath, and turned to go, when out of the corner of her eye, beyond the northern guard tower, she saw something.

A man—a knight in armor. On a horse.

She abandoned pen, ink, and parchment and skittered down the stairs. The eastern tower was useless; she needed a guard tower on the north side if she wanted to be seen. She ran across the courtyard as fast as she could go.

A sudden stabbing pain in her thigh announced the presence of a thorn. Or was it just a reminder pain, like Sand occasionally got in his wrist? She clutched her leg but otherwise tried to ignore it.

Up the guard tower stairs.

Out the top.

She leaned over the edge. The man and horse were close. She waved. He waved back. Her heart nearly stopped.

The knight rode closer.

"Don't get too close!" she called.

He lifted his visor. "I'm aware of the thorns," he called back, and she froze. The voice. She recognized that voice, though it was deeper and slower than when she had known him before.

"Sir Bleyz?" she called down, tentative.

He reined in his horse. He crossed himself, but remained silent.

"Sir Bleyz—you conducted me to and from the Abbey of Saint Armel many years ago—and you were supposed to guide me to the court of the Duchess, when it was time."

He crossed himself again. "Are you a ghost?"

"No!" *Yes*. "No, I was . . . I have awakened, Sir Bleyz."

"You were dead, my lady! Forgive my saying so."

"You've called me 'my lady'—then, you recognize me?"

"Lady Perrotte."

"Yes. And . . . And I *was* dead, Sir Bleyz. But I am not. Now. Any longer."

"My lady—" And there were tears in his voice. "Your lord father . . ."

Her heart clenched. "I know, Sir Bleyz. I know he has passed on."

Sir Bleyz bowed his head a moment.

"How is it you came riding past here?" Perrotte called down. "Have you come to free me?"

"A rumor came to my ears. No one believed it, but I had to know. And now . . ." He crossed himself again. "I did not think a girl truly dwelled within the castle walls, and now that I find that it is you . . ."

He wiped at the corner of his eye. Was he weeping? She frowned. He had conducted her from the abbey, true, but they had never been especially close.

"My lady, it is good to see you. I am at your service."

"Then please, help me think of a way to get out of here!" she called.

He shook his head. "My lady, you are far safer in there. I have no doubt that were you to leave, your life would be in grave danger."

"From who?"

"You know from who!"

She nodded. She did know. Jannet. "How is the countship? How goes my sister's rule?"

She could barely hear his scoffing laugh, but his shouted words were plain enough. "The Princess rarely comes to Boisblanc. The dowager Countess is in charge here, and she taxes the folk most severely, still trying to make up for the fortune lost inside there."

Fortune lost? Perrotte hadn't even thought of the treasury—had assumed it would be empty. Surely there had been time to empty it during—

"Tell me about the sundering!" she called.

Sir Bleyz's horse made a nervous motion, and Perrotte realized that the knight was communicating fear or tension to his mount. Was he simply afraid to be seen here by someone who might report to Jannet, or was he afraid of . . . her? A girl who should be dead?

"When your father returned to the castle, he had questions about your death. I guess they were not answered to his satisfaction! Some weeks later, he took the Countess to the chapel and made her swear on the holy relics that she had not killed you. I was there. As soon as she touched the saint's heart and swore her innocence, the sundering came. The castle shook—we had no time! We all ran away, carrying very little—those who tried to stay and save a few things, they were driven off by invisible beasts that clawed and scratched—"

Perrotte felt sick to her stomach. She couldn't even imagine the sundering, but she *could* picture Jannet in the chapel, her hand over Sainte Trifine's relic. She rubbed her belly, trying to soothe it.

"Once we were gone, the thorns sprang up. Many men have died trying to cross them."

She was silent for a moment, trying to regain control of her rebelling body. She felt hot and faint, ready to vomit.

"So . . . there is nothing you can do to free me?"

Sir Bleyz shook his head. "Nothing I know of! The Countess even once tried to breech the thorns with a siege tower! I can almost make out the shape of it—" He squinted off to her left. "If you were to get free from the castle, my lady, and you did not have an army in place, I think she would try to kill you again!"

She nodded. That sounded true.

"Doesn't everyone *know* she killed me?" Perrotte asked. "Wasn't there some sort of rebellion from the barons?"

She couldn't read Sir Bleyz's expression from this distance, but she thought she already knew the answer. Jannet was plenty vicious enough to quash any such rebellion. "She has us in a vise grip, my lady, and we have no *proof*."

"Other than the sundering of the castle!"

"I am the only living witness of her oath," Bleyz called. "And I've been in exile for years, lest she has me killed." He glanced at the rising sun. "My lady, I must fly! It is dangerous if any see me here. I will go to Nauntt and send messages to your barons who remember the Cygne name and would welcome your return. Look for me with the new moon!"

And with that, he spurred his horse and rode away from the castle.

"Wait!" she called, but it was to no avail. What good would it do to send messages to her loyal barons if she were trapped in the castle forever?

22

Hammer

SAND WOKE TO THE SCENT OF PORRIDGE.

He opened his eyes to find Perrotte sitting cross-legged on her bed, eating. She held out a bowl for him.

"Wha—at?" he asked inarticulately, accepting the porridge against his better judgment.

"We have a lot of mending to do today," Perrotte said.

"We do?"

She nodded and handed him a scrap of parchment. "I've been observing the thorns, and I think on days that you mend more, the thorns shrink."

He stared at the notations. "You've only got two notations here."

"I know. That's why you need to mend a lot today. And maybe none the following day, and I'll measure the thorns both days, and then! We may have a pretty good idea. But we need to test it."

He stared at her, trying to think through the theory. Could that be it? Could that *really* be it? Not fire, not cutting, not figuring out how to go under or how to go over—but *mending* might defeat the thorns?

"And then we need to take measurements," she said. "Because if we can't dwindle the thorns away before winter, we need to figure out how to deal with our food supply. But if we *can* get free by winter, we'll worry about food a lot less."

He felt left behind. "You think that *mending* the broken things makes the thorns shrink?"

She rolled her eyes at him. "Do you know what testing *means*?"

He rolled his eyes right back. "Yes. I test metal all the time, to see if it's pure, to see if it's—"

"Well, then! Stop acting like I've just suggested you figure out how to train bumblebees to fly you over the thorn hedge, and let's get to work!"

FIRST, THOUGH, THEY TOOK Merlin to hunt. Merlin collected enough larks that Sand could finally have lark stew; then the falcon was allowed to eat the sparrows she'd worked so hard for.

On the way back to the kitchen with their string of larks, Perrotte stopped and stared at the ground.

"Green. More green! Look!" She pointed at the earth.

He bent beside her to see a row of tiny, two-leaved green plants poking up through the earth. "Peas! That's where I planted peas!"

"You planted peas!" She clapped her hands. "I hate peas!"

Between the lark stew and the anticipation of the garden, things were looking up in the kitchen—until they discovered mold on some of the cheeses. And a funny rust on some of the dried apples. And then blight got into Perrotte's tisane herbs.

The worst discoveries were some rotting turnips, however; not because either of them mourned a lost turnip, but because, in the back of Sand's mind, turnips were their starvation rations, the option that stood between them and death. And also the rot smelled terrible.

"But how?" Perrotte asked. "I thought nothing rotted here!"

"Nothing lived and nothing died; but then you woke up. And the garden woke up."

She wrinkled her nose. "That makes no sense. Everything was dead before. It wasn't all just *sleeping*."

"Well, neither were you. You didn't just wake

up. . . .” He took a deep breath. “You *lived.*”

“So?”

“So . . . I guess death comes with life.”

She shook her head, but what could either one of them say? Before she woke, the turnips had lasted for twenty-five years. After she woke, they rotted in open air—though the ones still buried in the root cellar remained solid and dull and turnipy. For now.

Sand didn't know where the independently beating heart in the chapel fit into all of this living and dying, though. He tried not to think on it too often.

ONCE PERROTTE WAS FULLY recovered from her battle with the thorns, and all Sand's thorns had likewise been removed, they began to work in earnest on mending. If mending truly made the thorns shrink, they'd have to fix every single thing in the castle. A daunting thought.

They began their tests of the theory in the smithy, where Sand had the most skill. Together, they set up another forge, another anvil, and made certain Perrotte had her own piles of tools and equipment.

“It will go faster if you can pump the bellows for me when I ask, and on some larger pieces, I may need you to wield the sledgehammer.”

“Sledgehammer?” Perrotte asked, alarmed. “Aren't those terribly heavy?”

"Eight pounds or so. The artistry in blacksmithing is knowing where to hit, more than your strength of arm. So the way that works is, the master smith, or in my case, the smith with more experience, hits the piece with a lighter hammer, and then you, as the smith with less experience, try to hit the same spot with the sledge. That's all you have to do, just follow my lead."

She nodded, looking a bit unsure of herself, but didn't refuse or hesitate. "Very well. Anything else I should do, oh, master smith?" She gave him a funny little bow, tipping an imaginary hat to him.

He hadn't thought he'd sounded *too* imperious during his explanation, but he responded in kind to her gesture, saying loftily, "I'll let you know."

They worked steadily for hours. Sand taught Perrotte just a few of the endless secrets of smithing, enough that she could mend things with very little intervention from him. She had been reluctant at first, saying, "I think I should just help you; the magic of the mending lies in you, not me." But he told her that she would be a better help to him if she understood smithing well, and had a few projects under her belt.

While they worked, they discussed all the other things that needed mending in the castle, and pondered which things would defy mending altogether.

"Will those unmendable things count against us, with the hedge?" Perrotte fretted.

"I know as much about curses and magic as you do," Sand replied. "Probably less. You tell me—does magic care about the spirit of one's intentions or does it care about results? Is magic practical, and knows that not everything here can be fixed, or does magic expect perfection?"

"I don't know," Perrotte said crankily. "I guess we'll have to try a few things and find out."

"It took me five broken buckets to remake two. The wood that couldn't be made back into buckets was too shattered, and the metal that bound the staves together joined my scrap piles. It all went to mend other things, or to keep us warm, and so forth. I have to think that counts, even though there are three fewer buckets in the castle."

"I don't *know*," Perrotte repeated. She was mending spoons and other unbladed kitchen utensils, as they did not require the difficult art of tempering.

"For mending windows and the like, we don't have a glass furnace," Sand said. "Does the magic care that we don't have a glass furnace, or is the magic going to quibble with us about the windows?" He was making nails, because nails went fast and they would need many of them when they moved on to mending doors and furniture. "Though. Maybe we could—"

Perrotte shouted wordlessly, and jumped back from her anvil.

Sand looked up to see the face of her hammer, which had fragmented into three wedge-shaped pieces, fall completely away.

"What just happened?" she asked, staring at the hammer like it had turned to a viper and then back into a hammer.

"Your hammer wore out. The facing came off. Perfectly, I might add—those three pieces mean that it was good hammer, properly tempered."

"A *good* hammer? But it broke!"

"Yes, it did."

"How?" The word was anguished. "We're menders! We are *mending*! How can this break?"

Sand tried to sound comforting. "Some things just wear out, Perr."

She looked far more upset than a broken hammer would warrant, but Sand thought he understood. They spent so much time dealing with broken things or trying to fix them that it was a grave insult for one of their tools to betray them. A tool he had already mended once, in fact.

Would he be as upset if it had happened to him instead? Perhaps.

"I'll fix it," Sand said. "What's more, I'll teach *you* how to fix it."

"But that involves tempering—you don't want to teach me tempering; you said it was too hard."

"It's hard, but I never said it was *too* hard. You're smart, and we'll get more done if you understand tempering. I was just being lazy, taking the easy way, in not teaching you."

Sand put aside his nail rod, and began his lesson on the art of drawing a temper. As he explained how to test the steel, she interrupted: "I know, I know, testing! I teased you about testing, and now I regret it. But why can't it be easier, to be a blacksmith?"

"Well," he said slowly, "not all iron and steel is the same in quality. We observe it, we assess it . . . So we can make the right tool with it, not something that will snap or bend when it is used. In the end, we have to make do with what we've got, but at least we know what we have before we start work. That's why we test."

Perrotte's impatience had faded during his explanation. "It's a good way to live one's life," she said seriously. "To observe, to test, to assess, before trying to bend something."

Sand considered that, then nodded. "Sure. Though there's another thing people say about life, that they learned from blacksmiths."

"What's that?"

"'Strike while the iron is hot.'"

Perrotte frowned. "I've heard that before, and I always thought it meant to jump on an opportunity. That's how people mean it, isn't it?"

"Perhaps," Sand said. "But if you control the fire, you control *when* the iron is hot. And also, you can reheat iron. I always thought it meant that there was no point in trying to bend cold metal—so, don't try to make situations into what they aren't."

"Sand . . ." Perrotte was stoking the fire in her forge, arranging the charcoal to her liking.

He waited, but she said nothing more. "What is it, Perrotte?"

"Are you really going to go to the university, like your father wants?"

"I promised I would. What about you?"

"I don't know. I never wanted to go to court. I wanted to study astronomy and the natural sciences. I, for one, *dreamed* of going to a university to study. My old tutor made it sound like the most wonderful thing. Of course—" She jammed her poker deep in the fire and rooted around the coals. "Of *course*, women aren't admitted to universities. The best we can do is to go live near one, and hire tutors to come to us."

"It's unfair: You want to go to a university but cannot, and I do not want to go and must."

"I should cut my hair and pretend to be you," Perrotte said, then laughed.

"Well," Sand said, "that wouldn't really solve *my* problem. My father would know I wasn't at the university when I showed up in the smithy every morning."

"You could apprentice with someone else."

"I know." But he couldn't. That was no way to keep a bargain with God.

"I was going to court to get away from Jannet. She was sending me to court to get me away from her. It served both our purposes." She looked up from the embers. "I didn't really realize that until just now. Though . . ." She trailed off, and clamped her mouth shut, a distant look glazing her eyes. Her "memory of a memory" look.

Sand nodded, swallowing against a sudden lump in his throat. He had sometimes wondered if his father's burning desire to send Sand away was because Gilles didn't love him. He could understand a stepparent not loving their stepchild, as was clearly the case with Perrotte and Jannet—in spite of Agnote, who he loved and who loved him. He was sad for Perrotte, for not having an Agnote in her life.

"That's enough wallowing," Perrotte said, looking up from her fire. He hoped his face didn't show any of his feelings, so he busied himself with his own forge, as though he'd not been staring at the top of her head the last few moments. "That's enough wallowing. Come on. Let's get mending. We have some magic to test."

❧

Perrotte measured the thorns the next day, and found that they had retreated a goodly amount. The tops of the castle's tallest outer walls were now exposed by the shrinking thorn break. Sand found this hopeful; Perrotte reserved judgment.

"It has to be the mending," Sand said. "So we should just start again tomorrow."

"No," Perrotte said, drawing out the word and speaking to him like he occasionally spoke to his little sisters. "Look. The thorns are producing tiny baby raspberries that could be weighing the branches down. So, to test it *properly*, we have to take a day off. If the thorns still shrink, we'll know it's *not* the mending, and then we don't have to work as hard."

Sand found that puzzling. Why *wouldn't* they keep mending things? If the thorns came down, people would move back into the castle, and they'd probably rather things were mended.

But he agreed to resist mending that day. Instead, they worked in the garden. The odd things that Sand had planted all sprouted. And about a hundred things that Sand had *not* planted all sprouted as well, or came back to life. Vines that clung to the keep wall for support started to bud—Perrotte assured Sand that these were roses, and they would have rose petals to scent their wash water, and tart rose hips to snack on come autumn—if they were to be there in the autumn. A hazy green mist seemed to arise over the bushes and branches around the courtyard, as more plants unfurled buds or blooms.

"Too silent," Perrotte said the day they harvested the asparagus spears. They had agreed that they could not wait the full week to eat asparagus, so these spears would be only half the size they should be. But there were already new spears poking from the earth.

"How so?"

"No birds singing. Not a one."

They eagerly took the asparagus to the kitchen and passed it through a pot of boiling water, then a pot of fresh cold well water. "The quench," Perrotte said with a laugh, and then they fell to eating the fresh food, their lips smacking greedily. Sand had never loved the slight bitterness of the vegetable, but it was hard not to eat asparagus in a valley known for growing it. He'd often considered asparagus a burden, in fact—but right now, it seemed a gift.

The asparagus was gone before they knew it, and immediately, Sand wanted more.

As fast as the garden now grew, the food in the kitchen spoiled ten times as fast. The cheeses in the pantry seemed to have remembered their true age in one night, and were nothing but a web of fuzzy white threads the next morning.

Sand wondered if they might starve slowly on asparagus and larks and half-rotten turnips. It was never quite *enough* food for the both of them, and they went to bed hungry that night.

"We're sharp-set," Perrotte told him. "A proper falconer keeps his birds this way, a little bit hungry always, a little bit keen on food, so that the falcons will want to hunt."

"I would not do well as a falcon," he told her.

The next day, they discovered the thorns had not shrunk at all during the rest day. This was enough proof for both of them; they agreed to live sharp-set and mend the broken things in the castle as though their lives depended on it.

Which, in fact, they did.

Ember

The first time Perrotte met Anna—before Jannet, before Anna became the Duchess of Bertaèyn—Perrotte had been left in the nursery with Anna and her baby sister while their parents visited. When the nurse was busy with the littler girl in an antechamber, Anna had convinced Perrotte to climb out the bedroom window with her.

"I do it all the time," Anna said, one leg over the windowsill. She pulled herself outside, and clung to the vines on the castle wall. "Come along!" she ordered Perrotte, peering in the window.

Perrotte did not hesitate, though perhaps she should have. She'd never been a girl who climbed things. She plunked her bottom onto the windowsill, threw her legs over, and scrabbled to find footholds. She thought she had footing, so she knotted her fingers in the vines and lifted her body away from the windowsill, intending to swing around and face the wall.

She had vastly overestimated the security of her purchase, however, and her foot slipped off the vine and down into nothingness. The jagged end of a broken branch, hidden among the vine's leaves, scraped a line of hot pain down her thigh. Fear washed over her, and she scrambled to find a place for her feet.

"Good heavens!" came the nurse's voice from the window. A hand shot out and seized Perrotte's arm. The nurse hauled her inside and tossed her to the carpet. Anna was seized next, and thrown down beside her. The nurse closed the casement, all the while scolding them—did they think they were birds, monkeys, or squirrels?

Anna stayed down on the carpet beside Perrotte. Perrotte, trying to catch her breath from the fright and the pain, as well as the horror of being scolded, stared at Anna. Anna stared back, her eyes lit with strange delight. She grinned. *Anna's having fun!* Perrotte realized with a start. *And she thinks I'm having fun too!*

There had been no other moment like that. And Perrotte did not think that climbing out windows, being scratched by branches, or getting in trouble was fun, so when it came down to it, she and Anna didn't have much to build a friendship on, did they?

And yet, in all the ways that the nobly born counted friendships, Perrotte and the future Duchess were considered close friends. Their families relied on each other, and they themselves did not detest each other. Who knew how they might have come to regard their friendship if Perrotte had ever arrived at court?

Perrotte considered how different her friendship with Sand was in comparison. Certainly, their time spent trapped together, working for a common goal, made their bond more intense. She found herself thinking often of Trifine's resurrection by Saint Gildas. Gildas had not only avenged her murder but he'd brought her back to life. She wondered how Saint Gildas and Sainte Trifine felt about each other. That had to be an intense bond, too.

But beyond all of *that*, Perrotte genuinely liked Sand.

So it made her sick to think about not telling him the truth about Sir Bleyz. But every time she convinced herself to reveal the truth to him, something stopped her. Something that knew that Sand would not approve of how she planned to depose Jannet.

THEIR DAYS OF BEING sharp-set continued. The ancient food spoiled and spoiled, and the garden grew and grew. They swooped down on any new food like Merlin on a ring pigeon. They ate spring onions, borage, garlic scapes, rampion, and parsley, and more asparagus, dandelions and leaf lettuce. Mints sprouted, so they drank tisanes and chewed mint leaves.

Trees and plants bloomed, and bees flew over the castle wall to drink the nectar, but didn't stay. Sand was wistful, wishing aloud that the bees would set up a hive within the castle wall, so they could collect the honey.

Daily, Perrotte measured the thorns. "We have to work faster, or we'll starve," she said. "We're peckish now, but it's spring. Even if we have a bountiful summer and a good harvest, we won't have enough to save for winter, and no means to preserve it anyway. We've no swine, cattle, or fowl. We can't make sausages. We can't collect eggs. We've no spices or salt to preserve anything. No vinegar to pickle anything."

"We can dry apples and pears and cherries," Sand said.

She shook her head. "That won't be enough, not nearly enough." She eyed the unripened fruit on the hedge. "Dare we eat the raspberries when they ripen?"

"Are you suggesting we eat cursed fruit? Vicious fruit? Attacking fruit?"

"The harvest would be a problem," she agreed. "We have to get out of here."

"We're mending as fast as we can," Sand said.

"And it's working," Perrotte said. They had exposed nearly a foot of the outer walls. "I just don't know about the timing." She stopped herself from saying, *Perhaps Sir Bleyz can send us food, catapult it over the wall.*

Sir Bleyz. His plan to foment a rebellion on her behalf confused her. They hadn't known each other that well before she died. He'd been newly a knight, and new also in her father's service. He had conducted her to the convent, and they'd barely spoken.

But when he came to bring her home from the convent the day before Christmas, she had found herself babbling aimlessly to him. Her relentless chatter was probably from relief over leaving the convent. First, she talked freely about her father's letter to her, with the plan he had outlined that she would become a lady-in-waiting to the Duchess. Sir Bleyz, a very chivalrous young knight with a magnificent shock of black hair, let her talk as much as she liked.

Her chatter flowed so easily, though, that she found herself making up stories about her life for him. Lying, in fact. She told him how the nuns had been loath to see her go, and had wept when she took leave of them. "I went to each one, and gave them all a token of my favor—a handkerchief, a scarf, a nice ribbon—of course they cannot wear anything fancy with their habits, for they are nuns, but it is nice, when you have nothing lovely, to look upon something pretty."

She didn't know why she lied to Bleyz, but he was new to the Boisblanc household, and she thought maybe he would actually believe that she was both beloved and cherished by the countship and her family, and she was not in fact unwanted and unfavored.

The stories took on embellishments. She told him next about how, though her father insisted that she go to court and wait on Duchess Anna, it was against her stepmother's pleading. "Jannet's heart is breaking over my departure," she told Bleyz. "She told me once that she would keep me in her purse if I were small enough, so she could just open it up, any time of day or night, and look inside and gaze upon my face."

She then proceeded to tell Sir Bleyz all her plans for court—she made up no few stories there, either. "Duchess Anna is so thrilled that I am coming to attend her," she lied next. "She writes me letters three times a day, in hopes that I will be able to come to her sooner."

It wasn't a total lie that the Duchess looked forward to Perrotte joining her at court; there had been a letter from Anna, written by a scribe, that formally welcomed her to Rennes. The letter mentioned the supposed fun they'd had together when they were small—but did not mention the latter two occasions that they'd met: Anna and her parents had attended the Count and Jannet's wedding, and Perrotte had gone with the Count and Jannet to Anna's father's funeral.

A sobering memory of truth didn't stop Perrotte's story, though. That was how the idea of the scented shoes had begun—she told Bleyz about the new fashion she planned to start at court. Sir Bleyz surely knew about scented gloves, didn't he? Well, imagine scented shoes!

Her fantasies all spiraled down to the nothing from which they came once they reached Castle Boisblanc. Her father wasn't even there; he was attending the Duchess. Jannet didn't come down to greet her, being newly delivered of a daughter. No one had sent the news of her new sister to Perrotte in the convent, and Sir Bleyz hadn't seen fit to tell her. She was allowed to peek in at the wet nurse and let the baby clutch her finger briefly, but that was all.

A sister. Perrotte was still the heir to Boisblanc, then. For now.

The lack of fanfare at her return was a small relief in a way, though she knew then that Sir Bleyz must immediately understand how much she had lied to him on their journey from the convent.

He'd probably known from the beginning, if she had to admit the truth to herself.

Now, twenty-five years later, he wanted to help her.

The more she thought about his final words as he rode away, the more she felt certain that he planned to use her resurrection to leverage himself back into a position of power. Did it even matter to him that she couldn't get out of the castle?

She couldn't blame him. He'd been exiled because he knew Jannet's secrets. Life in exile was hard. But even so, Perrotte didn't want him to use her.

The new moon was close. She barely slept in her bed at night, even compared to before. Her restlessness worried Sand, she knew.

Every night, she climbed the guard tower, and found herself ignoring the stars to instead scan the horizon for a light, for a sign that Sir Bleyz was coming. She often dozed up there, needing more sleep than she admitted to herself.

She dreamed often of her marsh beneath the world, the stars and grasses she counted there.

The night of the new moon, however, the dreams of her death shifted, and she found herself reliving the day of the red seed.

A dark-haired woman came to her in the marsh.

"Perrotte, the time has come for you to move on," the woman said.

Perrotte smiled. She'd had this argument before. "I will not drink. I will not go on."

"Are you afraid to forget? I was afraid to forget once," the woman said. "The thing is, to drink, you are only

giving up the strength of the memories, so it is not painful to be gone from the world. The memories remain. And the love remains, stronger than the day it was born."

"What love," Perrotte said, and it wasn't a question.

"Ah," the woman said, and clasped her hands in front of her.

"What happened to the woman without a face?" Perrotte asked.

"Politics." The woman sighed. "Now hear me: You may have given up the choice to go forward . . . but you can still go back. And sometimes to go forward, you must go back. Open your mouth, Perrotte."

A strange obedience stole over her, and Perrotte opened her mouth. "How odd," she thought. "I'm dead and I still have a mouth."

The woman held up a red seed, which glowed with life in the darkness under the world. She leaned forward, brushing back Perrotte's hair tenderly, then placed the seed under Perrotte's tongue.

Flavor filled Perrotte's mouth. Tart yet sweet. Moldering yet fresh. Dead yet living.

The woman leaned close and kissed Perrotte's cheek. "I have a message for you, Perrotte. Your mother loves you, and your saints love you. And they have asked that you live again."

Perrotte had closed her eyes, unable to bear her aching-full heart with open eyes—and then, and then, it was all gone, and she had awakened in the dark, cold stone crypt beneath the chapel.

Just as she came to life in the dream, she woke.

"My lady!" Sir Bleyz called, saluting her with a torch. She scrambled to her feet to look down. "I have been hard at work, moving secretly among the barons. I have told our most trusted allies that you live, and this has brought hope again to them!"

Her mouth was dry. She swallowed. "It has?"

"The Cygne line is much missed among the people, both low and high." He paused. "As is the Boisblanc line."

"My sister lives, I thought!"

"But your stepmother rules. And you are the true phoenix—from the ashes, you have risen!"

"But I—"

"Your army can be ready with a week's notice. We can march on the Countess at Góll Castle and depose her!"

Góll was a hunting lodge turned castle that her father had not liked very well, but it was the second largest and second most defensible of the Boisblanc castles. So that's where Jannet now lived, and presumably where her father had died.

Perrotte swallowed against the lump in her throat that this last thought created.

"The war of this reclamation will be swift—none

will oppose you!" Sir Bleyz called.

War? She would declare war on Jannet?

Reason and emotion fought within her. The door in her mind, where the secrets of her death lay, popped open. She still would not look inside, but something slipped out in that moment—an ember, a burning brand, something alight. It rose within her, a line of fire from the pit of her belly, passing through her heart until it burst from her mouth in an angry, triumphant cry. "Yes! Yes! Raise my army. I will claim my land!"

24

Door

THE THORNS WERE FADING. SHRINKING. THINNING. Every measurement that Perrotte took confirmed this, and she took many measurements from many angles, climbing this tower and that, using a sighting stick, and recording all her observations.

By day, she worked side by side with Sand—in the smithy, in the kitchen, in the carpenter's shop, in the garden. They mended stools with hammers and chisels, wove baskets, stitched leather, sewed bedsheets, stuffed mattresses, rehung doors, repaired latches, coopered barrels . . . Many things neither of them knew anything about, but through careful examination of broken objects and the use of what Sand called "the smith's imagination," they often found a way to move forward.

But the key to their success in repairing things was really Sand's mending magic. The only problem was, Sand wouldn't admit that he had that magic. Not aloud. Not to her. But he did admit it, tacitly, by making sure he assisted in everything that she couldn't do perfectly. Certainly, with all her practice, Perrotte could turn out many basic tools and implements that were whole and functional in the end. They were not beautiful, but she thought she might become quite good at smithing someday.

But in the crafts that neither of them understood, the difference was clear. Perrotte's lumpy carvings turned magically smooth and useful if Sand even took a moment to chisel a few gouges near the end of the task. She was the better tailor, from years of practicing embroidery against her will, but when she tried to sew pages together back into a book, she just created an awkward mess until Sand punched a few holes and pushed through a few threads—then, *voilà*! A perfectly repaired book.

She might have been jealous, except it was so very clear that it made Sand uncomfortable and perhaps even a little scared.

And because she felt guilty, she didn't push him. She knew she should tell Sand about Sir Bleyz. About the army that he rallied on her behalf. But she thought—she was quite certain, in fact—that Sand wouldn't approve.

So she only spoke with Bleyz in the night, leaning out from one of the guard towers. She never told him why she only wanted to talk at night, but he preferred it too; no one from the village would see him approach the castle, see her lean out of a tower, and report the whole thing to the Countess. They both knew, though never spoke directly about it, that if the Countess discovered Bleyz's doings, he would be executed.

She found it difficult to plot a rebellion from shouting distance, but they managed it. Bleyz reported in every few nights about which barons he had approached. All agreed to war. All were weary of the hard times since the sundering of the castle. The countship was poor. The Countess's taxes were as high as she could set them, and stayed that way, year after year. She pushed the *corvée* to its limit, requiring her vassals and her vassals' vassals to labor in her fields and on her roads longer than any other lord in Bertaèyn. She forced them to surrender ever-larger portions of their harvests. She overcharged for the use of her mills, her ovens, and her winepresses. And she had closely and freely allied herself with France, not only supporting the King against Breton lords, but marrying her daughter to a prince of France.

Every instance of mismanagement or injustice that Perrotte heard strengthened the ember in her heart. She wanted revenge. She wanted justice. She wanted Jannet on her knees, pleading for her life.

Sir Bleyz worried about funding the army, until Perrotte checked the treasury and found it to be as well-stocked as the rumors suggested. The coronet and sword of Boisblanc were gone. Clearly, some money had been taken away. But many money chests remained, reminding Perrotte of broken eggs, with silver deniers spilled like egg whites, and golden francs like yolks. It would have been impossible to gather all the coins together and carry them off during the castle's abandonment, with invisible beasts attacking the stragglers. The thorns had kept anyone from coming back.

Broken coins spent as well as whole ones. Perrotte scooped up bag after bag, night after night, and threw them over the hedge for Sir Bleyz. The lost wealth of Boisblanc would buy Boisblanc back. Jannet would be deposed.

When *that* thought crossed Perrotte's mind, she stopped in her night's coin scooping. An emotion coursed through her, something between sorrow and dread, something that prickled like a hedge full of thorns trying to get out from deep inside her. Perrotte stumbled, then fell, landing hard in the pile of coins around her.

Against her conscious will, the door in her mind burst open.

And everything Perrotte had been hiding from herself came out.

AFTER HER LESS THAN triumphant return from the convent, Perrotte had comforted herself with going down to see the shoemaker's apprentice, to ask him if he would scent a pair of slippers for her as one might scent a pair of gloves—just as she had explained to Sir Bleyz while weaving her stories for him.

She had known Gilles since his apprenticeship at Castle Boisblanc began, a handsome boy who always lurked behind his master. She couldn't remember when she started being friendly with him, or when friendliness had changed to friendship.

It was not proper, to be friends with an apprentice shoemaker, but Gilles *liked* her, or pretended to. All the other boys she'd ever met, peasant or noble, apprentice or page, had been respectful or frightened or fawning or reserved. No one else had ever smiled at her, or asked her questions about her life. Gilles did that, whenever his master wasn't looking and Loyse wasn't paying attention.

So she went to him then, with her plan for success at Anna's court, and asked him for help, all unknowing of what ill would come of it.

She had stopped in to check the progress of the work several times. At last, Gilles brought the finished slippers and gloves to the tower room, the night before she was to leave for court.

She was watching the stars. She had no astrolabe, no books, and no charts, but Raoul had come and opened the hinged roof of her observatory, and it was enough. She hadn't bothered to write her father about the disappearance of her astrolabe and other things. She hadn't let him know about the emptiness of her tower room. The few times she had complained about Jannet early on, he'd at first told her not to be inhospitable to her new mother; later, he had told her not to be a brat. So Perrotte had never complained to her father about Jannet again.

Footsteps sounded on the tower stairs, and Gilles's face appeared in the opening, lit from his candle. He climbed to her level, smiling uneasily.

"What's wrong?" she asked.

"I'm not pleased to be here," he said baldly, but when she scrunched her nose in confusion, he explained. "I am unfond of heights." He plopped a bag down between them. "Your gloves and dancing slippers."

She clapped her hands and opened the bag. She pulled out the shoes first, kicking off her fur-lined slippers and sliding her toes into the soft leather. They fit perfectly, almost like a second, but tougher, skin. They were not as soft as her squirrel slippers, but they were comfortable in a different way. She wriggled her toes in them, then got to her feet and danced around the room. It wasn't quite as she imagined, with every footfall releasing an obvious puff of perfume, but they would do.

"Try the gloves too," Gilles said, and Perrotte danced back and pulled those on too. She spun around the room again, carrying on in an imaginary *basse danse*.

She stopped, panting. "Fast shoes," she announced.

"Pardon?" Gilles asked.

"They dance so quickly, I'm already out of breath!"

"Ah," Gilles said, nodding. "Certainly. Sit down, and rest a moment."

She sat beside him and yawned gapingly. "I'm tired," she said.

"Then I should go."

"No! Stay. I won't see you again for a long time, after tomorrow." Maybe not ever. If Jannet ever managed to have a son, would Perrotte ever return to Castle Boisblanc?

At least she would see her father at court from time to time.

"I suppose not," Gilles said. "But still. I should go."

"Why?" she asked, yawning again. "Do you think I'm going to go to sleep here, and need some privacy?"

"Mayhap. If you wish to sleep here, perhaps you should. Just . . . close your eyes."

It did seem an attractive prospect, to close her

eyes. Her vision blurred. Tiredness crashed over her like a wave. Her muscles relaxed of a sudden, and she toppled over. "Gilles?" she slurred. "What's happening . . ."

"Shhh. Just go to sleep, my lady. Let yourself fall."

That was when she knew—knew that Gilles knew something. Had done something. She fought the tiredness, trying to sit up. She managed to push herself upright, even shoved to her feet.

"What did you *do*?" she asked, stumbling toward him.

"Lady Perrotte." His voice was pleading. He was standing now, his arms were reaching for her, his hands were on her shoulders, he was trying to push her down—she jerked away.

"What did you *do*?" she asked again.

"I—nothing bad! Nothing wrong! You are going to go to sleep, my lady. Gentle as anything. Go to sleep, and dream pleasantly for a long time."

"I wasn't tired," she told him, fighting to understand what he meant, fighting to think how to explain to him why it was that she was *not* going to sleep.

"Be still, you don't want to fall and hurt yourself," he said, reaching for her.

She pulled away from him, but the movement overbalanced her. She stumbled and hit her head against the wall. Gilles cried out. Her blurred vision turned black and sideways for a moment. She lost track of up and down. She fell to her knees, then collapsed completely. Her head hit the floor and a light sparked behind her closed eyes. Gilles shouted again, grabbing her arm.

She tried to protest, to tell him how wrong he was to grab her, to tell him how she knew, she *knew* he had poisoned her slippers or gloves, but it all came out as an incoherent, garbled howl. She had lost her ability to stand. She had lost her ability to talk. Her vision was gradually fading back in from black and sideways, but it was slow to return, and everything remained a blur.

She wanted to cry. She wanted to scream. She wanted to use words and fists. But she couldn't. Her body wasn't her own anymore.

From beyond the blur of her vision, Gilles cursed. "She's dying!"

Farther off, a woman's voice answered. "What did you *do*?"

"Only what you told me! You lied, my lady. This wasn't gentle."

25

Coins

A shrill scream woke Sand. He sat bolt upright.

"Perr?" he asked into the darkness, but she didn't answer. He couldn't hear her breathing, and when he reached for her hand across the corner of their mattresses, he touched nothing but fabric.

The scream had come from far away. He leaped up, lit his candle from the fire's embers, and went in search of her.

She wasn't in the library, her old room, or the kitchen. Nor the chapel. The last place he expected to find her was the crypt, and when he didn't find her there, he truly began to worry.

She was close enough that he'd heard the scream, so he presumed she must be in the area of the inner courtyard. But she had not screamed again. He called for her in the great hall and then started searching the keep, room by room.

He noticed a tattered tapestry had been pushed aside, and a small, broken door once hidden by the fabric was open. The faint light of a candle came from within. He heaved a sigh of relief, and entered the room.

It was the treasury. He swallowed hard, his mouth suddenly dry. He'd never thought himself particularly greedy, but here lay more gold and silver than he imagined existed in the world, let alone an amount he ever expected to find in one room.

Perrotte sat on a pile of coins, a leather bag grasped tightly in one hand, staring at the ceiling.

Was she having some sort of fit?

"Perrotte? Perr? Are you all right?" He placed his candle holder near the door and knelt beside her. Sharp edges of broken coins poked his knees, and he shifted uncomfortably.

To his relief, her eyes moved to meet his. She gasped and grabbed his arms. "Sand. Sand." She wrapped her arms around his neck and held on to him tightly.

He wasn't sure if she was crying or not; if so, she was nearly silent. But then the hot tears hit his neck, and he knew. It was sort of foul. He was pretty sure she was leaking snot onto him, too. But he put his arms around her in return. The world was too big and the castle too small to worry about the foul sensation on his neck while his friend was weeping. He held her tight.

Eventually, her arms loosened and her body relaxed away from him. He let her sag back onto the pile of coins.

"What's wrong, Perrotte?"

Her mouth worked, trying to form words, before she closed her eyes and shook her head.

He sat for a long moment, frustrated and fearful. "You don't have to tell me, of course," he said at last. "But it will make you feel better. My grandmère likes to say, 'A burden shared is a burden halved.'"

Perrotte opened her eyes. Now she scowled at him. "Oh? And you've halved all your burdens, have you?"

"You know my heart better than anyone living, at this point."

Her eyes dropped to the candle flame, which she watched for a few moments. A small line creased between her eyebrows as she looked down at the candle. His father's forehead had a line like that, made permanent by repeated use over the years. Agnote would pretend to try to wipe it away with her thumb. She called it his worry line.

"Is that it?" Perrotte asked quietly. "Those are

all of your burdens? You want to be a blacksmith but your father wants to send you away?"

"That's far from *it*," he said sharply. Anger rose within him that she would be so callous. "I fear that I'm a witch. I worry for my sisters, if my father wants to send them away as he wanted to send me. I am sad for my grandparents, who lost a daughter to fever and a son to war, and now have no one to pass their secrets on to. I fear we will never escape this place, and we will die here before our times."

Her laugh was brittle.

"What?" he asked, appalled that she should laugh at his fears.

"One of us *already* died before her time." She stood abruptly and shook away the coins whose ragged edges clung to her skirt.

He tamped down his anger. She wasn't thinking properly. "Perrotte . . . ," he said. She looked down at him, waiting. "You screamed. It woke me. What happened? Did you remember something bad, like you did in the tower?"

Perrotte offered him a hand, her eyes steady on his. "I did."

He took it and rose to his feet. "Well?"

Their hands parted, and fell to their sides.

"Well, Sand, I was murdered."

Sand's whole body tensed. He found himself

panting for breath as though he'd run miles. His legs wanted to crouch, his hands wanted to become fists. He was ready to fight. But who would he fight with? Perrotte?

He forced his legs and hands straight and his breath to slow. He was shocked by Perrotte's news, but not *surprised* at the same time. Because it made sense of a strange story: How could a girl so young and so healthy die so suddenly? Certainly, she was just as likely to have died of some plague or disease as anyone, including his own mother—but she would have remembered falling sick. And castles did not sunder themselves over natural deaths. He was certain of that.

No, he wasn't surprised. What did surprise him, however, was the sudden, violent rage that filled him, and how all he wanted to do was find the person who had killed her, and—kill that person back. Murderous rage, he'd heard this feeling called, but he'd never realized how hard it was to bear, how he was bursting with it, how he felt it in his eyes and ears and down to his toes. Rage filled him to the brim, and it felt like any movement would tip him and he'd spill this disastrous emotion out into the world, using words or fists—or a knife if he could find one.

His rage chose fists. He turned and pounded one of the broken money chests in the room, breaking it wide open. Coins fell, pelting the floor in a hard, swift rain. Perrotte may have called his name, but all sounds had meshed into one, and he wasn't sure.

Sudden embarrassment at his outburst pulled his rage back from the edge. He cringed away from the money chest he'd been pounding, and pulled his fists into his sleeves. He gulped for air, filling his belly with breath, then let it out in a slow, ragged rush.

He took a physical step away from Perrotte, his feet crunching on the half-coins below. He swallowed painfully, his throat suddenly parched.

"Yes, well," Perrotte said, eyeing him closely. She hadn't moved during his explosion. "And sometimes a burden shared is a burden doubled."

"Who?" he asked.

Perrotte was silent.

"Who murdered you?"

"Who do you think?"

"The Countess."

Perrotte turned away, speaking to the wall. "She and my father married when I was seven years old. It never occurred to me then that it might end like that, that it *could* end like that. Mothers love you, don't they? Mothers protect you. Even if you are a bad child. Even if you don't deserve it." She held herself stiffly, arms folded tight, looking very narrow and alone.

"I'm so sorry, Perrotte. Even if you *were* bad, you didn't deserve it."

"Of course I didn't." Her voice was hollow, unconvinced. He had no idea what to do for her. "Perhaps you should go back to sleep," she told him.

Anger had burned through him like a wildfire, and now he felt ash-ridden and raw. His hand was raw too, bleeding lightly from a half-dozen fine cuts caused by the rough edges of coins and splinters of wood that he'd smashed his fist on.

It was the opposite of his nature, to feel so wild. Perhaps it was having been practically raised in a smithy; perhaps it was because he had been tending fires under his father's eye for six years; but Sand had the most appreciation for a purposeful fire, not one that was out of control.

He had to help her. He had to make Perrotte's life better.

"How can I mend this?" he asked.

"You can't. Just go to bed, Sand."

He didn't believe that. Everything could be mended. He just had to figure out how.

26

Star-taker

It had not been her intention to lie to Sand, but Perrotte could not tell him that his father killed her. Though she had no doubt that Jannet had ordered the deed done, Gilles had made and delivered the poisoned slippers or gloves—she wasn't sure which, and perhaps it was both. *You lied, my lady. This wasn't gentle.*

Perhaps she should have told him—not just about Gilles, but also about Bleyz and the rebellion. But his rage was too much for her to bear. The small glimpse she'd seen had frozen her in place with fear—this wasn't *Sand*, was it?—but also, she'd been . . . just a bit . . . annoyed. This was *her* problem, not his. She was the one who'd been displaced and murdered.

She waited, standing stiffly in the middle of the treasury, until she could no longer hear Sand's footsteps. Rubbing the tense muscles in her jaw, she cast about, looking for the leather sack she'd brought in with her. When she found it, she scooped coins into the sack haphazardly and tucked it into her bodice.

She climbed her favorite guard tower with a tight throat. She felt on the verge of tears, yet no tears fell. She signaled with her lantern, covering and uncovering the light three times. Then she waited, still rubbing her jaw, until Sir Bleyz's torch approached. He called softly to her; she waved, and didn't speak, just threw the pouch of coins out over the hedge as hard as she could. It landed well beyond the thorns.

Sir Bleyz dismounted and picked up the sack. He looked inside, then stared back up at her. "This will do very well, my lady!" he said. He tilted his head to one side. "Six times this amount would hire a company of Swiss pikemen."

Perrotte swallowed hard against the pain in her throat. "Come back tomorrow night, I'll have it ready for you."

Sir Bleyz saluted her as though he were a knight about to take the field for the joust. Words of praise and gratitude tumbled from his lips, but she didn't care. She turned away and left the tower.

She was tired, but she did not feel that she could

return to her father's room. She crept down to the kitchen, blew out her lantern candle, and curled up on the warm spot on the hearthstones. The only noise was the whisper of the fire, and the occasional tap of Merlin's talons on the rafter.

Perrotte fell asleep.

SHE WOKE WHEN SHE sensed Sand nearby. She hadn't heard him enter the kitchen, but the swish of his clothing and the soft padding noise of his stocking feet so close to her face, back and forth, back and forth as he found food, must have disturbed her slumber.

She kept her eyes shut.

He left before long, and she breathed a sigh of relief and sat up. Not much later, she heard the telltale noises of his work in the smithy.

Her throat still hurt, like there were words stuck in it.

She should tell Sand. If not about his father, then at least about Bleyz and her barons and her Swiss pikemen.

She heated water to wash up, but untying her hair, brushing it, and retying it felt like too much work, so she just left it alone, and went down to the smithy.

Sand was working the bellows when she arrived. Perrotte just stood and watched.

He pulled one of the pieces of metal out of the

fire, quickly hammered it against the anvil at a sharp angle, straightened the angle, hammered some more, and replaced the item in the fire. He began the same process with the other piece of metal. He moved with a strange, urgent energy. She had never seen him like this.

Perrotte didn't think Sand had seen her in the doorway, he was so focused on his work. But he turned his head and barked, "Come here. Hold this piece."

She didn't like his tone, but as long as he was using it, she didn't feel bad about not confessing to him. She took the tongs from him, holding the metal exactly as he instructed.

"When I tell you to put it in the fire, lay it in right where the coals are brightest and hottest. Go in sideways—this is a welding fire, and there's only a small opening to reach the coals," he said. "Up to about halfway—here." He pointed at the spot on the iron bar. "Pull it out as soon as I tell you, then hold it just like this. I'll do the rest. But don't move it yet."

He pulled over a small box of white powder, and sprinkled some of the powder over the flattened, notched end of the metal he'd just worked. He did the same with the other piece. "This powder is called flux. Now, put your piece back in the fire."

They put both their pieces into the heart of the fire, then Sand pumped the bellows with strong, steady strokes. Perrotte peered in at the white-hot burning coals, mesmerized by the fierce light that seemed to bore straight through her eyes and into her brain.

"Does the metal match the coal yet?" Sand asked.

"No . . . not really."

He worked the bellows some more, steady and strong.

"Close," she told him, and now he pumped the bellows with vigor.

He craned his neck, staring into the fire. "Now."

She pulled out the metal piece and held it on the anvil as he'd instructed. Quick as a hare, he brought out his piece, fitting it over hers so that the notches aligned. Then he brought his hammer down in one powerful stroke. A bright spark shot out between them, almost crossing the smithy. The tongs jarred Perrotte's hands as Sand struck twice more.

"Open your tongs." He pulled the metal away from her to put it in the fire again. The two bars were one complete piece now.

How could he *ever* argue that his mending wasn't magic?

"It's not magic," he growled, as though he'd heard her thought—or maybe she'd spoken aloud. "It's just welding. Almost any smith can do it."

She cocked her head, trying to figure out what he was making.

He heated the metal again, brought it out and began to expertly bend it into a circular shape. He worked the piece for some time, alternately flattening it and making the ends meet. He notched both ends, as he had done before when the piece of metal had been two bars; then he added more flux, and welded the ends together. He'd made a complete circle.

Perrotte's heart sank a little when she realized he hadn't asked her for her help with this weld, but then Sand pulled from his ash pile two more complete circles. She leaned forward to examine the circles—then her breath caught.

"Sand," she said, becoming still. Her fingers reached out to touch, but he swatted them away.

"Dark heat!" he reminded her. "It's quite hot still."

"Is it—is it an armilla?"

Sand looked confused. "No. It's an astrolabe!"

She wanted to laugh, but knew how rude that would be—even though she would be laughing from delight, not out of ridicule.

"An astrolabe is flatter than this," she said. "You're planning to put this all together, so all the metal circles link up to look sort of like a sphere, and it sort of spins, right? That means it's an armilla—an armillary sphere."

"No, it's an astrolabe. Like you had, once, until—" He bit down on the words, and reached inside his tunic to pull out a folded sheet of parchment. He handed it to her. It was a diagram of an armilla for certain, but it was labeled "spherical astrolabe." Perrotte could see where Sand's confusion came from.

"Oh, I see," Perrotte said. She had possessed a flat astrolabe, not an armilla—but her stomach stirred with excitement. What did it matter, the name Sand called it? She'd always wanted an armilla. "Yes, I guess that's a different term for it. Sand! Can you really make this?"

He nodded. "The details might take some time to get right, but I can get the basics together pretty quickly, I think."

"And . . ." She hesitated, not wanting to sound greedy.

"It's for you," he said.

She thought her face might fall off from grinning so broadly. If they hadn't been surrounded by hot metal and fire, she wasn't sure she wouldn't have tackled him with a hug. She settled for laughing with joy and clapping her hands.

Sand was frowning. "It's not an astrolabe then, like the one you had?"

"It's better," Perrotte assured him.

They spent the day working on the armilla—which Perrotte decided to always refer to as her spherical astrolabe, as a sort of thank-you for Sand's astonishing gift. It was a tool much harder to come by than her old astrolabe; her father had never agreed to let her have one.

"Astrolabe means 'star-taker,'" Perrotte told Sand.

"Mm-hm," Sand said placidly, neither excited to know it nor uncomfortable to learn this. He was in his element, peaceful and productive, making something new with skills he understood. She might have been jealous if she hadn't been so excited.

"And I know the perfect motto to put on the side," she announced.

"Oh?"

"'*Mens videt astra.*' 'The soul sees the stars.'"

"I like it," Sand said. "That is so much more *your* motto than either the phoenix or the swan mottoes."

Perrotte laughed at the truth of this, and spent the next hour babbling happily about astronomy. Sand just nodded and kept working, occasionally directing her to help with this bit or that of the forging.

They ate and hunted Merlin and went back to work, ate again, then went to sleep. The heaviness in Perrotte's chest was gone because they were still friends. But the pain in her throat returned, because though they were friends, she still could not bring herself to tell him her last secrets.

PERROTTE WOKE AFTER A few short hours of sleep. She slept longer each night, she realized, and she had some hope that, by the time she was twenty or so, she might sleep through the night and only experience the regular sort of insomnia that she'd had before she died.

She went to the treasury by lantern light and gathered money for the Swiss pikemen, then took it up to the guard tower. She parceled the coins into several twists of cloth that she could throw easily, then waited for Sir Bleyz.

She and Sand would have to pause in their armilla—no, their *spherical astrolabe*—project and get back to the mending. They needed to bring down the thorns and get free of this place. She couldn't let Bleyz go off and fight her battle for her. She needed to be there, to assert her place as Countess, to bring Jannet to justice, and perhaps above all, to prove that she was not dead.

She signaled with her lantern. Sir Bleyz came. They spoke briefly, and she threw him the money. He departed. She was watching his torch retreat into the dark fields below, when a footstep scraped behind her.

She whirled, aiming the lantern's light at the noise.

Sand's voice was ragged. "War, Perrotte?"

"War," Perrotte answered fiercely. "I told you I would beat plowshares into swords."

"That was to cut your way out of the hedge!"

"I believe I said that I would then run my enemies through," she said, and she stepped around him, intending to go downstairs. She was never going to let herself be trapped in a tower again.

He stood aside and let her pass but followed her. "War, Perrotte! People will die. People with families, people with—"

She whirled on him, her lantern unsteady between them. "People who can't pay their taxes? People who can't afford the Countess's mills or her ovens or her winepresses?"

Sand crossed his arms. "They'll pay with their lives—people armed with pitchforks and poorly forged swords!"

"Yes!" Perrotte said. "That is the price of rebellion! People risk their lives. And when the thorns come down, I'm going to go out and risk the same. If I lose the war, do you think I'll live even a *day* past laying down arms?"

He was deadly quiet for a moment. "It doesn't matter. The hedge isn't coming down," he said with eerie calm. "I'll not mend another thing in this castle. *No one* dies. Nobody's brother or father or son falls in this war, and *you* don't get executed, either, Perrotte. We will just stay here. Live here. Forever."

"So we die here together of starvation or old age? No, thank you! I'll keep mending things. You've taught me enough. I may not have the magic, but I can mend it all!"

"You'll never get the chance," he said, snatching the lantern from her hands and dashing it to the stones.

Army

IT COULD NOT COME TO WAR.

It could not come to Perrotte's second death, either.

The thorns must never come down.

He strode to the smithy and grabbed the sledgehammer. He knocked aside the bricks of his forge with a few heavy swings. Embers tumbled out onto the loose sand floor and burned ineffectively alone. Bricks crumbled and fell.

All he could think about was Perrotte's head on a chopping block, and his grandfather's smithy, empty of the son lost to war. Sand turned and swung a weighty blow at the smithy door.

Perrotte was shouting: "Stop, Sand, stop!"

He turned to her, panting. "You started it! You can stop it. Will you stop it?"

"Yes! Yes! Don't do this, Sand. Don't undo all our mending!"

"Isn't war just as bad as this? Worse?" He gestured at a broken anvil in the corner, lying on its side. "Just as destructive, but to more than just *things*."

She was standing between him and the astrolabe, he noticed. He wondered if *that* was the real reason she wanted him to stop. But since it was breaking his heart to destroy the smithy, he lowered the sledge.

"You'll stop this knight from raising an army?" he demanded. "You won't go out there as soon as the hedge is down and get yourself killed?"

"Yes, Sand," Perrotte said. She wasn't crying, though her voice broke. He admired her strength of will.

He dropped the big hammer to the floor and stared at her. He hoped—how he hoped—

A distant *boom* interrupted his thought. Perrotte's head whipped around.

"Is that—" Sand began.

"Cannon fire?"

He had no idea.

They ran out the door, racing to the nearest guard tower.

Beyond the thorns, beyond the asparagus fields, stood a small army.

Sand squinted. He could make out a line of cannons aimed at the castle. Above them hung a puff of smoke, not yet dispersed in the still air of morning.

"Phoenixes!" Perrotte snarled. "Everywhere phoenixes, not a swan in sight."

Sand frowned, looking at the phoenix-spangled banners of the Boisblancs in the distance. He was so used to seeing all the phoenixes around the castle entwined with silver swans, that it only then occurred to him that the swans were unusual in some way. He'd never seen the swans before he'd awakened in the castle. The Countess must have removed the Cygne swans from everything in the countship over the last twenty-five years.

"What are they doing?" Sand asked, bewildered. He craned his neck this way and that, trying to figure out where the cannonball had hit.

In the distance, he sighted another puff of smoke. An instant later the *boom* arrived, a cannonball fast on its heels.

The cannonball flew into the hedge, and the thorns absorbed the projectile almost silently.

Sand would have laughed with relief if he hadn't seen another smoke puff in the distance.

This time, the cannonball struck the wall in the thin bare space where the thorns had receded. The wall crumbled, and the thorns moved yearningly toward the broken spot.

"If they destroy the castle walls with the cannons, will the thorns just come and . . . kill us?" Perrotte asked. "Is that her plan?"

Sand shuddered. "That's diabolical."

"Well, what else can *she* do? She can't cut her way through the thorns and take back the castle. The standard tactics for breaking a siege are useless to her. Starving us out won't work—we can't surrender, anyway, because of the thorns. She can't wait for our guards to grow careless—we haven't any. She can't bribe any doorkeepers—we haven't those, either. Destroying the walls is her only way of destroying us."

They braced themselves for the next hit, but no further smoke puffs rose up from the line of cannons.

In the distance, a mounted knight rode slowly out, bearing a white flag on the end of his lance.

"They won't shoot more. They want to parley," Perrotte said. Then she brightened. "Wait here!"

She ran off, and Sand waited, watching the knight approach. Perrotte returned shortly, clutching a book that had been reordered but not yet mended.

Perrotte hunkered down with the book, flipping over a few pages, scanning them quickly. "Here. 'A garrison of two hundred men armed with forty-eight hand crossbows, two great crossbows, and about forty thousand arrow and bolts, can hold off an attacking force of several thousand.' Oh, and . . ." She scanned the next few lines. "We'd need a few trebuchets and cannons, too."

It had never occurred to Sand to mend any of the defensive weapons of the castle. They were never his priority. And they still weren't.

"How does *that* help us?" Sand asked. "We don't have two hundred soldiers. We have . . . us."

"You could repair the great crossbows," she said. "That would be a start. It might be enough to keep them wary of us."

"Don't we have the thorns for wariness?"

"Better to have the crossbows *and* the thorns."

He nodded. In the distance, he heard unintelligible words. The knight was shouting something. Sand gestured at Perrotte. "Stay down. Don't let them see you, not just yet."

"Parley!" Sand could make out the words as the knight drew closer. "I want to talk with whoever is in the castle!"

Sand leaned over the edge of the guard tower's wall, showing his face. "Well?" he called.

"What is your name?"

"Alexandre, son of Gilles Smith."

"And what are you doing in that castle?"

Sand glanced back at Perrotte, feeling a funny half-smile creep over his lips. What was the best answer?

She gave him an answering smile, and a shrug. Then she motioned: *Go on, then.*

"I'm mending it," he called down.

This, of course, was not an expected answer, and the knight was silent. The knight was too far away for Sand to read his face.

"And to whom do *I* speak?" Sand asked.

"Sir Jos, son of Lord Helori."

Behind him, Perrotte swore. Sand glanced back.

"He was a *baby*," Perrotte whispered.

"So you don't know anything about him."

Perrotte shrugged. "He had the worst colic!"

"Not helpful!"

Perrotte shrugged again.

Sir Jos called. "How did you get into the castle, Alexandre, son of Gilles Smith?"

Sand shrugged. "A saint kidnapped me from his shrine and put me into a fireplace here. So I guess the answer is, a miracle of Saint Melor. Or so I think. He has not told me."

"If you are trying to antagonize him, you are doing a good job," Perrotte whispered.

Sand scuffed his shoe at her. "I'm just telling the truth!"

"You're very good at telling it in the most maddening way possible."

"Thank you?" Sand looked back at the knight,

who was getting too close to the thorns. "Keep your distance from that hedge, Sir Jos!"

But Sir Jos did not watch his distance, and quick as anything, the thorns reached out and snagged the horse's forelegs. The horse did not like this, and tried to rear back. The thorns were too strong, of course, and the horse thrashed and screamed. Sir Jos tumbled to the ground. He jumped to his feet and cut the branches, freeing the horse, who bolted for the horizon.

But while Sir Jos had worked to free the horse, he had not protected himself. The thorns reached for him and pulled him into their center.

28

Parents

SAND DOUBTED THAT THE ARMY WAS PLEASED THAT their representative, sent to parley under the white flag of truce, had been eaten by a magic hedge.

The army sent in two more knights to try to reclaim Sir Jos—this time not bothering with a flag, accompanied by a whole cohort of archers to cover them. They promptly lost those two knights as well.

When four new knights came forward, Sand shouted down: "Don't draw any nearer! You cannot defeat the hedge!"

"We will send a priest next to cast out the demons you have summoned into this hedge, evil sorcerer!" one of the knights called.

"Really," Sand said, looking down at Perrotte.

"Could there be a more willful misinterpretation of this situation?"

"To them, it looks like the hedge is protecting us," Perrotte said. "It might be a reasonable conclusion. As much as I don't want to give anyone loyal to Jannet any sort of credit for intelligence or . . . anything."

"What is your name?" a knight called up.

"Alexandre, son of Gilles Smith." Sand was growing bored of this question, it being the third time he'd answered it that day.

"And what are you doing in that castle?" the knight shouted.

"Mending it," Sand called. "Still."

"We demand your immediate surrender of the castle!"

"We cannot leave this castle any more than you all can get in!"

"We? Who else is in there with you? What fell companion aids you in your sorcery?"

Sand could have smacked himself for saying "we." He decided to ignore the question. "Listen! This castle is a trap! I am not here willingly!"

The knights moved closer to the hedge, but with a great deal more caution than the first three knights. They were able to avoid the thorns when the hedge grasped for them, but the bramble had spooked them. The knights retreated, galloping back to the army.

"What now?" Sand asked.

"I bet Jannet will come out now," Perrotte said.

But Perrotte was wrong. The day wore away and no one came for several hours—but the next people sent to parley were known to Sand.

"Oh, no," Sand whispered, his heart pounding in his ears. "They sent my parents."

Perrotte refused to hang back any longer. She popped up to peer through the crenel, squinting against the full spring sunlight, but staying somewhat out of sight behind a stone merlon. She was silent as Gilles and Agnote walked slowly toward the hedge, alone.

"Father? Agnote? Stay well away from the thorns," Sand called.

They obeyed, keeping far back. They looked up at Sand, shading their eyes, and Sand's heart swelled. He had missed them so much.

"You look thin!" Agnote called. "Are you not eating?"

"There's not much to eat," he answered.

"How did you get in there, son?" Gilles asked, far more gently than Sand expected.

"I was at the shrine to Saint Melor, and I left him some nails. I do not remember what happened next, but I woke up here, in the fireplace."

Gilles ran his hand through his hair, a gesture of frustration that was so familiar to Sand in this strange place that he felt like he was in a dream.

Agnote asked, “Who is that skulking in the shadows next to you?”

Sand didn’t think Perrotte would come out. Neither of them wanted to reveal her presence to the army. He was ready to deflect the question, but she stepped forward into the crenel and stared down at his parents.

“Hello, Gilles Shoemaker,” Perrotte said, not loudly.

For a moment, the world seemed to hold its breath. In that instant, Gilles’s face drained of blood. Sand noticed moss growing in the corners of the tower where shadows kept the stone damp and cool. In the distance, a cuckoo sang.

Gilles crossed himself.

“What is it?” Sand heard Agnote ask his father. “What is wrong? Who is that girl?”

“A ghost,” Gilles said, swallowing hard.

“Not a ghost, Papa,” Sand said. “Perrotte has . . . awakened.”

Perrotte poked him hard on the shoulder.

He whispered, “Don’t you think it would be easier to tell the world that you were asleep than it would be to say that you died and were resurrected?”

Perrotte darted back behind the merlon, and yanked him out of sight after her. “Easier for who? Easier for you?”

“Easier for both of us?”

"Pretending that I was just asleep and not *dead* is not going to be easier for—" She stopped in the middle of that sentence, shaking her head. "Yes, fine. Maybe that will be easier for me, in some ways. Tell that story. It will definitely be easier for *him*."

"Why does it need to be easier for my *father*, of all people?"

"Because . . ." She put her hands to her face, pressing her knuckles into the soft flesh of her cheeks. She dropped her hands and reached for one of his. "Because, Sand, it was your father who made and brought the poisoned slippers that killed me."

He had imagined, ever since it happened to Perrotte, what it must feel like to be stabbed with a hundred or a thousand of the hedge's thorns. It felt just like this, in his imagination.

His father had killed Perrotte.

His *father*.

He closed his eyes. He wanted to suggest that she didn't really remember, though he knew she did. He wanted to suggest that maybe she was lying. But he knew she wouldn't.

It made so many things make sense. It answered why Saint Melor had chosen him. His family owed a debt, for the sins of his father.

He slumped down to his bottom, eyes still closed, back against the guard tower's wall. He heard a thud as Perrotte slid into the same position beside him.

"I'm sorry I didn't tell you," Perrotte said. "It's been hard to be honest with you, while I've been hiding that. I'm sorry I didn't tell you about Sir Bleyz and the rebellion, too. And I want you to know, you were right. I should not bring war to the people. I have forgotten the madness of the War of the League."

Sand ignored that. "How did it happen? How did you die?"

Perrotte told him about the scented slippers and scented gloves, and how Gilles had prepared them for her. Every word seemed to fall through Sand's chest and strike his heart, one sickening blow after another.

Eventually, the story ended. They sat there in silence for a moment, until Sand heard his name called from outside the castle. He forced himself to his feet, to look down. Agnote was there, hands cupped around her mouth. His father was nowhere in sight.

He shouted down, "If they sent you to convince us to leave the castle, tell them: We are trapped by the thorns. If they sent you for any other reason, you can tell us tomorrow. I love you, Agnote. Tell Avenie and Annick that I miss them."

"Sand!" Agnote called. "Come back!"

But Sand had turned away. He left the tower, and did not look back.

29

HEAD

SAND FLED, AND PERROTTE LET HIM GO. POSSIBLY, she wanted to be alone with her thoughts as much as he did. Sand wasn't sure that he'd done the right thing, telling his parents that Perrotte was alive, but he didn't know what else he could have done. He hated lies of omission, more now than ever.

He went to the smithy and restacked the bricks of his forge. That made him feel much better. His mind stumped the same question over and over in a tired, worn-out pattern, like mules circling a grinding stone: *How can I fix this? How can I fix this? How can I fix this?*

Bring down the thorn hedge and go to war. Leave the thorn hedge and be destroyed. One path led to war. One path led to injustice. Both ended in Perrotte's death, probably, and likely enough, his own as well.

And . . . his own *father* had killed Perrotte. Maybe Papa was coerced, maybe he was lied to, maybe he was bribed, but the guilt had been on his face, and Sand didn't know how to bear it, or how Perrotte could bear being around him, the son of her executioner. She had been so broken in the castle's treasury when she told him about her murder.

He had to fix her.

How did you fix a person, though?

"Everything can be mended," he muttered. He drew just short of punching a wall. It was so unlike him, and unlike every smith he knew. Smiths were gentle folk; all their aggressions were spent on shaping metal.

He thought about firing up the forge then, and beating his frustrations into something useful, but he *wouldn't* mend anything that might bring down the thorns faster.

His feet knew better what to do than he did, and he found himself in the chapel. He approached the relics.

He opened Sainte Trifine's silver reliquary briefly, and stared in grim wonder at the sight of the beating heart. He closed it.

Anything could be mended. Everything could be mended. The heart was proof. He could mend Perrotte. His father. The whole situation with the

Countess. He just had to figure out *how*.

The other reliquary drew him, the golden box that held Saint Melor's fragmented skull. The story about the saint's silver hand and bronze foot tugged at his imagination. If he were to mend the skull, what metal should he use? If bronze was for feet and silver was for hands, then wouldn't gold be the metal for a head?

"You're not mending anything, remember, Sand? The hedge." He paused and shook his head at himself. "And Perrotte's out of sight for a few minutes, and you're talking to yourself again."

Talking to himself was bad, but Sand had to admit that the hedge wouldn't fall because he mended *one* more thing in the castle. The amount of mending he had left to do in order to bring down the hedge was . . . No—certainly *one* more thing wouldn't matter.

And the possible benefit was enormous. In the stories, Saint Melor's head spoke. If Sand mended it, quite possibly it would speak again. Sainte Trifine's beating heart was proof of the presence of *something*, but it could not answer his questions.

If anyone was the master smith of this situation, it had to be the saint who brought him to this castle. Saint Melor could show Sand where to apply the sledge. Saint Melor had to know how to mend everything. Why else would Sand have been brought here, if not for this?

❧

REMOVING THE SKULL FROM the chapel felt like a kind of sacrilege, but so did setting up a workshop in the chapel. In the end, with slow footsteps and a great deal of reverence, Sand carried the skull of Saint Melor in its reliquary down to the smithy and perched it on his anvil. He built a hot fire around a partially intact, thick crucible that he filled with broken-up bits of the golden reliquary, and waited for them to melt in the blistering heat.

In the meantime, he arranged the pieces of the skull carefully, envisioning how he would fit each one back together. The skull had not merely been broken in half—it had broken along every major seam of the skull, into twelve large pieces.

The whole time he worked, the back of his neck prickled, and at times, he thought he felt other hands guiding his own. The invisible hand on the right felt colder than the one on the left, and Sand shivered. Immediately, the sensation died away, but it returned as he moved on to the next piece.

When at last the gold was molten, Sand cautiously dipped the edge of one skull fragment in the gold, and then pushed it against the matching edge of the other piece. He waited for the gold to cool. The mend held, probably more due to his mending magic than any skill or knowledge: the pieces stuck together, with a seam of gold running between them. Carefully, he did this with the remaining pieces. The jaw, however, needed to move, yes? So Sand quickly tapped out a pair of golden hinges with a very small hammer, and then made tiny steel nails with which to attach the hinges. With great delicacy, he hinged the jaw.

He carried the skull back to the chapel, where he knelt, gazing upon the mended skull, waiting for it to speak.

It did not speak.

Sand crossed himself and prayed, then waited.

The skull did not suddenly plump with flesh. Sand was glad of that. There were no eyes to open, and so Sand could not guess if any spirit were filling the void. And while he stared at the skull, he realized that hinging the jaw had been pointless, since the whole of the skull sat on the jaw, and nothing short of a true miracle would allow the jaw to move and speak. A human head, he realized, mounted on the neck and allowed the jaw to dangle and close at the will of the speaking human. If he rested his own head atop his chin, he would not be able to speak.

He stood to leave, berating himself for his foolishness. Then it occurred to him: He should ask a question.

He turned back to the altar. "Saint Melor, hear me!" He cleared his throat, feeling ridiculous. "I have a question. How can I mend my problems?"

He felt silly. He really did.

But then the skull spoke.

The jaw did not move. He'd absolutely wasted his time with the jaw. But in spite of that, a voice did emanate from the skull, a voice that he heard not through the air, but from within the bones of his own skull—deep, deep inside his ears.

Some things are not meant to be mended.

The sound made his head itch, but deep inside where he could not reach. He dug his finger into his ear canal, but came out with only a bit of wax and no relief from the itching. He swallowed and gaped and yawned, even going so far as to stick a finger to scratch at his tonsils—but this only made him gag. It was maddening, but eventually, the itching faded enough to bear it. Sand shook his head, like a dog shaking off water.

"Some things are not meant to be mended?" Sand asked. "But then why did you—or Sainte Trifine, if it was she—bring me here, if not to mend?"

Some things are not for you to mend.

Again, the itching drove Sand nearly mad. He rubbed his throat, swallowing heavily, and forced himself to cough.

"You don't understand," Sand said finally. "Perrotte—you brought me here to mend Perrotte, didn't you? And this castle? Well, I can't fix them alone! I don't know what to do! I don't know how to make anything better!"

Some things cannot be mended.

Sand put his hand over his ears, trying to block out the itching voice, but it was no use. He kept his fingers out of his ears and mouth, however, having learned—if it could be called learning—the futility of that. Though he felt hard-pressed not to chew on one of the chapel's candles, for he thought that the lumps of wax would feel very pleasant on the way down, and that they *might* scratch the itch within him.

He left the candles alone. "Can't you at least tell me why?" he asked, plaintive.

The skull didn't answer.

"Why was I brought here, when I am *useless*?"

The skull didn't answer.

"Can't you tell me *anything*?" Sand raged, climbing to his feet.

Finally, the skull spoke again.

Some things just are.

"Argh!"

Sand spun around. Perrotte stood at the door of the chapel, holding her ears.

"What is that? And why is it doing what it's doing?"

"It's Saint Melor's head," Sand said. Then, "It's, ah, talking."

The annoyance faded from Perrotte's face. Her eyes went wide, and she came forward as though pulled by an invisible rope.

She knelt beside Sand, yanking his arm to bring him back to kneeling too, and assumed an attitude of quiet prayer.

Sand braced himself for the skull to speak again, but the moments slipped past, and the skull was as silent as Perrotte.

Finally, he nudged her with his elbow. "If you want the skull to talk, you have to ask it a question."

"But that is not what she has prayed for," a voice said from behind them.

30

Saints

Beside her, Sand yelped in surprise. Perrotte rose trembling to her feet and turned to face the voice.

Two figures stood in the dimness of the chapel, a faint glow emanating from their white raiment. A woman with dark hair stood beside a boy about their own age. For a flicker of a moment, the strangers' aspects changed; shadowy scars appeared across both their necks, and one of the boy's hands gleamed silver. But the signs of their bodily infirmities fled as soon as they appeared, and Perrotte half wondered if she had imagined them, then decided the marks were meant to ensure that the visitors would be recognized.

Sainte Trifine and Saint Melor.

Sand moaned, very quietly, and crossed himself. He'd recognized the saints too.

Crossing herself seemed like a good idea, actually. Perrotte did so too.

"Why did you bring me here?" Sand blurted.

But the saints did not appear offended; they just regarded Sand with eyes both calm and dark. "You know why," Sainte Trifine chided.

Sand shook his head. "I have *ideas* why. I don't *know*."

Saint Melor didn't appear to like this response. "Knowing was never promised to you."

Sand subsided. Sainte Trifine was kinder, her expression warm and sympathetic. "You know more than you think," she told him.

Perrotte shuffled her feet, and now the saints gazed upon her. Their attention was not comfortable. She took a deep breath. "I prayed for the removal of the thorns," she said at last.

"You did?" Sand exclaimed.

Perrotte spoke to the saints and him both. "I did not expect to receive a visitation."

Saint Melor's eyes remained on her, assessing and impartial. Her scalp prickled. She shifted from foot to foot, waiting.

But it was Sainte Trifine who spoke. "The thorns are none of our doing," she said.

Perrotte's breath hitched. "They're not? But—you destroyed the castle—you raised the thorns."

Sainte Trifine shook her head. "It is true that I sundered the castle, when your stepmother laid her hand over my heart and swore that she had not killed you—"

"But she did kill me," Perrotte said fiercely. "It was Gilles's hand, but *her* will."

Sainte Trifine's face was rueful and sorrowing. "I do not think it was her will. I confess I should have looked into her heart then, but the lie, the false oath taken on my heart, angered me so; a lie meant to cover the slaughter of a Cygne daughter no less . . . It was my impetuous doing. I have long regretted it."

Perrotte rubbed her forehead with her thumbs, frowning. "I don't understand!" she cried. "She *murdered* me. You punished her. What is there to regret?"

"She was punished, but my actions also punished an entire generation of your family and your vassals," Sainte Trifine said. "Who knows what courses their lives would have taken if I had done differently? I did not know that the sundering would be compounded by the thorns, and that being cut off from the wealth of the countship would plunge the countryside into such poverty—which in turn caused your sister to marry a French prince for his wealth, and thus lose Bertaëyn one more inch of its independence from

France. I have much to make up for."

Perrotte's thoughts were frozen.

"That is why," Sainte Trifine said, her pale hand extending to Melor, "we brought Sand to this place, and we enhanced certain of his abilities—we gave him mending magic."

Perrotte felt Sand tense beside her, rocking forward on his feet. He'd gotten his answer after all—and more.

"But the thorns are neither of ours," Sainte Trifine said.

"Who, then?" Perrotte demanded. "Who has trapped us here?"

Saint Melor said, "The thorns are from the earth *you* were laid in, Perrotte."

"Wait." Perrotte's hands flew to her cheeks. "The thorns are mine? I control the thorns?"

Saint Melor shook his head. "The thorns are not one person's magic. Do not read intention in the thorns. They are a wilderness created by rage and sorrow."

"*My* rage, though—*my* sorrow?" Perrotte crossed her arms, holding her upper body tight against the sudden trembling that had overtaken her.

"No. Not just yours," Saint Melor said.

"Not only rage and sorrow, but fear, as well, and guilt," Sainte Trifine said. "The thorns grew not from your feelings alone, Perrotte. There is more grief and rage and fear in this castle than one girl could create. Many people grew these thorns. But only from within the castle can they be taken down."

"By mending things," Sand said.

Saint Melor turned his head with regal slowness, and Perrotte remembered: Saint Melor would have been a king had his uncle not stolen his inheritance. "Mending the castle is an important part of it, Sand, but it is not the only part."

Sand's lips thinned as though he were thinking hard. He nodded stoically. Perrotte wanted to poke him. Did he understand what Melor meant, or was he just accepting that he couldn't understand in his Sand-like way?

Sainte Trifine said, "You are so angry, Perrotte, and you have much to forgive."

"*Forgive?*" Perrotte exploded. The saint was right, she *was* angry. None of this was fair. The world wasn't fair. Armies weren't fair. Revenge wasn't fair. Jannet wasn't fair. *Her stupid father wasn't fair.*

No one was blameless in this, but most of the time, she was angriest at her father for marrying Jannet, for letting Jannet kill her, for being dead now.

And Bleyz. Bleyz must have done something very wrong, for Jannet's army to be camped out in the asparagus fields.

And Gilles, who had let himself be duped by Jannet—for he must have been duped—how could he have been so stupid?

Every once in a while, she was even angry at her mother for dying, and leaving an empty place for Jannet to occupy.

"You chose anger over Heaven, Perrotte. You would not forget and move on," Saint Melor said, and placed his thumb on her forehead, between her eyebrows.

Her vision blacked out, and memory flicked through her mind like lightning bolts: *The fields of white lilies, the banks of the slow-fast river, and the souls who drank and forgot.*

And: *The red-mawed woman, and the white tree, and Perrotte's refusal to drink.*

And: *The dark-haired woman who came to her in the marsh, the red seed that glowed with life, and the reminder of her mother's love.*

The memories faded, and Perrotte found herself standing with her eyes shut, rocking back and forth on her feet slightly with her heartbeat.

"It is time for you to break with your past, as you should have broken with it when first you died," Trifine said.

Perrotte opened her eyes, flinching. *I don't want to die*, Perrotte thought. Her heart was a fist. This was the end. She'd never been meant to be resurrected, and now she must undo the mistake.

"No, Perrotte," Trifine said kindly. "We do not ask you to face death again now, but to face life. With forgiveness."

"How do you—?"

"I can see into human hearts, Perrotte."

She knew—she knew in the core of her—that the saints spoke the truth, even though she didn't understand everything they said. But there was something else she knew.

"I don't want to forgive," she admitted. "I can't. It will—" She broke off.

"Forgiveness is not death," Trifine said. "It is life."

"For who? Whose life? Forgiving allows people to get away with murder."

"Whose murder?" Melor asked, in the same tone her tutor had used when she was supposed to know the answer already.

"Mine," Perrotte ground out.

"Murdered, and yet, you live." Melor raised his palms toward her, as if presenting her the world.

She grimaced.

He smiled.

Trifine said, "Jannet never intended to kill you, Perrotte. She only wanted to put you to sleep for a very long time."

"*Only?*" Sand spoke up. "What does *that* matter? Putting someone to sleep so long that their loved ones die and the world moves on without them—that's very evil too!"

Trifine nodded. "Of course. But it is just far enough from murder to assuage the guilt of a woman who yearns for Heaven."

Perrotte burst out, "So I'm supposed to forgive Jannet because she didn't *mean* for me to die? That makes her worthy of my forgiveness?"

Saint Melor said, "No, Perrotte. Forgiveness is not for her worth, but yours."

Trifine stretched her hands toward Perrotte. "Child, you do not forgive because the person who wronged deserves it. You misunderstand the point of forgiveness entirely. The only cage that a grudge creates is around the holder of that grudge. Forgiveness is not saying that the person who hurt you was right, or has earned it, or is allowed to hurt you again. All forgiveness means is that you will carry on without the burdens of rage and hatred."

"The choice belongs to you," Melor said. "To both of you. Now: approach us."

Sand half turned to Perrotte; she could read the fear and awe on his face. He grabbed her hand tightly, and she squeezed his fingers, as if saying, "I am here, I am beside you."

They stepped forward together, closer to the saints. Melor made the sign of the cross over both of them. Sainte Trifine bent down and bestowed a kiss on each of their foreheads, then also signed the cross over them.

"We will be near, no matter what happens," Trifine said.

Free yourselves, and go, with our blessings.

The voice was from everywhere and nowhere, and it filled her full. Perrotte covered her head with her free arm, holding on to Sand with her other hand as if he were her hope of life, until the voice faded from her skull. When she lowered her arm, the only remnants of the saints were their relics on the altar.

31

Siege

SAND AND PERROTTE STARED AT EACH OTHER.

"Did you see? Their feet didn't touch the ground," Sand whispered.

"I wasn't looking at their feet."

Sand's chance to respond was interrupted by another cannonball hitting the castle walls.

"I believe the army wishes to speak with us again," Sand said.

"Or else the bombardment has started in earnest."

They raced to the guard tower and climbed up to look out. Sand was correct; the cannon fire had been a greeting. Another group of knights had come to parley—and this time, they had a prisoner.

Sir Bleyz, armorless and bound, was held between

two of the knights.

"To the trespassers in Castle Boisblanc, and the pretender claiming to be Perrotte of Boisblanc: Know that the traitor, Bleyz of Redon, will be executed for his crime of fomenting rebellion among the barons of this countship, lest the squatters vacate the castle by dawn."

Sand glanced at Perrotte, who shrugged helplessly. "Um, it's going to take a little longer than dawn," he called down.

This appeared to surprise the knight who was shouting the ultimatum up to them.

"How long?"

"Maybe by winter?" Sand said. After all, that had been their previous estimate on when they could finish mending the castle.

The knights making parley were too far away for Sand to read their expressions, but they didn't *seem* to think this was good news.

"I will return at sunset with an answer to your counteroffer!" the knight said. "Be here, or we will fire the cannons again!"

"We'll be here!" Perrotte cried.

She left the tower, and Sand followed. They met at the foot of the stairs.

"I'm not wrong, am I?" Sand asked, suddenly uncertain what Perrotte wanted. "You really do want to leave the castle? You prayed for the thorns to be down. The Saints all but told us to go. But Perrotte, if you want to stay here forever, I'll stay with you."

Her eyes moistened when he said that, but she shook her head. "I have to try to save Sir Bleyz," she said.

"And if they execute him anyway?"

Perrotte shook her head, knotting her fingers together. "We can't stay here forever. I think—I think it's time to live in the world."

Sand nodded. "Yes. I think you're right."

They stood awkwardly together for a moment. Sand thought: If she were his sister, he would just hug her. She looked like she needed comfort. But the awkward moment passed when Perrotte said, "Anyway, if we stay, *she* will just pulverize the walls and let the thorns take us, and—oh, Sand, I don't know how to bring down the thorns! I'm *trying* to forgive. Honestly, I'm trying with all my being."

Sand looked at the sky. "We have until sunset to come up with a plan, I guess."

Perrotte said, "If *she* just wants the wealth that is trapped in here, we could just . . . give it to her. Then she'd go away."

He frowned. "Are you sure that's all she wants? She tried to kill you, Perr. Or put you to sleep for a long time, anyway. Do you even know why?"

Perrotte let out a whoosh of breath, and started

walking toward the kitchen. "I would have to guess that once she had a daughter and not a son, she wanted to make sure her daughter would inherit instead of me. But she could have had more children, and tried again for a son and heir."

"Perhaps not? Agnote is a midwife. Sometimes, women have babies, and their midwives know right away that they can't have any more children. . . . She could have had a childbed fever or too much bleeding, something like that."

"Maybe. I never heard even a rumor of it, and the servants will talk about things like that." Then Perrotte gasped. "Oh! How long after the sundering did my father die?"

Sand shook his head. "I don't really know. Fairly soon, I think—within the year?"

Perrotte closed her eyes, and her voice was pained when she spoke. "Papa was dying. He tried hard to hide it from everyone, but he was much reduced from the man he was before the League War. When he married Jannet, I remember him saying something like, 'At least when I'm gone, you won't be alone.' Oh, Papa." A tear slipped down her nose.

Sand really wanted to hug her then, even held one arm out to welcome her close—but she just took his hand as if that was all he offered. He was comforted that he could offer her something, though; her hand clutched his as if he were saving her from drowning.

"How was your father so wrong about her?" Sand asked.

Perrotte shook her head. "She was so annoyingly *pious*, I would never have thought she was dangerous to me."

"Really?" Sand frowned.

"Really. When she first married my father, I—foolishly—told her I loved her. I didn't really, but it seemed like the right thing to say to my new mother. She told me not to lie, and that she would not lie to me either. And as far as I know, she never did lie about anything, up until the point when the castle was sundered. Well. *If* she lied then. Sainte Trifine said something about intention, and I thought she was trying to excuse Jannet, but maybe she was trying to explain something about her—and the sundering." Perrotte shook herself, then looked guiltily at Sand. "I failed to tell you about the sundering as Sir Bleyz explained it to me," she said, and proceeded to relate the tale.

So many pieces fell into place with that story. Sand's mind reeled, thinking about invisible beasts harrying stragglers out of the castle.

Unbidden, Sand's stomach growled.

"I'll go hunt Merlin," Perrotte said.

"I can—"

"You should probably consider how to repair some

of our defensive weapons," she said gently. "Either we'll need to mend them when we mend everything, or we'll need to mend them to hold off our enemies."

SAND WENT TO THE armory. He no longer believed that mending mere objects would bring the thorns down entirely. Though maybe the magic of the mending wasn't of the material *things* of the castle; maybe the mending was, and always had been, of Perrotte.

Except . . .

Some things don't need to be mended. The words echoed in his mind.

Some things are not for you to mend.

You get used to things, Sand realized, thinking about winter. Agnote made him a new goatskin coat every autumn, which at first never felt like it kept out the cold. Sand always shivered and cursed winter at its start. But as the weeks passed, Sand found himself turning into the wind, letting it knife through his coat, through his very bones. Even though he recognized he was cold, he knew he was but a few steps away from a warm fire, and so he welcomed that bracing chill—because it was so unlike summer, and spring, and autumn.

When winter finally faded away, he always missed it a little.

Was winter broken? He'd never thought of it in

those terms, but he hated winter so much at the start of the season when he was always so cold, and so angry about being cold, that yes, if you asked him then, he would have said: Winter is broken.

But winter was necessary. Why else would the world have it? The trees seemed to welcome the season, from the way they changed colors before they dropped their leaves and went to sleep. Winter was part of a cycle, like day and night, life and death. Winter *was.*

Some things are not meant to be mended. Some things, even though uncomfortable, maybe even horrible, were things you needed to pass through. For winter, you put on your goatskin coat, thought ahead to summer, and knew that you could not mend it, even if you tried.

Some things are not for you to mend. Sand had not been brought to the castle to mend Perrotte's mind or soul. He was sure of that, because he did not have the ability to do either. He was, at the heart of it, a blacksmith. Not a scholar. Not a saint. He was a smith. He was here to do things that only a smith could.

It came to him then, in that moment, staring at the giant crossbows in the armory: a mad, strange idea—a way to mend the castle itself.

PERROTTE APPEARED IN THE armory with a roasted lark and some asparagus. Sand ate them, staring at the great crossbows he'd been working on so feverishly when she came in.

"What can I do to help you mend those?" she asked, and he shrugged, and pointed out some things while he snapped down the food. She set to work, and when he was done eating, he joined her.

"You're repairing all four of the great crossbows?" Perrotte asked. "The book on warfare I found said we only needed two or three, and Sand—there are only two of us. I'm not sure that's enough to man more than one crossbow."

"You're right," Sand said, but he was having a conversation with himself in his own mind. He wiped his brow. "We really only need two—we can move them."

"That's not what I—"

He shushed her. He could barely hold the whole of this mad idea in his head. All he could see was what needed to be done next, and then he did it, the whole plan only glimmering at the edges of his awareness. His mind ticked over, doing mental equations, thinking about angles, and praying that his magic was up to the task.

"Maybe I should get to work on mending the crossbow bolts for these fellows?" Perrotte asked. "It can't be too hard to mend them, they're just like giant arrows—"

"Yes. No, don't mend the ones we have, forge them out of iron. Yes, we'll need four of them, with loops on the end, like the eye of a needle—but wide enough for rope to pass through." He showed her the size by making a circle with both his hands.

"But won't that make the bolts fly wrong? I'm not sure what the point is," she said.

He gestured impatiently. "Are you helping or not?"

"It's my castle," she said, offended.

"And I'm the one mending it."

"But why? Why needle eyes? Also, won't we need a *lot* more than four bolts?"

"No. Just four."

Dimly, he heard Perrotte question him, and he didn't answer.

He felt himself being shaken by the shoulder.

"Sand! You're acting very strange. Tell me what's going on."

His eyes focused on her. He had worked in a manic daze, not wanting to stop lest he lose the whole plan before he understood it. He forced his mind to return to normal paths. He still didn't know how to explain the plan, but he had to try.

"I'm going to make a very large chain," he said. "I'm going to need your help with the welds."

"Why?"

"Well, this chain has very large links," he said, spreading his hands to illustrate the size.

"You don't say. And to what end, Sand? Are you making an anchor for a great ship? It's very impractical to make something so big here, miles from the sea-coast."

She was teasing him. He liked it.

He was going to miss her.

"No," he said, finally understanding her question. "We can use the chain to mend the castle. I think that will bring the thorns down, once and for all, more effectively than mending all the little bits inside the castle."

"That's madness. You have no proof that will work."

He thumped his chest. "No. But I feel it here."

She twisted her hands together. "It's a frightening thought. That you'll do one great act of mending, and then—we'll be free."

He understood this. The thorns were their protection as much as their cage. Uncertainty faced them beyond the castle walls. Even though he knew his magic was from the saints, that didn't mean there wouldn't be an accusation of witchcraft. And Perrotte's future was extremely perilous, far more than his own.

"We'll need to bargain for your freedom tonight," he said. "We need to look strong. We have the wealth of the countship in the treasury, and they think we can control the thorns, so we have a position of power, in a way." Sand decided not to mention his fears about accusations of witchcraft. "All I face for my own peril, when we leave, is going to university. But your peril is greater, and I couldn't live with myself if, through my actions, you died—*again*."

She shook her head. "You aren't going to university."

"Yes, I am."

"No. Your father owes me a life, and I'm going to take yours as payment."

The words might have sounded like a threat, taken by themselves, but said by Perrotte with her steady gaze and her wry half-smile, Sand understood they were not.

"What—what would you do with my life?"

"Give it back to you."

He swallowed past a sudden lump in his throat.

"Like you did for me," she said. "I'll also offer you a forge. If I own *anything* when this is all over, any bit of land, I'll give you a smithy of your own on it. And a master blacksmith to take you on as an apprentice, if your father doesn't see reason."

Sand said hoarsely, "I know mending magic isn't good for much when it comes to rescuing people from prison, but I'll figure out how to use it to free you. If you're taken prisoner."

She nodded. "But if I die—" She turned her face away for a moment. "I don't think I want to be born a third time, Sand. Just . . . let go."

"I don't promise that."

"Well, you have to." She turned back, glaring at him with wet eyes. "It's not your choice to make."

He stayed silent.

She glared at him. "Yes, of course, your actions *are* your choice. But it's my body and my life. So it shouldn't *be* your choice. So therefore, it's not your choice. Honorably and rightly, it is not."

It took all his willpower to nod and mean it, to not secretly tell himself in the back of his mind that he would lie to her, that he would make the promise and then break the promise. *No. No lies, not to her, not to yourself.* "I promise," he said bitterly, but meant it.

Perrotte nodded. "Good. But I don't plan to be taken prisoner or executed, Sand. Whatever agreement we make with that army needs to be ironclad, and bound by impartial witnesses, someone who'll protect us when we're free and in Jannet's grasp."

Mending

SUNSET CAME, AND PERROTTE AND SAND CLIMBED the guard tower to parley.

Unexpectedly, Gilles ran behind the men who approached with the white flag. Two women rode with them as well: Sand's stepmother, bound and gagged, and Jannet.

Perrotte's whole gut lighted with fear at the sight of her father's wife.

"That's Agnote. What are they doing with Agnote?" Sand fretted.

Perrotte shook her head, feeling faint. "I don't like this. I don't like any of this."

"You can do it, Perr," Sand said, and took her hand.

She looked down on the assembled people and waited, expecting Jannet to say something. Her father's wife had grown older, but was far from withered and ancient. Perrotte realized with a jolt: Jannet had been very young when she married the Count.

Jannet said nothing, and Perrotte got tired of waiting.

"Our demands!" Perrotte said. "We will surrender this castle one week from today. Provided that there is a witness from the court of the Duchess of Bertaèyn to oversee the peaceful exchange, we will bring down the thorns, and leave the treasury intact for you. In return, you must let us go free, as well as your prisoners, Sir Bleyz and . . . Agnote?" She glanced at Sand.

Jannet didn't move. She wasn't looking up at Perrotte at all, in fact. Her hands were clasped around a rosary, and her lips moved constantly in silent prayer.

Perrotte stared at her.

Jannet gave one nod.

The knight out front said, "We accept these terms!"

"The witness you choose must be known to Perrotte or Sir Bleyz!" Sand shouted from beside her. "An impartial witness and a person of unimpeachable character!"

Another nod from Jannet. "Agreed!" the knight said.

It was done.

Perrotte left the tower, going slowly. She felt dizzy with pent-up grief and anxiety.

Sand took her hand. "What on earth did Agnote do that she's a prisoner?"

Perrotte shrugged. She had no capacity to speculate on anything.

"We need to get to work," Sand said.

THEY WORKED TOGETHER IN companionable, urgent silence, as late into the night as they could. Sand wedged four of the biggest anvils together in a tight cluster, and took apart four forges, rebuilding them into one enormous forge.

The first link of their giant chain was bigger around than Sand's upper arms.

When Sand finally called a break for sleep, Perrotte stretched her back, wiping a hand across her forehead, then shook the kinks and pains out of her hammer arm, before finally rubbing her tong hand. She'd never worked this long at the forge.

They slept. Perrotte slept as long as Sand for a change, but he didn't sleep as long as usual, either. They got up and went back to work. They brought each other water and food. Sand went and looked at the army periodically, and brought updates; Perrotte would not go. They gave up on sleeping in beds, just making pallets on the floor of the smithy, and slept in snatches.

Days passed. They kept track with hash marks in soot on the wall, afraid they'd miss their deadline.

They forced each other to take breaks for Merlin's sake, if not their own. They climbed the towers and hunted the falcon, watching the army in the distance. Rain came. Rain went. Sand and Perrotte worked metal side by side at the forge, groaning with fatigue, drowning in chain.

"We're out of metal," Perrotte said at last.

"Hardly," Sand said, and together they went through the kitchen and the rest of the rooms and stole back all the steel and iron implements that Sand had repaired over the weeks he'd been in the castle, and turned those things into chain as well.

"Pretty soon now, we *really* will run out of metal," Perrotte said, while they munched on onions roasted at the forge.

"Soon," he agreed, and swallowed his last bite.

"You never asked me what it was like to be dead," Perrotte said conversationally as they got back to work.

Sand, too distracted by the trial that lay just ahead, nodded, and was more forthright than she expected. "You are right. It seemed rude. Also—" He shuddered. "It's frightening, honestly."

"It wasn't scary at all, to *be* dead. Much scarier

to die." Perrotte pumped her bellows fiercely. Sand made an objecting squawk.

She slowed down. Too much air did odd things to the metal and interfered with welding. Sand had told her this several times over the week. "Sorry, I forgot."

"When I was younger," Sand said, "I thought it was too much heat that ruined a weld. And Grandpère and my father both let me think it. Oh, they gave me hints. Grandpère wondered aloud how there could be too *much* heat in a process that required sparkling white metal. So I thought maybe the trouble lay in the metal heating too fast. And they let me think that, for a while. But I started doing everything based on that, and my father reminded me that there are *four* elements in the world."

Perrotte pumped the bellows and tried to figure out what Sand was trying to tell her with his story.

"I worried over that comment for days," he said. "I pumped the bellows slower and slower during heating, and failed *all* my welds. I thought about the elements over and over. I figured: fire was obviously not the answer. I couldn't be on the right track with that theory, if my father had to remind me that there were *four* elements. Earth, well, that was the element from which we draw iron, and perhaps that was the issue, but what *about* earth? Everything in blacksmithing is about earth! Even more than it's about fire! Water?

No, no—the problem had nothing to do with water, because the quench was long after the welds failed.

"So I pumped the bellows and thought. That's when it came to me. Air. Air had to be the complicating factor. Certainly, air from the bellows feeds the fire, but air also rushes over our steel as we heat it. I wondered: Could too much *air* really complicate the issue of welding?

"I asked Papa, who grunted. That always means I've finally found the right answer. I asked him: Why didn't you just tell me? He said, 'If I tell you, you'll just forget at some critical point. If you figure it out for yourself, you'll always remember.'"

Perrotte watched her heating iron. "You think you've explained too many things to me, while you've taught me smithing? And not let me figure enough things out for myself?"

He shrugged. That meant yes.

She nodded. She agreed. But they hadn't had the time for her to learn slowly, to figure things out for herself.

"It doesn't matter—you aren't planning to be a smith," he said.

She thought about the work they'd done on the spherical astrolabe. She could see working on things like that for the rest of her life, and she would always be grateful to Sand for what he'd taught her. And for what she hoped he would continue to teach her. And for what they might learn together.

"Well?" Sand asked.

"Well what?"

"What was it like to be dead?" Sand asked, and grinned. "Enough time passed that I thought it would seem spontaneous if I asked now."

She told him. About a field of lilies, and a woman without a face, and stars in a marsh.

"But what about Heaven?" he asked.

"Well, if I had been in Heaven, I don't think I could have been brought back to life," Perrotte said.

"It sounds like a dream."

"It mostly feels like one too. But now it's time to weld."

She lifted the incandescent metal out of the fire and brought it to her anvil, while he swung around the other side to meet her with his sledgehammer. She held the link in her tongs, indicated the spot she wanted with a light tap, and waited while he brought the sledge down.

The spark of welding shot between them, and she sighed.

"What?" Sand asked.

"Whatever happens," Perrotte said, "I mean, unless our plan fails and Jannet has me executed or locked up for life, which is actually pretty likely if things go wrong—but whatever *else* happens—will you still be my friend?"

She asked the question in a voice that was trying not to be plaintive, but no matter how brave she tried to sound, she knew he could hear the sadness and fear and loneliness beneath.

Sand regarded her carefully. "I'll always be your friend, if you'll allow it. My lady."

"Ugh," she groaned. "Please. Never call me that again." But she smiled.

"I'll always be your friend, Perrotte," Sand repeated.

"And I yours, if you allow it," she replied.

TWO MORE LINKS AND they were done with the chains. Then came the rope making, but eventually, they finished with that, too.

The crossbow bolts came out well enough, with their weird needle-eyes on one end. The arrow tips on the end of the bolts didn't look as good as they should, but Sand assured her that they would work for his plan.

Sand directed her to tie ropes to each end of their chains: four ropes, two chains. Then they attached the ropes to each of the four crossbow bolts.

Together, they moved the crossbow to where Sand pointed. He aligned and realigned the weapon, sighting this way and that.

Perrotte fidgeted.

"I don't really know how crossbows work, I guess," he said.

"You knew enough to repair them."

"It's a bit different to shoot."

"Well, what's the worst that can happen?" Perrotte asked. "We might have to try again?"

Sand checked one more time, and fired.

The bolt flew out, rope trailing after, and sped into the open window at the top of the tower. Sand's aim had been good, his planning worthwhile, and his imagination better. Perrotte waited while Sand ran up the stairs and started hauling up the rope, the chain trailing after. On the other side of the tower, the rope dropped out another window, and Perrotte ran to catch it, and help pull. Her muscles strained, but the chain came up, threading through the tower windows.

Sand did the same thing with the other chain and another tower on the other side of the split keep.

"I can't believe it worked," Perrotte said.

"It worked."

"I can't believe how much of those chains *I* forged!"

"You forged a lot of that chain," Sand agreed.

"And now . . ."

"And now."

The next step was fiddly. They moved the

crossbows into place and staked them there. The plan involved using the winches of the great crossbows to wind the ropes taut, to draw the chains tight around the towers, and, eventually, to pull the towers together, sealing up the crack between them.

The winding was long and arduous, and in the end, Perrotte could not get the winches wound quite as far as Sand could, so he had to take over for her.

"But that's right and proper," Perrotte said. "You're the one with the mending magic."

Sand shrugged, and kept winding, grunting with effort, while Perrotte watched.

"It shouldn't work," Sand muttered. "I don't think it will."

"It's magic," Perrotte reminded him.

"It is magic. And there's the other piece."

"The forgiveness piece." She sighed. "I could forgive your father, I think. For your sake. But I really don't know how to forgive Jannet, Sand. When I think of just not hating her, of not being angry . . ."

Sand glanced at her over the edge of the winch, grunting as his muscles strained to turn it. He stopped, bent over with hands on knees, and panted a moment.

She handed him a cup of water, and he drank it down. Sweat dripped into his eyes, and he wiped it away. "Perrotte," he said.

"You want me to turn the winches with you?"

Sand nodded. "Yes. I want that. But also . . . in regards to forgiveness . . ." He put the cup down, speaking to the ground as he said his next words. "You have an imagination. Use it."

She didn't know how to answer that. He moved back to the winding winch, and she moved to the opposite side. They threw their weight against the wooden handles, and continued winding, tightening the ropes and chains around the keep.

"Imagine your life!" Sand cried. "Imagine what it would be like if you forgave her!"

Perrotte closed her eyes, pushing on the handles of the winch, rotating it another few inches. And then another. Her palms ached, as well as her legs and shoulders.

Perrotte directed her thoughts away from the pain in her body. Forgiveness. Forgiving was as hard as turning the windlass, but she supposed . . . she could see how to forgive her own mother for dying. Her father for marrying Jannet. Gilles for being duped. The path to those kinds of forgiveness seemed etched out before her on the floor of the castle in her mind. But where did the path to forgiving Jannet start?

The windlass ground forward. Across from her, Sand grunted unhappily.

What would it be like? To be free of the pain and grief she felt, the anger that welled in her every time she thought about the thing that had happened to her, the death she'd received, the years and people she had lost?

Another few inches.

What would it be like to remember the past without wanting to scream and to cry? Without feeling like a burden rested on her shoulders and her heart?

A few inches more.

Would life feel like it did when she stood shoulder to shoulder with Sand at the forge, creating the spherical astrolabe? Engrossing. Involving. Full of possibility and joy and friendship?

She had thought she was already pushing against the handles as hard as she could, but she found a well of strength in her legs. Thighs burning, she leaned in harder.

"It's moving! Keep going!" Sand shouted.

With a sudden rush, the windlass moved a full turn. Ropes creaked. Above them, the stones of the keep groaned and shifted, moving back together.

Beneath their feet, the ground shook.

The whole world rumbled and writhed. Perrotte was thrown to her knees. The next few moments were a blur of motion. That dreadful itching inside her head made by the voice of Saint Melor returned. Only this was worse, a hundred times so.

And maybe the Saint *was* speaking in that moment;

she thought that she heard words, words that she couldn't quite understand, but that nonetheless told a glittering, vivid story that made her giggle, made her weep, made her feel content, even though she would never be able to repeat the story or remember any of the details. The unheard words were like a half-glimpsed world beneath the surface of the sea; the waves parted and showed the lands beneath the deep to her for one long, shining moment. Just as suddenly, the waves crashed together, and the world beneath disappeared.

Perrotte huddled down, hands over her head, and still the earth bucked beneath her like the angriest of horses. The itching went on and on; the Saint's voice called her name like the clear note of a bell, over and over, and Sand's name too, and—

It all stopped, the movement and the voice and the rumbling. The only sound now was her own heartbeat in her ears.

Perrotte uncovered her head.

"Sand?" she called, and her voice sounded clear and tiny, as though it came from a thousand miles away but was spoken through a perfect, magic trumpet.

He hadn't been thrown far. He was looking at her, cheek pressed into the dirt. "Did you do it? Did you forgive her?" Slowly, he got to his feet.

"Not . . . really? No. But. But maybe I started to."

She too climbed to her feet.

He stared over her head. “Look.”

She spun to look at the keep.

The chains had fallen slack. The cracks were gone. The broken castle wall and the rift in the ground were perfectly and completely mended.

33

SISTER

ALL WAS SILENCE FROM BEYOND THE CASTLE WALLS. Perrotte stumbled over to Sand. Hand in hand, they walked like drunkards toward the castle gates, neither of them capable of treading a straight line.

"Not the portcullis," Perrotte said. "Not until we know."

Sand just nodded, and together they pulled open the castle's wooden gates, leaving the metal grating of the portcullis in place.

They looked straight out over the asparagus fields. There were no thorns in sight.

A clump of mounted men rode toward the gates, white flag flying.

Sand glanced at Perrotte. She met his gaze steadily. "Still not lifting the portcullis. But I'm glad the thorns are gone. Also," Perrotte said, "I just want you to know? I may tell some pretty egregious lies in a moment."

"What?"

"No one out there knows the limits of your magic—"

"I don't really know the limits of my magic—"

"—or that we can't bring the thorns back, so just . . . follow my lead."

"I don't think—"

"Sand! It's life or death. A bluff may be called for."

"I know it's life or death! And I don't want to be burned at the stake! Or tried for witchcraft at all, really, even if I were found innocent."

"I'm not going to tell them it's *your* magic," Perrotte said.

"That's not entirely—"

"Shh. Here they come."

The parley group came within earshot. Agnote, still bound, was pulled along behind. His father followed at a distance. Sand was able to see faces and expressions more clearly now, and read how worried his father and Agnote looked.

Why was Agnote *gagged*?

The dowager Countess was nowhere in sight.

The parley group was led by a young, well-dressed woman. The woman stood in her stirrups and raised her hands. "I am Rivanon," she announced.

Beside him, Perrotte gasped. Sand noted that this Rivanon had Perrotte's clear, hazel eyes and flossy hair. There was no mistaking that she was Perrotte's half-sister.

But where was the Countess?

"Have you come to broker a peace?" Perrotte called belligerently, obviously expecting that Rivanon had not.

"Yes," Princess Rivanon called back. She gestured at Agnote. "My mother took this woman captive, when she came to speak on behalf of her son and you. She said things that my mother . . . did not like."

Perrotte stared at Sand, who shrugged. Agnote was the kindest person he knew—unless you hurt an animal or a child. Then, she was easily the most frightening person he knew. If the Countess had made threats against either Sand or Perrotte . . . And in fact, the Countess *had* made a threat against the both of them, when the Countess had fired a cannon at the castle, so it was too late. The Countess had gotten on Agnote's bad side.

"I am releasing her, as a show of good faith," Princess Rivanon said, and gestured. Agnote was unbound and ungagged by two soldiers.

Agnote straightened her spine and walked slowly toward Sand. His father embraced her in an eyeblink. The two hugged, then moved to the portcullis together.

Agnote and his father reached for Sand through the bars. Sand gave them his hands. It felt so good to touch his stepmother's small, cool hands, and his father's large, warm ones. It wasn't a hug, but it was close. They smiled wanly at him.

"Sand," Perrotte said quietly.

He nodded, pulling away. His parents stepped aside.

"Where is your representative from the court of the Duchess?" Perrotte asked Rivanon.

"The Duchess herself, actually," Rivanon said. "She who is also your queen. Queen Claude."

The horses parted, and an even more elegantly dressed woman rode forward. Sand swallowed hard, his throat suddenly dry, and he sank to his knees there in the castle's entrance tunnel. The Queen of France! His parents knelt too, and Perrotte beside him.

"This *will* be an honest peace," the Queen said after she raised them up again with a gesture. "And honestly kept. By what miracle that young Perrotte lives again, I know not; but my mother counted Perrotte as her friend, and I will protect her friends."

Rivanon scratched her nose uncomfortably.

The Queen arched an eyebrow at the Princess. "I am aware of your own mother's concerns that this is not the true Perrotte, but let us act in good faith for now. If she is an imposter—which I must say, seems as unlikely as her resurrection, given the circumstances of those thorns—we will discover it soon enough."

Perrotte hesitated. "So I'm to be allowed to live?" she asked.

Rivanon looked stricken by this. "You are my sister!"

"And your mother was my stepmother," Perrotte replied. "These names for relationships do not matter."

"I agree; it is the relationships themselves that matter," Rivanon said.

Sand could see that comment had scored a point with Perrotte.

"I am going to call for a tent to be set up here at the castle gate," Rivanon said. "For privacy during our negotiations. Me on my side of the gate, and you on yours."

Perrotte hesitated only a moment, and nodded. "Sand's parents will be there, as well as the Queen," she informed the Princess.

Rivanon agreed, then rode away to organize the meeting.

Perrotte stepped back, to give Sand and his parents some solitude.

Sand pressed his forehead to the portcullis bars. Agnote leaned in to kiss his right cheek, and to his surprise, his father leaned in to kiss his left. Sand closed his eyes, inhaling the scents of rosemary and chamomile from Agnote's hair, and charcoal and lavender from his father's clothing.

"What happened to you?" Sand whispered to Agnote.

His father said grimly, "She said some very intemperate words to the Countess, and she's lucky to be free."

Agnote pulled back to look at Sand. She touched his forehead assessingly. "I remain uncontrite."

Sand became aware that the others were watching this reunion, and he flushed. Perrotte, in particular, watched with distinct longing on her face. Agnote followed Sand's gaze. She curtseyed to Perrotte. "My lady."

Perrotte took that as a sign to come over. She nodded to Agnote—but her eyes were on Sand's father. "Gilles," Perrotte said, and her voice caught.

To Sand's shock, his father fell to his knees before Perrotte, clinging to the portcullis. "I'm so sorry," he said, and Sand was even more surprised to realize his father was *weeping.*

Sand shifted from foot to foot, uncomfortable to see his father this way. Agnote's arm slid around his father's shoulders. "He never knew that he'd been sent to kill you, Lady Perrotte," Agnote said. "But he has regretted it every day of his life."

His father nodded silently, without looking up.

Perrotte shrugged unhappily. "I—I did not think he'd done it intentionally," she said.

Gilles pulled himself up. "I did—I did not mean for it, no."

"We should get some stools for this meeting," Sand said, wanting to give his father a little time to compose himself.

"Yes," Perrotte said, and brushed at her sooty clothes. "I should change into my . . . other gown."

The dress she had been buried in, she meant.

Sand and Perrotte hurried away from the gate. "We should ask for food," Sand said.

"No. That would be telling them how easily they could starve us out."

He nodded, but the notion that he could eat something other than onions, larks, and asparagus had him a little bit excited—even as his stomach churned with nervousness and fear.

After washing up, changing into clean clothes, and filling their purses with coins from the treasury,

Perrotte chose two of the finer stools Sand had mended, and called Merlin down from the rafters of the kitchen.

Perrotte said, "If the castle changes hands, it may change hands quickly."

"Won't you want anything else from here?"

She looked around at the broken things, at the mended things. "We hadn't gotten very far in making the spherical astrolabe, and all the rest of my things went missing or were destroyed long ago. Is there anything *you* want?"

Sand shook his head. He knew he'd do better with a fresh start on the astrolabe, and the best things he'd mended here were Perrotte and Merlin. He wasn't leaving without them.

"Wait. The relics?" he asked.

"The relics belong with the castle," she said. "And the saints will watch over us wherever we are."

34 Negotiation

THEY CARRIED THEIR STOOLS AND THE FALCON BACK down to the gate, to find that the view beyond the portcullis had become the interior of a sumptuously decorated tent. Perrotte perched Merlin on a stone outcropping.

Agnote and Sand's father had been given camp stools near the portcullis, but off to the side. A table had been pushed against the portcullis, and on one side of it sat Rivanon, hands folded. Somewhat behind her and to the right, on what looked to be an actual throne, sat the Queen.

A tense round of new greetings followed, then Sand and Perrotte sat on their stools.

Lady Rivanon coughed delicately and began. "The

first thing that I must establish: My mother wishes me to say that she did not kill Lady Perrotte. As all can see."

Perrotte cocked her head. Sand could see the anger blazing in her eyes—but she kept her temper in check. "No," she said simply. "I was killed. I was *dead*."

"My mother wishes me to state that she not only did not kill Lady Perrotte, but she never had any intention of killing her. The, er, potion on the shoes and gloves was meant to put Lady Perrotte into a lengthy sleep only."

Gilles nodded. "The Countess told me that the intention was that she fall asleep. But Perrotte *died*."

"But clearly, Perrotte did not die," Rivanon interjected.

Sand frowned, trying to figure out if Rivanon actually believed this or if she were merely performing a part as written by the Countess. But either way, it was a convenient fiction, and if Perrotte were not considered to be resurrected but rather just reawakened, then maybe he would be less in danger of being accused of witchcraft.

"I *did* die," Perrotte said.

"So it is your contention that you died," Rivanon said, to Sand's annoyance.

Sand said, in as deep a voice as he could muster: "Let's move on." He sent Perrotte a pleading look.

"Even if Jannet intended for me to only be put into a 'long sleep,' I think it's clear that her plan was the theft of my inheritance of the Boisblanc lands and titles in favor of you, her daughter."

Rivanon bowed her head in assent. "So the question, as it stands, is who is the rightful ruler of Boisblanc?"

"It's me," Perrotte said without blinking.

"Except that you died," Rivanon said. "In which case, it is not you, but me."

Sand bristled, but Perrotte put a hand on his arm. She remained silent. "Well played," she said at last.

Rivanon nodded heavily, as though she were not pleased herself by her maneuver. "I am prepared to offer you lands and money," she said. "Far away from here."

"To leave your mother effectively in charge of Boisblanc?"

Rivanon said calmly, "It's what she would like."

"Well, I don't like it. Give *her* lands and money far from here, and if you will not rule Boisblanc yourself, let me be your regent and not her."

The Princess's smile was pained and regretful. "She is my mother. She is old; she took good care of our father when he was ailing until he died. How can I exile her? How can I take away the only thing she has ever lived for?"

Behind the Princess, Queen Claude's mouth grew lemon-tight, but she did not speak.

"You are too young to be my regent, anyway," Princess Rivanon went on. "You are but thirteen!"

Perrotte's hands moved restlessly in her lap, but only Sand could see this; her back remained straight, her expression uncompromising. He could also see she didn't like any of this discussion—Sand didn't either—but at least no one was talking about taking Perrotte prisoner, and certainly, no one had mentioned executions.

Rivanon leaned toward Perrotte across the table. "But, I can promise you, once you've reached your majority, you can come back. And here and now, I will make you my heir."

Perrotte frowned. "And what of your own children?"

"My firstborn son will be my husband's heir, should God grant us children. If I have a daughter, she could inherit here—" Rivanon shook her head, uncertain.

"The Cygne line must return to Boisblanc." Perrotte gestured behind her. "One way or another. That is part of what caused the sundering."

They fell to discussing an intricate system of alternating inheritances and marriage alliances cemented unto the sixth generation. Sand frowned, not sure why he was so uncomfortable thinking about Perrotte's children's future marriages, but he *was*.

Merlin decided she was done perching, and flew to the table. As negotiations wore on, she walked back and forth, occasionally unfurling a wing to stretch it before tucking it back into position. The falcon provided a welcome distraction as she marched to and fro, but it was brief.

Though he felt lost within the negotiations, Sand was astonished that no one argued about any of the odd, magical things that had happened, either to the castle or to Perrotte. Everything was being reduced to mundane issues of inheritance law.

Perrotte stood abruptly some time later. "A break," she said. "Let us take a break."

"I'll arrange for refreshment," Rivanon said, and left with the Queen.

Sand's father and Agnote remained in the tent.

"Why isn't Jannet here?" Perrotte whispered fiercely to Sand. "Why isn't she here, looking me in the eyes?"

Sand glanced at his father, who still appeared wretched. Sand murmured, "She sent a boy to kill you, Perrotte. I don't think she's very brave."

Perrotte's eyes widened. Unfortunately, it seemed his father had heard his statement, for he leaned now against the portcullis with one hand over his eyes.

"What's wrong with him?" Perrotte asked.

Gilles lowered his hand and looked at her. "You could be my own daughter, at this point." He tilted his head at Sand. "You're my son's age."

Perrotte gave him a sharp, impatient nod. "And?"

Sand held very still, hardly daring to breathe—wondering what his father was going to say.

"I can never be sorry enough," Gilles said. "And I've been sorry every day of my life. I left the castle that day. I ran away from my master."

Sand started. He'd thought his father had been in the castle when it was sundered.

"I ran and ran, after they told me you were dead," Gilles went on. "But no matter how far I tried to go, I couldn't leave sight of the castle. My feet wouldn't carry me." Gilles shrugged. "I knew I was cursed for what I'd done to you. I could only run in circles around this place. I ended up on Sand's grandfather's doorstep, and—well, he saved my life, I guess. Gave me something to do, something to learn, even though I didn't love it. It took a long time to love anything, because I knew I had lost my right to a happy life for my sin. I can't say I loved blacksmithing, but that's what made it safe to do, you see. And I couldn't say I loved Sand's mother, though I tried; but she loved me, and I hoped that would be enough for the both of us."

Both Agnote and Sand flinched when Gilles said

that. But he continued, looking past Sand now. "But the secret is, you love your children. That just happens, I guess, or it did to me. You have no choice. You start to love again. I finally understood how to love Sand's mother, after—" He gestured at Sand.

Agnote stood behind her husband, hand across her mouth while tears streamed over her cheeks. He continued. "When your children are born, you pray to every saint you can find that they won't share your curses. Sand went missing and I hoped he'd run off and gotten free, like I wanted. When I found out where he'd gotten to"—he waved an arm around, indicating the broken castle—"I thought, 'It's the worst thing that could happen, they've punished my son for my sin.'"

Perrotte made an annoyed noise, and Sand's father looked shocked.

"Really, Gilles!" Perrotte said. "I only *wish* the saints or God or whoever punished wrongdoers as strongly as you've punished yourself. Do you think *Jannet* has gone through these kinds of agonies over what she had you do? Anyway, Sand came here, or was brought here—and I don't think it was some punishment, but maybe all of our salvations—and he woke me from the dead. And he started mending this castle. And we were a bit hungry, and we got into some arguments—but I think, overall . . ." Now Perrotte put her hand on Sand's arm. "It was the only way. Maybe even the best way."

Sand knew what she meant, and he didn't think he would ever be able to explain it any better than she just had.

Agnote wiped her streaming eyes. "I'm glad you two had each other," she said. "We go around our whole young lives, some of us, *most* of us, looking for the place we fit. When you find that place, you keep it; when you find those people you fit with, you keep them." She took Gilles's hand.

Perrotte's fingers tightened on Sand's arm, and she smiled at him. Her smile faded when she said, "I really thought Rivanon and I would see each other and instantly know. That we could love each other, or that we could count on each other. But . . ." Perrotte sighed and turned to Sand's father.

"I do forgive you, Gilles; I forgave you for your part in my death as soon as I understood that you hadn't meant to do this to me, though I guess I might still be angry that you were duped by Jannet."

"Thank you," he said hoarsely.

"But you owe me a life, Gilles Shoemaker-Smith," she said. "And I'm going to claim Sand's from you. He doesn't want to go to university. He wants to be a blacksmith."

Sand's father sighed. "He has the smarts."

"So? He doesn't have the inclination."

"I was only trying to send him away so he wouldn't get caught up in the curse on me."

Perrotte shrugged. "Fair enough. But it doesn't matter now. The worst you feared has happened, and now the worst you feared is over. Yes?"

"Yes," Sand's father said, nodding. Sand met his father's eyes; he saw that his father understood what had happened in the castle—not the details, but something of the importance of the ordeal. Sand took a deep breath, feeling the muscles across his shoulders ease, just a little. He had proven something to his father, by surviving, mending, and freeing himself and Perrotte.

They fell silent for a moment. Agnote went to the tent flap and peered out, then made a tsking noise.

"What?" Gilles asked.

"The Queen is discussing something furiously with the Princess," Agnote said. "I wouldn't wonder that she is saying the dowager Countess has no right to be allowed to continue on as Princess Rivanon's regent here, but . . ." She shook her head.

Perrotte said evenly, "Jannet's family is old and powerful. There may be political considerations to deposing her." Her fingers were bloodless where they clutched her arms, belying the evenness of her tone.

"That's unjust!" Sand burst out.

Perrotte's lips thinned, but she just shrugged stoically. "Mistress Agnote? What did you say that got you imprisoned by Jannet?"

Agnote grimaced. "I don't remember half of what I said," she confessed. "I certainly told her she was a terrible parent who didn't deserve children, stepchildren, or her own fleas. Anyway, considering what I said and who I said it to, it was a very brief imprisonment."

Perrotte stared at Agnote. Agnote held her spine straight and lifted her chin. Then Perrotte clutched her belly and started to laugh. "Sand told me once that you were the kindest person he knew. He never told me you were so funny and brave! I'm glad I got to meet you."

Agnote flushed, smiled, and curtseyed, all at once. "Thank you for saying so, my lady." She peeked out the tent flap again. "They're coming back."

35

CASTLE

PERROTTE AND SAND STOOD, WAITING FOR THE Queen and Rivanon to enter the tent and sit down. But servants entered first, passing cups of watered wine and bowls of grapes to them through the portcullis. Sand tried not to drink and eat too greedily, but when grapes were followed by cheese and bread, it was hard not to moan and slurp happily.

"Now that we are refreshed," Rivanon said some time later, "what say you to our agreement?"

Perrotte asked questions about the location of the lands that were being offered to her until she inherited Boisblanc. She was being given temporary dominion over a small barony deep in Burgundy, and the land belonged to Rivanon's husband.

"You want me to leave Bertaèyn?" Perrotte exclaimed.

The Queen spoke. "I think we can do better than that. There is a castle that belonged to my mother on the edge of the ocean that now lies empty—that is in the lower country, not Haùtt-Bertaèyn, but it is still within the duchy. It will be quite different than what you are used to, and you must speak Breton, not Gallo, to the people who live there."

Perrotte nodded. Sand was alarmed; he wasn't very good at speaking Breton.

"Does it have a tower that could be turned into an observatory, and a good smithy?" Perrotte asked.

The Queen nodded.

"I can accept those lands and those terms," Perrotte said. "Now for the rest of my demands." Rivanon and the Queen both raised eyebrows at her, but she went on. "I require: for Sand to be safe and happy, of course; Jannet's not allowed to throw him or any of his family into prison."

Sand whispered, "Please don't put my name in the same sentence as 'prison.'"

She ignored him. "I also require a steady stream of the best tutors in natural philosophy. Oh, and cloudless nights and an endless supply of parchment."

"All but the cloudless nights, I will grant you, sister," Rivanon said. "Is that all?"

Perrotte looked at Sand. "Is that all?"

Sand imagined Perrotte free and well fed and observing stars with a tutor. He imagined himself working in the smithy, learning from his father and grandfather. And betimes, they would see each other, until he was old enough and had learned enough to go to her and be her smith.

It was a pleasant future. More pleasant than most he had contemplated his whole life.

Nonetheless, he leaned forward to whisper in her ear: "*Is* that all? Use your imagination!"

Right there, in the midst of negotiations, Perrotte closed her eyes, seeming to look inside herself. Her lips curved into a smile. She opened her eyes and said to Rivanon, "And any woman or girl who wants to learn with a tutor of the natural sciences may come and join me in my studies. We will need more than one tutor, in fact, if our population grows."

Rivanon raised her eyebrows, but conceded.

Sand had to hide his beaming smile. Perrotte was barred from entering a university—but no one could stop her from creating one of her own. His heart swelled for her.

The rest of the negotiations went swiftly. All was agreed. A scribe was summoned to write out the contract; Rivanon signed and sealed the document, and Perrotte did as well, through the portcullis bars. Then the Queen's signature and seal were added as well, to show that the agreement held royal approval.

The deal was struck, and their freedom was secure.

Servants swiftly took down the tent. Sand raised the portcullis. Outside the gatehouse, he found Perrotte waiting with Merlin on her arm. She extended her free hand to him, wearing a hesitant smile, but her eyes were worried, wary, and not a little anxious. He understood. But the Queen was there. The Queen would not allow this fragile peace to be broken, would she?

He took her hand. Together, they walked through the gates of the castle and into the world.

Outside, the air was no clearer, and the sun was no brighter. And yet, the world was greater than they had yet known it. They looked at each other. Neither of them had any words.

Then, Sand's father grabbed him up into a rough embrace, and held him tighter than Sand ever remembered being held. He breathed deeply, a sigh of profound relief.

"Well mended, son," his father whispered into his hair.

"Thank you, Papa," he said, and turned his head to the side when he heard a flutter of wings. Merlin had taken flight and now perched calmly on the carved stone crest of the phoenix and the swan above the castle gate. She looked down at them, waiting.

She'd had to fly off because Agnote had grabbed up Perrotte in a warm hug too. Sand only briefly wondered what "my lady" thought of his stepmother's overfamiliarity, but Perrotte's eyes were closed, her arms were around Agnote's abundant waist, and she was smiling.

Rivanon called Perrotte's name, beckoning them over to where she stood with the Queen. Sand and Perrotte parted from Sand's parents, and the four approached the Princess and the Queen.

Merlin swooped down and found Perrotte's shoulder. Perrotte winced slightly, but bore the falcon's grip.

"That is an astonishingly friendly falcon," Princess Rivanon said.

The Queen agreed, and they admired the bird for a time, as they had done during negotiations. It eased the tension by giving them something neutral to discuss. Perrotte just smiled at Sand; he wondered if she would ever explain that Merlin was as resurrected as Perrotte, or if the falcon would just remain part of the secrets of the Sundered Castle.

"Avenie and Annick are staying with Grandpère and Grandmère," Gilles said in a low voice, just for Sand's ears. "We should go and retrieve them soonest. Do you think we are almost finished here?"

Perrotte and Sand's eyes locked. She had overheard. She looked somewhat desperate, her lips pursing grimly. Sand was about to burst out, "No, no, I'm not finished with Perrotte, and I never will be," but at that moment a small mounted party rode toward them from the distant army. They did not carry a white flag; the siege was over and truce was unnecessary, Sand reminded himself, but still, he found them ominous.

A priest on a donkey came first, followed by the infamous Jannet, who carried a cross high in front of her face, like it was her penance. They were flanked by ten or so men.

"They're going in for the treasury," Rivanon said.

A knight followed this procession at a distance: Sir Bleyz. He was free now. He came and knelt before the Queen, the Princess, and Perrotte.

"I am in your service, Lady Perrotte; I will go where you go."

Perrotte looked torn, but in the end, she spoke her mind kindly. "How did they find out about your rebellion, Sir Bleyz?"

"The broken coins! They gave us away. Everyone who knew anything about the sundering knew immediately where they'd come from." He sighed, shaking his head.

"Rise, Sir Bleyz," Rivanon said, as the last of her mother's party entered the castle gates.

Merlin flapped suddenly, lifting off Perrotte's shoulder and screaming a loud, high *kee-kee-kee* call. Beneath their feet, the earth trembled. Sand grabbed Perrotte with one hand, whoever he could reach with the other, and ran away from the castle walls—were the walls falling? Or was it something worse? All he could think of was the story of Saint Gildas throwing sand on the castle of Sainte Trifine's murderer, and the earth swallowing the castle whole. They had to get away.

A clanging slam came from behind them. Sand tossed a harried glance over his shoulder. The portcullis had dropped shut.

Perrotte had started running too, and now led him; the other person Sand had grabbed pulled away from him, slowing and turning. It was Princess Rivanon. If the ground weren't still shaking, Sand might be embarrassed, even worried about having placed hands on royalty without permission. Sand halted, dropping his hands and also turning.

Beside him, Princess Rivanon clutched at her mouth. Perrotte swore.

Thorns. The earth trembled with the force of thorns rising from the dirt, and climbing up the castle walls—the air was filled with the creaking noise of their swift growth, as the plants swarmed upward until they reached a full man's height above the outer walls.

"What have you *done*?" Rivanon cried, looking at Sand and Perrotte.

"This is no magic of ours!" Perrotte said.

Sand's parents stood a little way off with the Queen and Sir Bleyz, panting and staring at the thorns. The Queen's servants and courtiers pelted toward them, concerned for the Queen's safety.

"No, Your Highness, no—it's not our magic," Sand told Rivanon, his mind twisting and turning. He had to explain everything the saints had said about the thorns and mending and forgiveness. The ideas were a jumble within him, and he fought to make the words come out right. Then, like a blessing, he felt a breath in his ear, and he became calm.

Sand turned to look, but no one was beside him. Was it the breath of a Saint that he felt? Words came to him as though they'd just been whispered in his ear.

"The thorns are not one person's magic," he said, his voice large and surprising to himself. Everyone looked at him. "The thorns are a wilderness created by rage and sorrow, by fear and guilt. Many people grew these thorns."

The earth stilled at last, and yet everyone stared at him until Merlin landed on Perrotte's shoulder once more.

"Well—!" Rivanon said, brow furrowed. She looked confused and helpless, but she wasn't blaming them for the thorns at least. "Release my mother, then! You brought down the thorns before. Do it again!"

Now Perrotte stepped forward. She appeared as tranquil as Sand had felt with the Saint's breath in his ear, and he wondered what she felt now, and what she heard.

"Only from *within* the castle can the thorns be taken down," Perrotte said, her voice strong and pure as a bell. She glowed slightly, as the Saints had done during their visitation.

"How?" Rivanon asked, her voice nearly a wail. "You've already mended the keep!"

Sand said, "There is much within the castle that is still broken. And . . ." He glanced at Perrotte, doubting himself now that the surety and calm of the Saints' whispers had gone.

"It's up to your mother," Perrotte said. She was still calm. "She will have to make her own peace with what she's done before she can free herself."

Sand half expected Rivanon to order him or Perrotte or both of them into a dungeon, but the Princess just took a deep, shuddering breath, and nodded. She accepted this? With so much less argument than Perrotte and he had accepted it?

The voice in Sand's head was smaller and less itchy than Melor's voice had been, and he did not think anyone else could hear it: ***We told you we would be near, no matter what happened. This is our blessing.***

When he saw the small smile on Perrotte's face, he knew that she had also heard the voice.

Some of that old magic that made people ignore the castle seemed to be at play; already, the Queen had turned away, and even Agnote and Sand's father were standing with their back to the castle, placidly, as if just waiting for Sand to finish his business with the Princess and Perrotte.

"They're too high; I can't even talk to her like I talked to you," Rivanon said, tears slipping down her cheeks. "The thorns are much higher than before you brought them down."

Sand glanced up at the towering thorns. "She's not alone. She has companions," he said, thinking of his lonely weeks, before Perrotte came back to life. "Her priest and those knights."

Perrotte nodded. Rivanon did not look soothed.

"Though—what if the food stops growing?" Sand asked, struck. "They might starve to death."

Rivanon made a wordless sob, but Perrotte shook her head. "The red seed," she said. "The *red seed*, the one that brought me back to life, also brought the castle's life back. While the thorns were not entirely from me, I think that the, the *lifelessness* might have been. My part of the curse, if you will; I was dead, and the castle was dead."

Sand nodded, satisfied. "So it's all entirely up to them. To the Countess, that is. Good." That seemed just. More just than Rivanon sending Perrotte to Burgundy and leaving the dowager Countess to rule. He couldn't be sorry for the Countess trapped in the thorns. He would leave that sorrow for others.

The Queen joined Rivanon and Perrotte. "I believe this turn of events may change *some* of the terms of the contract you negotiated today; I would suggest we rest ourselves, take some time for reflection and prayer, and sleep on what those changes might be. We can reconvene tomorrow to discuss those changes, and to present candidates for a worthy overseer of Boisblanc while you are with your husband, Rivanon, and before Perrotte comes of age."

Rivanon swallowed down her tears, and nodded. She went to give orders to her servants.

The Queen turned her lovely doe-like eyes on Perrotte. "Do you feel sorry for the Lady Jannet, there, trapped inside that castle?" she asked with mild curiosity.

"Yes," Perrotte said. "I can *imagine* how it feels."

The Queen made an enigmatic smile. "My mother said you were the only girl she ever convinced to climb out a window with her."

"I was the *only* one?" Perrotte said, startled.

"I look forward to hearing your version of the tale."

"Yes, Your Majesty," Perrotte said, and curtseyed.

"Very good, then," the Queen said, and bustled off with her courtiers and servants.

"You climbed out a window with the Queen of France?" Sand asked.

"She wasn't the queen then," Perrotte said. "And I didn't enjoy it."

"It had to be more fun than being trapped in the castle," Sand said.

She glanced at the castle. "That's a different thing altogether."

Sand regarded the bare thorns that had retaken the castle. This hedge had no leaves, no blossoms, no tiny yellow-green raspberries. Fun didn't enter into it, but their time in the castle behind the thorns had given them each other.

"What I *am* worried about," Perrotte said, "is how we'll restore the countship with its wealth still trapped inside that stupid castle." She kicked a stone into the thorns. It disappeared without a trace.

Sand patted the full purse at his waist. "You have a little to start with. But we should've taken more."

"I didn't want to be greedy," Perrotte said. "That will teach me." Her smile was ironic.

"Perrotte?" Rivanon said, returning. "May I invite you to Góll Castle for the night? The Queen is staying there . . ."

Sand's heart fell. This was it, then; the beginning of their time apart.

Perrotte looked at Sand, hesitating. "I would be pleased to join you at Góll Castle, Rivanon, but not just yet. I—I need to go with Sand."

As quickly as it had fallen, his heart rose. A late spring wind ruffled his hair, bringing the sweet scent of flowers from far across the asparagus fields. Sand smiled at Perrotte.

"All right." Rivanon sounded only a little unsettled, but not hurt. She stepped forward, hands clasped, and bent down to kiss Perrotte on the cheek. Their flyaway, golden-brown hair briefly mingled, caught in the wind. "Until we see each other again, sister," she said gently.

Perrotte smiled painfully, an expression trapped somewhat between sadness and shyness. "Until tomorrow," she said.

Rivanon left, servants and knights trailing after. Sir Bleyz remained, and saluted Perrotte. "I am your champion, my lady," he said formally. "Where you go, I follow."

Perrotte said something pretty in response to this, while Agnote spoke in Sand's ear: "Is Lady Perrotte planning to sleep at our house?" she asked anxiously. "Or is she just staying to supper? She knows we're not noble nor rich, and that our house is not large nor sumptuous?"

Sand said, "She knows. And we'll figure out what happens later. She just wants to be with us for now."

"Good, good," Agnote said, appearing comforted. "It's good for her to be with us. Among people who